IMPERFECT
PRETENCE

IMPERFECT PRETENCE

Ann Barker

ROBERT HALE · LONDON

ISBN 978-0-7198-1560-7

Robert Hale Limited
Clerkenwell House
Clerkenwell Green
London EC1R 0HT

www.halebooks.com

2 4 6 8 10 9 7 5 3 1

For Paul and Susie whom I love to bits,
And for my dear friend Ruth – you're for keeps!

Typeset in Sabon
Printed in the UK by Berforts Information Press Ltd

Chapter One

'Damn! I always try to forget about that.' Max Persault drew his heavy black brows together, and surveyed the scene which now confronted him as he stood on the deck of the *Lady Marion*. The Pool of London, which they had just entered, was so crammed with vessels, that in places it was possible to cross the Thames by clambering from ship to ship.

Truth to tell, he was irritated rather than surprised. For the past eleven miles, they had been aware that the wharves on either side were filled with all kinds of craft, being loaded, unloaded, or simply lying at rest. They had observed other ships leaving, no doubt with their holds full of every kind of cargo, their destinations as far flung as China or the Americas. Nor was the *Lady Marion* the only vessel making its way upstream. They had overtaken more than one other, although thanks to the efficient design and good condition of their own ship, they had not been overtaken themselves. Even so, no amount of speed and efficiency could alter the fact that they were now in for a considerable wait.

'Don't we all?' answered the weather-beaten wiry man who was steering the ship skilfully through the crowded waters, in order to find a place where they might drop anchor. ''T'ain't the busiest port in the world for nothing, Cap'n Max.'

'I suppose we should think ourselves lucky that we've nothing on board that will spoil,' Max answered. 'Some of these poor devils must be sweating blood at the thought of their ruined cargo.'

'And no place to land it, 'cept over there,' agreed the other, indicating the dock which lay along Billingsgate on the south side of the City of London. This area, called 'Legal Quays', was where imported cargo had to be inspected by Customs.

'It's enough to turn a man into a free trader,' Max replied with feeling. 'D'you know, Abe, I'm more than half convinced that men take to smuggling just to avoid the tedious wait involved in standing by.'

The other man chuckled. 'You could have a point,' he agreed. 'What say we crack open a bottle of that fine wine you've got down below?'

Max chuckled. This was an old joke of which Abe Collings never tired. 'What say we leave my cargo where it is, and go ashore for a pint of ale when the ship's safely stowed?' he replied.

'Right you are, Cap'n Max.'

Abe Collings was the Master of the *Lady Marion*, whilst Max Persault was the owner, both of the ship and of the cargo she carried. Max owned two ships, this one and another, the *Lady Ruth*, which was presently at Southampton.

The sea was in his blood. His father had been a lieutenant in the Royal Navy when he had met the Honourable Marion Barry, younger daughter of the Earl of Cristow. His Lordship had not been enamoured of his daughter marrying such an insignificant person, but Marion had been determined. Fortune had also favoured the young couple, since Marion's older sister, Eleanor, had secured an alliance with the eldest son of the Duke of Haslingfield some ten years before. The earl was therefore prepared to be more lenient with regard to his younger daughter. His leniency was rewarded when young John Persault gained, in quick succession, his captaincy and a substantial amount of prize money.

The couple were blessed with just two children, Max and his younger sister, Ruth. Mrs Persault was always uneasy when her husband went to sea, and never really happy until his safe return. After he had left the service she had breathed a huge sigh of relief. Ironic, then, that he should have lost his life whilst out with his family on a simple river-boating trip. He had seen a child from another party fall into the water, and had dived in to rescue him. Perhaps there had been an undercurrent, or hidden weeds on the river-bed. Whatever the reason, he had failed to return to the surface.

He had left his grieving wife and family comfortably provided for. There had been no material need to move from the house overlooking Porlock Bay which Captain Persault had bought following his departure from the navy. After her husband's death, however, Mrs Persault declared that she would never willingly look on the sea again, and moved with her family to stay with her father on his estate – mercifully landlocked – and comfort his declining years.

Max was only ten when his father died, and his sister Ruth five years younger. Although they had both grieved sincerely and deeply, the kindly if distant guardianship of their grandfather and the novelty of a new home had done much to divert their minds. Together, they had explored delightedly, relishing the chance to indulge in the kind of country pastimes which had not really been their lot in Devon, where the family garden had been so much smaller.

Max had inherited his father's fascination with water, and was delighted to find that one of the benefits of their new home was a trout stream, where a venerable countryman taught them to fish. There was also an ornamental lake where Max ventured to take his sister for rides in a boat, carefully avoiding his mother's eye.

Unfortunately, on one occasion, Ruth had become so excited that she had fallen out of the boat just at the edge, and Max himself had got soaking wet pulling her to the shore. Neither of them had come to harm, and all might have been well had they succeeded in getting back to the nursery without their mother finding out. As luck would have it, she had been walking along the corridor when they had made their entrance, dripping over the carpet and grinning sheepishly.

The consequence had been a hysterical outburst, followed by their both being confined to the nursery for the next day on bread and water. Max was kept there for a further day because he was older and should have behaved more responsibly. After that, he had refrained from taking a boat out on the lake.

At Eton, he had made friends with a boy whose parents lived near Southampton. Making sure that his mother never knew how close to the coast the Pilkingtons actually lived, he took advantage of Mr Pilkington's kindness by going sailing with him on his yacht whenever possible.

After leaving school, he had assisted his grandfather in managing his estate, but this situation could not last. Upon the earl's death, the estate, which had been tied so fast in an entail that the earl could not break it, went to the Crown. Nevertheless, Max found himself the earl's heir with regard to any unentailed wealth, with a comfortable if not lavish sum at his disposal.

His mother had wanted to remain in the same area, so he had bought a neat property for her in Leicestershire, not so near to her father's former estate in Warwickshire that she would be reminded of it every time she walked out of the door. Once he had settled some money on his mother and put aside a dowry for his sister, he looked about him for ways in which to make the modest sum which remained work for him.

Had it not been for his mother's anxiety, he would have gone to sea. Respecting her fears, however, he had resisted the lure of the ocean and, although he had invested in a ship of his own, he had set about finding a reliable man to take the helm whilst, for his own part, he had made it his business to study imports and exports.

Abe Collings had sailed with his father, and finding by chance that the man was looking for work, Max had immediately taken him on as the master of the *Lady Marion*. He had never had cause to regret his decision.

His life had undergone another change when his mother, at the age of thirty-nine, had married Sir Stafford Prince, a neighbour the same age as herself. To everyone's surprise, not least that of the new Lady Prince, she had almost immediately fallen pregnant, and a little over nine months after the wedding, had presented her delighted husband with twin sons.

This occurrence had had the welcome effect of making Her Ladyship much more placid and contented. Whilst her affection for her firstborn remained undiminished, her instinct to protect him became less significant when set against the dependency of the new, tiny lives in her keeping. When Max had ventured to suggest that he might go to sea with his vessel, therefore, she had greeted the announcement with only moderate alarm. 'Dearest,' she had said anxiously. 'You will take the greatest care, will you not?'

'Of course he will, my love,' Sir Stafford had said reassuringly.

'He is a grown man! Remember also that he will be with Collings! You know there is no man so reliable.'

'Yes indeed, but—'

'But nothing,' the baronet had interrupted in a firm, albeit kindly tone. He had smiled at his stepson, his blue eyes twinkling in his good-humoured face, before turning to his wife. 'Say "God speed, son, and don't forget to bring Mama a present."'

Lady Prince had smilingly complied, and Max had left, a prey to conflicting emotions. A tiny, unworthy and somewhat irrational part of him had resented the fact that he was no longer the only male who occupied a place in his mother's heart. The greater – and by far the more sensible – part had been delighted that she had found real contentment and peace of mind with a man who clearly adored her.

This had been made plain on his last whole day with the family when they had taken a picnic in the grounds of Sir Stafford's fine mansion, and the baronet had sat next to his wife whilst Max had rowed Ruth out onto the lake. There had been a tiny frown on Lady Prince's face as the boat had left the shore. Thankfully, at that moment the nursemaid had approached with two other servants, and Masters Richard and Benjamin Prince, and Her Ladyship's attention had been diverted.

'Do you feel supplanted, brother mine?' Ruth had asked him. She had inherited her mother's slender figure, fair complexion and strawberry-blonde hair. Just now, if the portraits were anything to go by, she was the image of her grandmother, Lord Cristow's wife who had died thirty years before.

Max had laughed, working the oars with ease. Only the camaraderie between them would have marked them out as brother and sister, for in looks they were nothing alike. If Ruth took after their mother, Max was like his father, not over-tall, with a square, powerful physique, thick, coarse black hair, and a swarthy complexion. 'Not a bit of it,' he had answered cheerfully. 'I'm eternally grateful to those two little fellows, for they have given me my freedom.'

'You will come back, won't you?' Ruth had said anxiously. 'I love the boys dearly; they are the sweetest little fellows! But you are my only full brother.'

'You won't get rid of me so easily,' Max had promised her.

It was of his womenfolk that Max was thinking as he looked across at the crowded quay. The ship had moored briefly further down the Thames, and Max had despatched a number of letters, among them communications to his man of business, and to his mother and sister. How delighted his family would be to hear from him! He was never able to give them more than very vague news with regard to his arrival until he returned to England. This particular venture had taken him away from them for nearly two years. Ruth would be twenty, and the twins two years old. How impatient he was to see them all.

Although he could certainly disembark now, leaving the tedious part of the business to Abe, it hardly seemed fair. He said so, when Abe suggested that he should do that very thing.

'You get along, Cap'n Max,' Abe assured him. 'Send that young fellow-me-lad of Boughton's along. He'll deal with all of this for you.' Boughton was Max's man of business.

Collings was still speaking when the sound of lively banter heralded the fact that a landlubber was coming aboard. In clerk's attire, with neat white wig, leather case and spectacles complete, he appeared utterly out of place as he looked about him, a harassed expression on his face.

'James Smithers! This is fortuitous indeed!' Max exclaimed, stepping forward, his hand held out; for this was the 'fellow-me-lad' to whom Abe had been referring.

The harassed expression disappeared, replaced by one of relief. 'Mr Persault!' declared the clerk, his slim white hand disappearing in the grip of Max's large, tanned one. 'It is good to see you safely returned. Welcome back, sir. Welcome!'

'I take it by your appearance that my letters have arrived.'

'They have indeed,' the clerk agreed, nodding. He indicated his leather case. 'I have papers here which should lessen, if not eliminate, the delay here, and I have instructions to remain on board ship. Mr Boughton would be glad of a brief word with you before you leave London.'

Max nodded. 'I'll look in on him then see about acquiring some new clothes before going to Warwickshire,' he said, adding ruefully,

'My mother will never forgive me if I appear before her dressed like this.'

Smithers, glancing at the loose-fitting trousers, well-worn leather shoes, homespun shirt, neckerchief and short jacket that was Max's usual attire on board ship, permitted himself a small smile. 'I should think that very probable, sir,' he replied.

'So, young sir, we're to have the pleasure of your company,' said Abe Collings, as he slapped Smithers on the back. 'Maybe it'll give you a taste for the sea.'

'I doubt it, Mr Collings,' answered Smithers, wincing a little at the vigour of the sailor's greeting, but standing his ground. 'However' – and he turned to indicate two sturdy-looking young men who had just appeared on deck, having managed to negotiate the difficult journey from the bank with a large hamper – 'I have here a taste of dry land that I think you'll relish.'

'You're a gentleman and no mistake,' Abe declared, rubbing his hands and preparing to investigate the contents.

Max smiled as he descended the companionway. His preference was to travel light, so within a very short time, therefore, he was back on deck with a few necessary items inside a drawstring canvas bag. 'My thanks for an excellent voyage,' he said, extending his hand to Abe.

'A pleasure, Cap'n Max,' the ship's master replied, gripping the other man's hand firmly. 'I look forward to the next time.'

'There's a carriage waiting,' said Smithers. 'Jenks and Hargreaves will take you to it.'

Max raised his brows. 'A carriage? From Billingsgate to Lombard Street? I may have been at sea but I haven't lost the use of my legs.' He turned to Jenks and Hargreaves. 'Your pardon, my dear fellows; I really don't need nursemaiding, you know.' With a nod in their direction, he threw his bag over his back, and swung easily over the side to the next ship.

'Mr Persault, sir!' exclaimed Smithers anxiously, taking a few hurried steps in his direction. 'You don't understand; Mr Boughton is not—'

'Goodbye, Smithers,' laughed Max, sketching a careless salute. 'I'll tell Boughton it was all my fault!'

'—in Lombard Street,' Smithers called to the empty air. He turned to Jenks and Hargreaves. 'Catch him up; make sure he goes to the right place, by any means necessary.'

Max heard the commotion and shouting behind him as he continued on his way, moving easily from ship to ship, relishing the physical movement that the activity entailed.

When he had first gone to sea in one of his own ships, he had been well aware that although he had learned much from Mr Pilkington, he was woefully ignorant about the workings of larger vessels. He had therefore instructed Abe Collings to give him the opportunity to perform every kind of task on board. As a consequence, he fully understood what his ships and his men were capable of; and all who served him held him in high regard. Over the course of that first voyage, he had kept watch in the crow's nest – the first time very fearfully, then later with increasing confidence. He had helped to haul in the sails, and had joined in manning the pumps; he knew how to repair, replace and splice ropes; he had played his part in loading and unloading cargo; he had also taken his turn at the wheel. There had been more than one occasion when, side by side with the rest of the crew, he had fought off a band of pirates. The notion, therefore, of being escorted to a carriage which would carry him the length of perhaps three streets seemed positively absurd.

Once on dry land, he looked about him, absorbing the sights and sounds of this part of London. In truth, time might easily have stood still since he had last been here. Although his voyage had taken him two years, it was longer than that since he had last disembarked at Legal Quay. Before setting off on this last excursion, he had spent a few days with an acquaintance who lived in Kent, and the *Lady Marion* had picked him up at Gravesend. Yet as he observed the comings and goings, nothing appeared to have changed substantially. The merchants, the scattering of fashionably dressed folk, the Customs officials, the working men, as well as the inevitable less savoury-looking individuals might well have been the very same. So, too, might the goods piled here and there, all impeding the progress of anyone who might want to make his way from A to B. He grinned wryly. Even had he had any intention of finding Boughton's carriage, the task would be well-nigh impossible amid such hubbub.

'Mr Persault, sir?' Max swore under his breath. His self-indulgent hesitation, brief though it had been, had sufficed for Jenks and Hargreaves to catch up with him.

He turned towards them. 'Well?' he said. He had never expected the two men to pursue him, judging that the sending of the carriage had been nothing more than a rather fussy courtesy.

'The carriage, sir, by your leave,' said one of them.

'Look—' Max paused. 'Are you Jenks or Hargreaves?'

'Jenks, sir.'

'Well then, Jenks, do you recall how easily I have just made my way from ship to shore?'

'Oh yes, indeed, sir, it was a marvel to behold,' Jenks replied.

'Excellent! You are clearly a man of action like myself, unlike the good Mr Smithers, who is, shall we say, a man of affairs?'

'I dare say I am, sir,' Jenks replied, thrusting out his chest a little.

'Then you must see how absurd it is for me to climb into a carriage, and be transported from here to Lombard Street, with all the attendant delays, when I might regain my land legs with a brisk walk that would probably take me half as long.'

'Aye, but orders is orders, sir,' put in Hargreaves, politely, putting a hand on Max's arm. 'Besides, sir, Mr Boughton ain't—'

Max glanced down at the hand on his sleeve, then looked straight into Hargreaves's face. 'Take your hand from my arm,' he interrupted tersely, lifting his chin. 'Understand this, Hargreaves: you may take your orders from Mr Boughton, but I do not. Stand aside.'

Max's muscular build, his air of authority and his position, usually meant that when he issued an order, men jumped to it. It only took him a fraction of a second to realize that, extraordinarily, Hargreaves was not going to oblige. 'Then I'll have to make you,' he said, springing back into a fighter's posture.

'Now, now, that'll do, sir,' said Jenks in a distressed tone. 'Mr Boughton didn't say we was to mill with you. Just as long as we get you there, sir, does it matter how? And besides—'

'No, it doesn't,' answered Max, his eyes on Hargreaves, who was preparing to square up to him. 'Which is why it makes no sense to me that you are trying to insist that I go in a carriage. Who sent you? Was it really Boughton?'

So saying, he made his first jab, catching Hargreaves on the chin. He had no doubt that he would be able to defeat the other man. His boxing skills had begun to take shape at Eton. Since leaving school, he had boxed regularly, and his square, powerful, muscular build made him admirably suited to the sport. A grin spread across his features. A little exercise such as this brief skirmish would afford was exactly to his taste.

It was not to be. He was just calculating where to hit Hargreaves next when something struck him over the head and he fell to the ground.

'That wasn't fair,' Hargreaves complained. 'I was only just getting started.'

'We're not here to stage a prizefight and attract a crowd,' the other man pointed out sarcastically. 'You know our orders. Now, hurry up and let's get him to the carriage before he comes round. I didn't hit him very hard.'

Fortunately for Boughton's two employees, Legal Quay was such a chaotic place that the odd bout of fisticuffs passed without comment. The carriage itself was waiting for them in Lower Thames Street. It was a well-kept, plain conveyance, without any distinguishing marks.

With the paid assistance of a passing sailor, who was given the tale that their friend had overindulged, and needed to be got safely home, they quickly bundled Max Persault inside, where a gentleman was already seated.

'Oh dear! I suppose it couldn't be helped?' he murmured regretfully.

'He wouldn't come of his own accord, sir,' Jenks answered. 'Nor listen to no explanations, neither.'

'Do you want one of us with you, sir?' asked Hargreaves. 'In case he should turn violent?'

'No need, no need, I shall be quite safe,' answered the gentleman in the carriage. Jenks closed the door, then climbed up beside the driver, whilst Hargreaves scrambled onto the back.

As he had said, Jenks had indeed only struck Max a glancing blow, and the carriage had barely started moving before he rubbed his head with a slight groan, and opened his eyes. 'What the deuce?' he exclaimed.

'I trust your head doesn't hurt too much. It really was your own fault, you know.' To Max's great surprise, looking solicitously at him from the seat opposite was his stepfather, Sir Stafford Prince.

Chapter Two

Had Max had the opportunity to consider who amongst all his acquaintance would have been the perpetrator of this outrage against his person, he would not have put Sir Stafford at the top of the list. The baronet had always seemed to be the most even-tempered of men, never given to violence as far as Max could recall. 'By all that's holy!' he exclaimed, frowning. 'This is a surprise indeed.'

'And one I regret,' Sir Stafford replied. 'Unfortunately, you would not come of your own volition.'

'I saw no need for a carriage ride from Legal Quay to Lombard Street,' Max answered. 'I still don't.'

'There is a reason,' Sir Stafford assured him.

'I'm not an irrational man, I trust,' said Max. 'A simple explanation – even the information that you were awaiting me in the carriage – would have sufficed. But I do resent being bundled in like a parcel, and I'll tell you frankly that the fact that it was clearly at your instigation makes it harder to bear.'

'I could not risk a delay,' the baronet answered.

'You make this matter seem to be of the gravest import.'

'Oh it is, my boy, it is,' said Sir Stafford, meeting his gaze.

'Then perhaps you might have the courtesy to tell me what such a matter might be?'

'I would rather wait until we reach our destination if you don't mind. Then there will be no necessity of repeating anything.'

Silence fell within the carriage, and Max looked out of the window. 'I take it that we are not going to Lombard Street,' he remarked.

'No, we are not. I think, if you will just exercise your memory for a few moments, that you will find that more than one person attempted to tell you so.'

Max recalled Smithers's desire to detain him, and the way in which he had interrupted both Jenks and Hargreaves. He grinned ruefully. 'Perhaps so. Are you able to tell me where we *are* going, or is that, too, of such import that knocking me on the head would be preferable to actually taking me into your confidence?'

'Yes, I can tell you where we are going,' answered the baronet placidly. 'We shall be paying a visit to a house in Lower Brook Street.'

'A visit? Not a visit of form, I trust.' He indicated his sailor's garb with a gesture. 'I'd have made more of an effort with my appearance had I known that I'd be in company.' Wholly unbidden, a brief look of consternation crossed his features. 'My mother—'

'Is safely in Warwickshire,' Sir Stafford replied reassuringly. 'As is your sister. No one will take exception to the informality of your garb, I assure you.'

'Just as well,' Max growled.

After another brief silence, Sir Stafford said, 'How has the voyage been? Have you accomplished all that you intended?'

He could not have found a better way of restoring harmony. He had always taken a great interest in Max's investments and business activities, and although the younger man was disinclined to be communicative at first, he gradually began to share with him the various experiences that had enlivened his most recent voyage.

Eventually, the carriage drew to a halt outside an anonymous-looking house in a street that Max did not recognize. Either Jenks or Hargreaves had put his bag on the floor of the carriage, so he picked it up before alighting, then glanced around. 'Lower Brook Street, I assume,' he remarked.

Fifty years before, the street had been almost entirely occupied by persons of quality. Now, with the expiry of short-term leases, some of the properties had been taken over by businesses, and the character of the street was much more mixed. There was no clue as to the kind of establishment that they would be visiting.

They were obviously expected, since the door opened at their approach, and the carriage, bearing Jenks and Hargreaves, started to pull away. They entered the hall, where Max handed his bag to a footman, who looked as if he might have taken it between finger and thumb had it not been too heavy. Max grinned. He had never found it difficult to mix with his fellow men, whatever degree they might be. 'Don't worry; there's no fish in it,' he said.

'So I should hope, sir,' answered the footman primly.

A slim, fair-haired man dressed in black came down the stairs towards them, with swift, light steps. 'If you would please follow me, gentlemen,' he said in an educated voice. They did so and, as they reached the turn of the stairs, Max looked down. Another man, a bruiser by appearance, entered the hall, and took his place on a chair, to one side of the front door. Max hesitated briefly, then continued up the stairs behind Sir Stafford.

They were shown into a room overlooking the street. It was a fine, square chamber, with a handsome desk and chair in one corner, a substantial cabinet with numerous drawers in another, and a large pier glass and table set between the two windows. The curtains and carpet were of a dull crimson shade, and there were several other chairs set in an old-fashioned style around the perimeter.

The room itself already had three occupants. Two of them were standing by the fireplace, whilst the third was looking out into the street, the light making it difficult to distinguish more than the fact that he was a tall, fashionably dressed gentleman. One of the two men by the fireplace came forward at once, his hand held out. 'Mr Persault, welcome.'

'Boughton,' Max acknowledged, shaking hands with his man of business. 'You're looking well. I trust your wife and son are in good health?'

'Well enough, thank you,' answered Boughton. 'Sir Stafford, welcome.' He turned back to Max. 'You must allow me to introduce Mr Hampson, my, ah, colleague. Mr Hampson, Mr Persault.'

Max looked at the other gentleman who had been standing at the fireplace. Like Boughton, he was dressed neatly and with care, in the style of a man of business. Even so, there was something about the way in which he carried himself that suggested that he was a good deal more than that. Boughton might term this man a colleague; he was surely no ordinary one.

'Mr Persault,' said Hampson. He was a quietly spoken man, probably in his forties, with a long bony face, and very keen grey eyes. 'This is most obliging of you.'

'Is it?' Max replied pleasantly. 'To be struck over the head, taken up in Boughton's carriage and constrained to ride in it across London? I'm glad you think so.'

'Constrained? Struck over the head?' exclaimed Boughton. 'How came this about?' he asked, turning to Sir Stafford. 'This was not part of the plan, surely?'

'Oh, I don't know,' said the man at the window, turning as he spoke. 'Once you begin dealing with such as my cousin, who is always readier with his fists than his brains, I would say such an occurrence would be almost inevitable.'

For a moment, Max was silent, transfixed by surprise. Then he hurried forward to greet the cousin whom he had not seen for over five years. 'Alistair! Good God!'

Max was about an arm's length away, when his cousin extended one white hand in which he held a long-handled elaborately chased quizzing glass, using it to keep the other man at a distance. 'One moment,' he said, indicating a mark on the sleeve of Max's jacket. 'Is that merely dirt or is it' – here he gave an elaborate shudder – 'fish?'

Max brushed the quizzing glass to one side. 'Damn it, why must everyone suppose that because I go to sea I have something to do with fish?' he exclaimed.

His cousin allowed the corners of his mouth to twitch slightly. 'In that case, if it is only dirt,' he murmured, allowing the glass to fall, stepping forward and gripping Max by the forearms. 'It's been too long, little cousin.' After a brief interval, he resumed his previous position, and looked Max up and down. 'Certainly too long,' he murmured. 'You sadly need my guidance, I perceive.'

'There his mother would agree with you,' remarked Sir Stafford.

'Some wine, gentlemen,' said Boughton. 'Mr Persault, I'm sure you would be glad of a glass after your misadventure. Then we can get down to business.'

'Allow me,' said Max's cousin, approaching a tray with a decanter and glasses which stood on the table between the windows.

As Alistair poured the wine, Max looked at him, remembering how they had first met. There were five years between them, so when he had arrived at Eton, a raw newcomer, unprepared for the rough and tumble of school life, his cousin had been a senior pupil.

Alistair Robert Maximilian Woollaston was then known by his courtesy title of Earl of St Edmundsbury. His father had died when his only son was still in the nursery, and Alistair had become his grandfather's heir. He was already tall at fifteen, and looked upon by the other boys as something of a leader. Max would never forget the day when, only a short time after his arrival, some older boys had been tormenting him in the dormitory by tossing one of his books between them. It had been a gift from his mother, and his tormentors had chosen to make mockery of the inscription. He had fought fiercely, but it was plain that he would be punished for his presumption, and his precious book probably destroyed to teach him a lesson.

All at once, the banter had ceased as another group of boys had entered, led by a tall youth with white-blond hair, whom Max had recognized as his older cousin. 'What is happening here?' Alistair had asked, his voice even, his head held high.

Despite the fact that Max's tormentors were as many in number as the others, they had all appeared to step back, and glance at one another, as if unsure of what to do next. Then Freddy Parish, who had taken a leading part in the horseplay, had said in a defensive tone, 'Just teaching this scug a lesson.' 'Scug' was the school term meaning someone of no account.

Max had barely known his older cousin, and what he did know did not make him optimistic. He had never visited any of the Duke of Haslingfield's estates, although the duchess had come to see her sister two years before, bringing Alistair with her. The older boy had already seemed to be almost an adult, and had regarded his younger cousin with some disdain. Max had no reason to believe that he would be any more cordial at school, and certainly did not expect him to intervene here. For a few moments after Parish had spoken there was silence. Then Alistair, in a movement which would become very familiar to Max over the years that followed, had flicked an invisible speck off his sleeve, and had looked directly at Parish.

'To which scug were you referring? Not my cousin, surely?'

Suddenly, from tormenting Max, some of the boys were falling over one another to explain themselves, whilst one or two managed to sneak out by the door behind them. 'Didn't know he was anything to do with you, St Edmundsbury,' Parish had said.

'Now you do,' Alistair had replied. 'Oh, and, er ... give him his book back.'

Max had fully expected to receive some sort of reprisal from this incident, and had been apprehensive for some little time. This anxiety had only vanished after he had ventured back to the dormitory alone on another occasion and encountered the same group of boys who had teased him before. Parish had said casually, 'Hallo, brat,' and that was all. His worst fears were over.

He had become a kind of pet adopted by Alistair and his friends, often running errands for them and performing chores; but also included in laughter and stories, and permitted to share treats, such as munching hot buttered toast, made on the fire in his cousin's study. By the time Alistair had left school three years later, Max had become well established with his own circle of friends.

Their paths had not really crossed during their adult lives. After school, Alistair had been packed off on the Grand Tour, an adventure which had lasted three years, whilst Max had gone back to live with his mother and sister, and give his grandfather whatever help he could with the estate.

What had Alistair been doing with himself, Max wondered. The slim, fair-haired boy of fifteen had broadened into manhood. He was a head taller than his cousin, although not as heavily built. Unlike all the other men in the room, apart from Max himself, he wore his own hair tied back in a queue. Like Hampson, he was dressed in sober black, but no one could have doubted that he was a man of fashion. The linen which appeared from below the cuffs of his coat was snowy white and dripped with rich lace. His black brocade coat fitted him to perfection, as did the breeches which matched it. A signet ring adorned the third finger of his right hand. Whatever he had been doing, he appeared to have sufficient funds, or obliging enough creditors, to sustain his activities. Remembering the wealth of the Haslingfield estate, Max rather thought that it must be the former.

When each man had been furnished with wine, Hampson raised his glass. 'To the success of our enterprise, gentlemen,' he said. Three of the five men raised their glasses to their lips. Only Max and Alistair refrained. 'You do not drink, Mr Persault,' Hampson observed.

'I am not prepared to share in a toast when I do not understand its terms,' Max replied. 'For all I know, your enterprise might be to murder me and conceal my body under the floorboards. You'll agree that it hardly started propitiously, at least as far as I was concerned. A fine fool I'd look if I drank to that.'

'And I do not drink if my cousin does not,' put in Alistair. There followed a brief silence.

'Very well, then,' said Hampson. 'Another toast; happiness and success to every man here.' This time, they all drank. 'Now,' he went on. 'To business.'

He gestured towards the desk, and approached it himself, clearly intending to take the chair that was set behind it. Remembering his cousin's effortless superiority, Max observed Alistair glide grace-fully towards the chair, and sit down on it with a brief word of thanks to Hampson, whose hand was already resting on its back. Smiling inwardly, Max picked up a chair and carried it over to the desk, and the other men did the same.

When they were all seated, Hampson said to Boughton, 'Would you like to explain, or shall I?' Boughton inclined his head as if to say that Hampson should continue. Hampson then turned to Alistair. 'Your Grace?'

Alistair waved a hand indicating permission; Max, on the alert because this meeting had been somewhat suspicious from the very beginning, immediately pricked up his ears. 'Your Grace? Is your grandfather dead, then?'

After a brief awkward silence, Alistair spoke in his usual soft drawl. 'Yes, he's dead, and at just the wrong moment. That's why we need you.'

'Me?' Max asked, his brows drawing together. 'Why should I be needed in such a case?'

'We need you to be me,' Alistair replied with the ghost of a smile.

Chapter Three

'To be you?' Max exclaimed. 'What the deuce do you mean?'

'Gentlemen, gentlemen,' said Hampson, in the tone of one who clearly felt that it was time he regained control of the situation. 'Your Grace, pray let me enlighten Mr Persault. '

'I'd be deuced glad if someone would,' said Max frankly.

'Very well,' Hampson responded, indicating to Boughton that he should fetch the decanter and refill everyone's glass. 'I don't know whether you are aware that your cousin has been spending a good deal of time on the Continent recently?'

Max nodded. 'In Italy, wasn't it?'

Alistair smiled faintly. 'Gambling, flirting and drinking my away around the courts of any princeling who'll have me,' he agreed, extracting his snuff box from inside his coat and taking a pinch.

'A useful fiction, cooked up for the benefit of the curious,' Hampson corrected. 'In fact, your cousin has been in France.'

Max looked incredulous. 'In France? Alistair, that's where they execute people who look like you.'

'I don't look like this when I'm in France,' Alistair replied.

'So what have you been doing?'

Instead of answering, Alistair got up from his place and walked back to his position at the window. Hampson glanced briefly at his back, then said 'His Grace's activities have been many and varied. Just now, he is procuring vital information concerning the remaining members of the royal family – principally the Queen and the Dauphin.'

'But surely, now they have executed the King, they will be satisfied,' said Max.

'They will not stop there,' Hampson told him. 'Remember the traditional cry—'

'*Le roi est mort! Vive le roi!*' said Alistair in perfectly accented French, without turning round. Max recalled that his cousin's grandmother on his father's side had been French, and that he had spent some of his formative years in France.

'Do you know how old King Louis XVII is?' Sir Stafford Prince asked his stepson. 'He is eight years old. Eight, Max! His father was executed in January. We have now heard just this week that he has been separated from his mother. For what purpose, do you suppose?'

Max stared at his stepfather. At the outset, the French Revolution had had its English supporters, who believed that reform of a corrupt system was desperately needed. The execution of Louis XVI in January of that year, however, had alienated many people's sympathies, obviously Sir Stafford's among them. The baronet had always seemed an amiable, even-tempered man, if anything rather indifferent towards politics. He sounded anything but indifferent now.

'Good God! You are going to attempt a rescue,' said Max, looking round at the assembled company.

'Mr Persault!' exclaimed Hampson urgently. 'We must not take anything for granted, even if we are in a safe house.'

Sir Stafford got up, walked to the door, opened it and went out onto the landing. 'Higgins?' he called. 'Is anything untoward?'

'All's well, sir,' the voice called back.

'Very well,' said Hampson, after the door was closed once more. He sighed. 'Something must be attempted. Louis-Charles should never have been king. He had an older brother who died in 1789, leaving Louis-Charles as the Dauphin. Now, with his father's untimely death, he is the uncrowned King of France and the hope of the royalists. The revolutionaries have killed his father. They cannot allow the boy to live.'

'Why should they execute a child?' Max asked. 'He cannot have offended against the state, surely.'

Alistair laughed humourlessly. 'What do you think was the charge against Louis XVI? High treason! Once France had been declared a republic, any monarch by virtue of his very existence would have to be a traitor.'

Sir Stafford nodded solemnly. 'Little Louis-Charles will be executed because of who he is, not because of anything he has done – unless we do something about it.'

'Yes, I understand,' said Max. 'What I do not see is where I fit in.'

'It's quite simple,' said Alistair. 'I returned to England to receive further instructions. It was while I was here that the death of my grandfather occurred. This means that I am now Duke of Haslingfield, with all the attendant responsibilities that the position entails. Fortunately, I shall not be expected to take my seat in the House until the autumn. However, my accession to the dukedom does make me more noticeable.'

'We have no way of knowing how many people connect M. Variens – as your cousin is known in France – with His Grace the Duke of Haslingfield,' Hampson put in. 'It is safest if we assume that some will have their suspicions. But if we can muddy the waters a little, then that might make His Grace's task all the easier, and gain us some time.'

'And we propose to do that by having you masquerade as me,' Alistair put in.

'I can't do that!' Max exclaimed. 'Am I the only one who has perceived a major stumbling block to this enterprise? Has no one looked at us side by side? I am nothing like Alistair. Not even a short-sighted person seeing me at a distance from the back on a gloomy evening would be fooled. How can this possibly be carried out?'

'Quite easily,' replied Hampson. 'We propose to send you to one of the duke's estates which he has never visited, and where he is not known.'

'I suspect you have one in mind,' said Max.

'Yes, I do,' said Hampson. 'The estate just outside Cromer would do admirably. There is a skeleton staff there. It's small, it's out of the way, and no duke has visited in years.'

'Then why the deuce should any duke wish to go there now?' Max asked.

Alistair raised an eyebrow. 'We great men have our whims, you know.'

'Do we indeed?'

Hampson cleared his throat. 'By your leave, gentlemen. With any luck, Mr Persault, you should be able to arrive with a severe chill and take yourself off to bed.'

'I've never had a chill. I don't believe I've ever had a day's illness in my life.'

'It's quite true, you know,' put in Alistair. 'The fellow is quite tiresomely robust – almost vulgarly so, in fact.'

'Well, you will just have to pretend,' said Hampson.

'There's no need for such measures,' said Sir Stafford. 'The place is out of the way. All he need do is live very retired.'

'For how long?' Max asked.

'Until His Grace appears.'

'Which will be – when?'

Alistair shrugged in a way that made it clear how easily he could pass for a Frenchman. 'When my task is accomplished; or at least until I can do no more.'

Max caught hold of his arm. 'Alistair, surely you must see how impossible this is?' Alistair glanced down at his sleeve. He released it, and the older man brushed it as if to smooth out the creases. 'Poseur!' Max exclaimed.

'Perhaps,' Alistair replied. For a moment, his mask slipped and he looked deadly serious. 'Max, I need to have someone to cover my back – someone I can trust, without even thinking about it.'

There was a brief silence. 'What do you say?' Hampson asked. 'Will you do this for us?'

Max stared at his cousin. 'Is there any possibility of your succeeding?' he asked.

Alistair returned his gaze. 'The chance is slight; I judge it to be worth the risk.'

'Your cousin's mission is a perilous one,' put in Hampson. 'I have absolutely no doubt that if you help us in this way, his position will be much safer, and his success and survival much more likely.'

Eventually, Max grinned ruefully. 'Then what can I say?' he answered resignedly. A collective sigh of relief passed through those assembled there, which he halted by raising his hand. 'There is one condition: Abdas Okoro comes with me.'

'Abdas...?' queried Hampson.

'Okoro,' Max finished. 'As my travelling companion.'

'This cannot be permitted,' said Hampson decisively.

'Why not?' Max asked. 'I doubt whether you will allow me to travel as I would wish – on horseback with the saddle-bags as my only luggage.'

'Certainly not!' Hampson agreed. 'You will need an entourage, of course.'

'Then Abdas can be part of that.'

'Out of the question,' Hampson declared.

Max stood up. 'Then you find someone else to undertake your masquerade,' he said, moving towards the door.

With the exception of the duke, the other men looked at one another in consternation. A small smile hovered over the duke's lips as he took out his snuff box and helped himself to a pinch.

'Mr Persault, you must see that this is impossible,' Hampson said in the kind of tone that might be used in reasoning with a six-year-old. 'We will only be employing trusted men to accompany you.'

Max stared at him for a long moment. 'Precisely,' he answered. 'You tell me that I can trust them, when I have never met them. I *know* that I can trust Abdas Okoro with my life. My cousin needs someone at his back whom he can trust. So do I. Deny me this, and you may kiss goodbye to my involvement in this scheme.'

Again, the men looked round at one another. Alistair put his snuff box away. 'Gentlemen, if my cousin vouches for this man, then you can be certain that he is to be trusted.'

Boughton cleared his throat. 'If I might be permitted to speak,' he said. 'I am acquainted with Mr Okoro in a business capacity, and judge him to be trustworthy.'

Hampson sighed. 'In that case, we agree to your terms,' he said.

Max lifted his arms, his hands open as a gesture of acknowledgement. 'Then I'm your man.'

'Mr Persault, we are in your debt,' said Hampson.

'Call him "Your Grace",' said Alistair. 'He might as well get used to it.'

'I suppose you realize I don't even look like a duke,' Max pointed out.

'That is true,' Alistair agreed, walking around him slowly. 'You look like a Thames bargee, in fact.'

'We can soon attend to that, Mr Persault,' said Boughton earnestly. 'We have arranged for you to be measured and for new clothes to be made for you.'

Max frowned. '*You* have arranged? You take a good deal for granted, by God.'

Alistair raised his brows. 'Haughty! That tone should do it,' he said.

'What of my mother and Ruth? They will be expecting me.'

'Leave them to me,' said Sir Stafford. 'I'll tell a story that will satisfy them.'

Max looked at him with a narrowed gaze. 'There's considerably more to you than meets the eye, isn't there?'

Being referred to as 'Your Grace' was not the only thing that Max found himself obliged to get used to over the next few days. Another was the quantity of clothes that the other men seemed to think that he should need.

'Your mother would be delighted,' Sir Stafford remarked, before he left for Warwickshire. 'What a pity I won't be able to tell her.' His story was to be that a return voyage to Spain could not be undertaken without Max's presence, since some delicate negotiation had to be conducted which only he could do with any authority.

'Pray send her my regrets, and assure her that I will wait upon her as soon as may be.'

'And looking as fine as fivepence, no doubt.'

'I shall look like a damned dandy,' Max grumbled later, as he was asked to pronounce on the fabric for yet another coat. 'Four evening coats! Five day coats, and breeches too – not to mention riding clothes! What the deuce do I want with it all? And as for shirts! Mind you,' he went on, looking down at his feet, 'I like the boots.'

'It is necessary to have all those clothes because *I* have that many clothes,' Alistair explained patiently, not for the first time. 'If you arrive looking like a brigand camping out, and with no more than a change of linen, no one will be deceived for a moment.'

There was a gentle knock on the door, and a discreet-looking individual entered. 'Your choice for the fabrics that I left with you, sir?' he murmured.

Alistair turned to the samples of fabric that had been laid out on the table. 'The maroon, I think, and the silver grey.'

'An excellent choice if I may say so,' replied the discreet individual, as he bowed and withdrew.

'You might show a little interest,' said Alistair mournfully after the man had gone. Max's response was a shrug. 'Anyway,' his cousin went on, 'you may console yourself with the thought that you need never buy another item of clothing as long as you live.'

'That is a great comfort to me,' Max assured him sincerely.

In truth, the thing that horrified him more than the clothes he was to wear was the fact that Alistair insisted on his getting used to his hair being powdered. 'Either powder, or we cut all your hair off and put you in a wig,' his cousin told him.

'Why?' Max exclaimed. 'I've never worn powder in my life.'

'To hide one's real hair colour makes an excellent disguise,' Alistair explained, 'especially when you are so dark and I am so fair. Once out in the provinces, where no one has ever seen either of us, you may do as you please.'

'That'll make a change,' Max muttered.

A third thing which Max was obliged to endure was the purchase of a number of items on his behalf, all financed by the ducal estate, including a coach and horses, together with a pleasure carriage and a gig, both of which were timed to arrive in Cromer two days after his own appearance. 'Why can't I ride?' he asked, when Hampson came to consult him upon the fittings of the said coach. His own horse, Filigree, was to travel with the later party, ridden by a groom.

'Because you are a duke, *Your Grace*, and you will be expected to arrive in style,' Hampson replied patiently. 'The less people find themselves questioning your actions, the less suspicion there will be about who you really are.'

'Indeed,' Alistair agreed. 'Really, Hampson, your patience has been remarkable, considering the recalcitrance of my oaf of a cousin.'

Max coloured slightly. 'You are very right,' he responded. 'I don't know how you've borne with me, Hampson. But I am what I am, and frankly, I've no interest in what colour the cushions and fittings of this damned coach are to be. Black, white, orange or pink with turquoise spots, it's all the same to me.'

'No, is it really?' Alistair asked him, his eyebrows raised.

Max laughed. 'Well, perhaps not pink,' he conceded. 'Otherwise, I'm quite indifferent.'

'Let it be green,' said Alistair, after a moment's thought. 'Sea green.'

'Aye, that'll do,' Max agreed with a grin.

Eventually, everything had been purchased that was judged to be necessary, and all Max's clothes had either been made, or were in the making, to be sent on to the address of the ducal estate near Cromer. He would also be taking with him some clothes for Alistair, to be available when his cousin joined him. 'You may be happy to wander around looking like a conscripted sailor, but I am not,' Alistair remarked.

The plan was that they would leave together in the new carriage. A coachman, a footman and two outriders had been newly employed for this mission. The backgrounds of the men had been carefully looked into. Nevertheless, all were starting work in the belief that Max was the Duke of Haslingfield. 'What they don't know, they can't give away,' Alistair remarked laconically.

For the same reason, the skeleton staff at present in residence would not be augmented until Max's arrival. 'At present, there is only a bailiff, a head groom and a caretaker,' Hampson explained, at a planning meeting attended by himself, Max and Alistair. 'The bailiff lives in his own cottage, and the groom over the stables. The caretaker is the only servant in residence.'

'It'll be a little difficult to live in style under those circumstances,' Max remarked with a grin.

'There has been no need of a steward or housekeeper in recent times,' Hampson replied, confirming by his manner that he had absolutely no sense of humour.

Max grunted. 'I assume they have been apprised of my coming.'

Hampson shook his head. 'No one has been alerted concerning your arrival,' he said.

'But what on earth is the purpose of that?' Max demanded.

'You will, of course, insist that a letter had been sent on ahead, which must have been lost,' Alistair explained. 'That will provide you with an excuse to throw your ducal weight about. It will also wrong-foot the bailiff, who will be falling over himself to oblige you.'

'It will also mean that you can make your own choice as to servants,' Hampson pointed out. 'My advice would be to manage with as few as possible for discretion's sake. You can always say that you will be sending for others from London.'

'You would be very well served if I took on enough for a royal palace and charged them all to your account,' Max told his cousin.

Joining them on horseback later would be Abdas Okoro. The African had made his home in Hampshire, not far from Southampton. During Max's absence, he had been supervising some work on board the *Lady Ruth* there as a favour to his friend. It was to the *Lady Ruth* that Max sent a letter with Hampson asking Okoro to support him in this enterprise.

Once the nature of the task had been explained to him, Okoro, who was always ready for a new adventure, willingly agreed, with the proviso that he would need to conclude certain business of his own first. Hampson furnished him with Max's itinerary, so that he could meet them at some point during the journey. The rest of the party would be informed that he was Max's secretary, who had been undertaking some business for his employer in another part of the country.

The party was to leave London through the Mile End Gate, passing through the village of Stratford. Their route would take them through Chelmsford, then to Colchester, where Alistair would leave the coach and travel on to where a ship would be waiting for him at Harwich.

'Harwich?' Max murmured, when he was told. 'Hardly the most direct route to France, surely?'

'Nor the most watched,' Alistair pointed out.

After Alistair had left them, Max and his entourage would continue on to Diss, thence to Norwich, and finally to Cromer. During the first part of the journey, Alistair, dressed far more plainly than was his wont, was posing as valet to the new duke – much to Max's amusement. He was less entertained when he discovered that at

Colchester, Alistair's own valet, who was travelling separately, would be taking his master's place.

'I don't need anyone to dress me,' he declared in exasperation.

'You do if you intend to look like me,' Alistair replied. 'If, on the other hand, you want to arouse suspicion by going round dressed with as much care as the lowest mudlark on the Thames, then by all means dispense with him.'

Max stared at him for a long moment, remembering that what was a rather tiresome subterfuge to him was a matter of life or death to his cousin. 'Sorry,' he muttered, looking away.

'You'll find he's more than a valet,' Alistair told him, after a brief pause. 'He's utterly discreet, completely loyal, and surprisingly handy with a pistol if need be. If he tells you something is so, then it is so. I'm loath to part with him.'

'If he's so valuable to you, don't you need him more than I do? Besides, I will have Abdas, remember.'

'I don't forget, and if he's all that you say, I'm glad that you will have him at your side,' Alistair replied. 'But I doubt if there are many blacks in Norfolk. You may need someone inconspicuous to go on an errand, and Barnes is very good at that. He can turn his hand to anything. I'd strongly advise you to get him to double up as your butler. That way, you'll always have complete control over who comes and goes.' He paused. 'Besides, I have to be able to act alone. It's the only way I can have a chance of coming out of this alive. Just be on your guard even when speaking to Barnes or Okoro. You never know who might be listening.'

'In Cromer?' asked Max incredulously.

'People talk,' Alistair replied. 'Cromer is not far from Blakeney and Wells, both of which can take bigger ships. It's even possible to bring larger vessels quite close in at Weybourne, which is only seven miles down the coast.'

'I'll be careful,' Max promised.

They set off very early from London, and, with a stop for refreshment just over halfway at Chelmsford, were in time to dine at Colchester. Given the need for discretion, they avoided visiting any of the hostelries in Chelmsford and instead decided to stop some two miles outside the town at a small place named Widford. They had been chatting idly as they drove, but shortly before they arrived at the inn, Max fell silent, a crease between his brows.

'What is it?' Alistair asked him. 'Having second thoughts?'

'And thirds and fourths,' Max agreed ruefully. 'Alistair, I'm very afraid I'll let you down. I'm no actor. If a group is ever got up to read a play, then I'm put in charge of moving chairs.'

After a brief pause, Alistair said, 'Listen, Max, what we need is for any interested observer to note that the Duke of Haslingfield has set off to inspect his Cromer property. On the journey, a display of your pomp and circumstance will establish the fact in anyone's mind that you have passed that way. No one in the vicinity of Beacon Tower will have any reason to think that you are other than what you appear to be. Rather than playing a part, you'll need the ability to think on your feet, and I know that you can do that.' He paused briefly. 'As for letting me down, I can't think of anything less likely.'

Shortly after this conversation, they arrived at Widford, where the carriage drew to a halt outside an inn called the Silent Woman. They both looked up at the sign which displayed a picture of a woman standing, rather improbably, since her head had been cut off. 'The only silent woman I've ever met,' murmured Alistair, as they prepared to alight. 'Remember, I'm the valet and you're the duke.'

He sprang nimbly from the carriage, and let down the steps with his own hands. 'This way, Your Grace,' he said, holding out his arm.

Max stared at him. Although he'd known this man for years, suddenly, it was as if he didn't know him at all. He had become a gentleman's personal gentleman; courteous, unobtrusive, conscientious. All at once, Max felt completely adrift. He had no idea of what to do or say.

'Your Grace?' Alistair prompted. His tone was perfect for the role. It was that of a servant whose master is not behaving as expected.

Still Max stared at him, and as he did so, he remembered a little outing that he and Alistair had enjoyed a few nights before. There had been a masquerade at Vauxhall Gardens, and the two of them had gone in masks and dominos. 'Watch how some of the fops behave,' Alistair had advised him. 'It may give you an idea or two.'

Together, they had sauntered about the avenues, sampling the arrack punch and wafer-thin ham, and observing the antics of those present. One fop had made a terrible fuss because he declared that his chair was dirty. 'Zounds! Look what a mark it has made on my new coat!' he had exclaimed. 'Dammit if I don't speak to the owner.'

The two cousins had grinned as various members of his party had tried to soothe him, one making matters worse by dabbing ineffectually at the almost undetectable mark on the man's blue brocade sleeve. Now, seized by sudden inspiration, Max took out his handkerchief and waved it. 'Take it away, Field,' he said in disgusted tones.

'Take it away, Your Grace?' repeated the 'valet'.

'Your hand, man,' Max answered. 'Your hand!'

'My hand, Your Grace?' ventured Alistair.

'Your hand, Your Grace,' mimicked Max. 'What are you, a damned parrot? Look at your hands. Dash it all, they aren't even clean!'

'I beg pardon, Your Grace,' Alistair answered humbly.

'So you should,' answered Max, strolling towards the inn door. 'You need to mend your ways, Field. I'm far from satisfied with your work; very far from satisfied.'

'That was good,' said Alistair when at last they were in the private dining parlour which he had insisted was essential for his master's comfort. They were bowed in by an obsequious landlord, anxious to make himself and his hostelry agreeable to a guest more illustrious than any he had entertained in at least a twelvemonth. 'Any casual observer couldn't fail to notice that the situation between us is not a happy one. All you need to do is to find fault with me at Colchester, dismiss me, and take on Barnes.'

'I was completely at a loss at first,' Max admitted. 'It was only when I remembered that fellow at Vauxhall that I managed to say anything.'

'My dear cousin, you were inspired!'

'Will you stay and eat with me, or ought I to send you to the kitchens?' Max asked.

'Keep me with you,' Alistair replied. 'The fewer people either of us mix with, the better.'

Chapter Four

'Well really!' Miss Church exclaimed, her fine hazel eyes flashing indignantly as she stared after the two men who had just entered the inn. 'Did you hear how that brutish-looking dandy raked down his servant? And in the public inn yard, too.'

'I dare say he deserved it, dear,' answered her travelling companion comfortably.

Unlike the men who had attracted their notice, the two ladies were on the point of leaving, having taken refreshment already. They were only waiting whilst their driver supervised the harnessing of the horses to their post chaise.

'I do not know how you can possibly suppose that, Aunt Roberta,' Miss Church replied, 'seeing that you do not know either man.' The younger of the two, she was slightly taller and slimmer than her aunt, who was comfortably rounded and in her mid-forties.

Holding back the retort that if she did not know the man or his master, neither did her niece, Miss Roberta Fellowes simply commented on the one remark that Miss Church had made with which she could quite truthfully disagree. 'All the same, Constance, I do not see how you can call the man brutish *and* a dandy. He can only be one or the other.'

Constance helped her aunt up into the carriage, then pressed a coin into the ostler's hand and climbed in herself. She looked at Miss Fellowes, her lips pressed firmly together. 'He certainly *was* both,' she declared. 'And as for his valet's hands, did you see them?'

Miss Fellowes shook her head slowly, a slight frown on her face. 'Certainly not at this distance, and I doubt if you could either,' she declared.

'They were spotless,' Miss Church answered, as their chaise drew out of the inn yard. 'Absolutely spotless.'

Constance Church was the only child of the Rev'd Peter Church and his wife Alice. Mrs Church had been the sister of Miss Fellowes and her brother Augustus, with whom Constance had made her home since the death of her father in 1791, two years before.

For the first fourteen years of Constance's life, she had lived with her parents in a small parish in Lincolnshire. Mrs Church was always fragile, and as soon as Constance was tall enough to unlock the cupboard containing the account books, much of the running of the household had fallen to her lot. When she was not thus occupied, her father would give her lessons, educating her as he would have done the son that he had never had.

Mr Church had appeared to be happy enough in carrying out his various parish duties. On the death of his wife when Constance was only fourteen however, he had given up his parish and moved to Cambridge to pursue a scholarly career.

Constance had always been closer to her father than her mother and, as far as she was concerned, he could do no wrong. So, trusting him completely, as she had always done, she had packed up their household effects and had set about making their home in the ancient university town.

The situation in which she now lived, in a country parish, mixing with country people, was much more akin to the place in which she had been brought up. Nevertheless, she missed the evenings when some of her father's fellow scholars would gather round the table, hotly disputing the American question, or universal suffrage, or problems with France, whilst she remained curled up in an armchair, occasionally interjecting some opinion, when most other girls of her age would long since have been in bed.

It had been from her father that she had gained her fierce sense of fairness. Whilst she was realistic enough to accept that, regrettably, revolution would probably not sweep through the country, levelling everyone, and bringing haughty aristocrats – like the one whom they had encountered in Chelmsford – to their knees, she saw no reason why the nobleman that they had seen – and what a misnomer *that* was – should be permitted to treat his employee in such a way.

What made it worse was that Aunt Roberta was quite right: a man could not be a brute and a dandy.

He had undoubtedly been turned out in the latest style. Dressed in a silk striped coat of violet with a high collar, a white waistcoat embroidered with silver and tight-fitting pantaloons, and with a tall crowned hat on his powdered head, he would not have been at all out of place in St James's Street. However, when the insufferable creature had made reference to his valet's hands, Constance's attention had been drawn to the hands of the nobleman himself. Here was the only flaw to his fashionable appearance, for he was not wearing gloves. As he had taken out his handkerchief to wave it in the air, she had noticed that his hands were tanned, square, and looked strong and capable. They were certainly not the hands of a dandy. They weren't even as white as the valet's hands, which had attracted such criticism. From this one small observation made quite by chance, she concluded that although he was definitely dressed like a dandy, he could not possibly be one. This meant that he had to be a brute. But what a brute he was!

'Constance, my dear? Where have you been? I declare, I must have addressed my last remark to you three times.'

'I beg your pardon, Aunt Roberta,' she replied, dredging up from her mind the very few fragments of information that she had picked up from what her aunt had just been saying. 'You were observing that Mrs Marriot looked better than you had expected.'

Miss Church and her aunt had just spent two weeks with a recently widowed school friend of Miss Fellowes outside Chelmsford. They had stabled the horses and post chaise at the Silent Woman in order to spare Mrs Marriot's small household any extra trouble, hence their presence in the inn yard.

Miss Fellowes directed a shrewd look at her companion. 'I was remarking that Mrs Marriot's *granddaughter* was getting on better, given the poor start that she had had,' she replied, a hint of asperity in her voice. 'I *knew* you were not listening.'

'I was in part,' said Constance placatingly.

'A very small part, perhaps. You need not think to pull the wool over my eyes. You were still thinking about that obnoxious man, and how to put him in his place.'

Constance laughed. 'Why do you know me so well?' she asked. 'It really isn't fair. It was a dear little baby, though, wasn't it?' It was in order to see the baby that they had postponed setting out that morning.

'A delightful creature,' Miss Fellowes agreed. 'I hope she continues to take after her mother. Her father is an excellent man, I am sure, and a first-class lawyer, but I think that that long nose and those thick brows would be very unbecoming in a female.'

They were proceeding at a smart trot. The road was generally quite a busy one, since it carried some of the London traffic. Unusually, on this occasion, they had almost reached Witham, which was nearly halfway between Chelmsford and Colchester, without meeting more than a handful of wagons, and single horseback riders.

'How agreeable it would be to be driving,' Constance sighed. She had been taught to drive by her father, and although she had never handled a team, was very well capable of guiding a pair of horses.

'You could never have driven us all this way in an open carriage,' her aunt pointed out. 'And Patch would never have managed the distance.'

Constance chuckled. 'After half-a-dozen miles, he would probably have turned back of his own accord,' she agreed. Patch was the Fellowes's venerable pony, brought into service for short distances when the gig sufficed. For this excursion, they had borrowed a post chaise and pair from Mrs Brewer, an acquaintance in a nearby village. Fred, the coachman, was driving it by riding one of the horses.

A gig passed them, travelling the other way. The driver, who was dressed as a clergyman, touched his hat politely as he caught sight of the ladies.

'How agreeable it is, my dear, to travel upon well-kept roads, where people are so polite,' Miss Fellowes remarked. The words were barely out of her mouth, when there was a sound of a carriage approaching them from behind at considerable speed, accompanied by two outriders. Seeing that the driver was clearly in a hurry, Fred took steps to guide the horses to the side of the road, and indeed had begun to do so when they were all alarmed by a blast on the horn from the oncoming vehicle.

'Have some patience!' Miss Church exclaimed. Mercifully, the horses appeared to be good-tempered and placid, and did not take fright at the noise. The carriage swept past them and as it did so, Constance caught a glimpse of a familiar crest on the side. 'It's him,' she said, losing control of her grammar in her exasperation.

'To whom do you refer, dear?' asked her aunt, retaining hers.

'The dandy brute!' Constance replied. 'Now why am I not surprised?'

'I don't know, dear,' said Miss Fellowes.

'Trust him to drive at such a wicked pace, to the danger of any other road users.'

'He wasn't driving,' pointed out Miss Fellowes reasonably.

'You can be quite certain that it was he who gave orders for the man to drive at such a speed. I hold him entirely to blame.'

'Yes, dear, I thought you might. Still, at least he has gone on ahead of us. As he is in such a hurry, he must have some distance to go, mustn't he? I should think it very unlikely we shall encounter him again.'

'Thank goodness,' said Miss Church heartily, as they continued on their way.

The ducal carriage arrived at Stanway, a small village outside Colchester, just as the light was fading, and drew up outside the Swan. They had set a smart pace from Chelmsford, since Alistair did not want to miss the tide at Harwich. As they travelled, they spoke little, for the most part resting in a companionable silence. As they drew near to Colchester, Alistair said, 'By the way, I've made my will.'

'Really?' said Max.

'You don't sound very interested.'

'In the nature of things you'll predecease me. I doubt it will be for another forty years at least.'

'Such touching faith in the success of my venture,' Alistair murmured. 'Nevertheless, I've done so. I've named you as executor. I hope that's all right.'

'I'm honoured,' Max replied, and meant it.

On their arrival at the inn, Alistair once more took on the

persona of Field, whilst Max, who was beginning to enjoy himself, swaggered into the inn as though he owned the place.

'My Lord,' murmured the landlord, bowing low.

Max stared at him, his chin high. 'I am Haslingfield,' he said. 'My servant should have sent ahead for lodgings for me.'

The landlord looked back at him in some consternation. 'I regret, My Lord....' he began.

'This is monstrous,' Max declared. 'Positively monstrous. Is it really beyond your ability to hold a room in reserve when it has been booked in advance?'

'I swear, My Lord,' the landlord protested, 'I have had no instructions from your lordship.'

'Evidently,' replied Max, his chin high. 'Otherwise you would be addressing me as "Your Grace".'

There was a faint snigger from the corner of the taproom. 'He's a bleedin' archbishop,' someone said.

Max could feel his mouth twitching. Had he been in their position, his attitude might have been the same; but he could not afford to let his performance slip. He swung round to face them, glaring at them from beneath his brows. Thus had he looked when he had confronted a pair of insolent sailors before knocking their heads together. Despite his dandified appearance, there was something about him that said he was a man to be reckoned with. The sniggering stopped at once, and the three individuals buried their faces in their tankards.

'I can put a fine room at your disposal, Your Grace,' said the landlord, after a baleful look at his other customers which promised reprisal later. 'I swear to you that I had no notice of your coming.'

'Field,' said Max in a dangerous tone.

'Your Grace?' murmured Alistair tentatively.

'Did you send ahead and reserve rooms for me?'

'Your Grace, I ... I....'

Max held up his hand. 'Enough! We will continue this discussion out of the gaze of the vulgar populace. Take me to this room of yours,' he said to the landlord. 'If it proves to be satisfactory, then I shall stay. If not....'

'If not, Your Grace?' the landlord ventured.

'I have the ear of the Prince of Wales. If it is not to my liking then no one who *is* anyone will ever stay here again.'

'This way, Your Grace,' said the landlord, indicating the stairs, and going ahead of this most difficult guest, who followed him, his unfortunate servant bringing up the rear.

After Max had pronounced the room to be tolerable, and had made some very exacting requests with regard to his dinner, the landlord withdrew, only just falling short of leaving backwards, as from the presence of royalty. Max looked at Alistair, his eyes sparkling, then hastily covered his mouth with a handkerchief as uncontrollable mirth threatened to prove his undoing. Alistair laughed silently, his shoulders shaking.

When they had both regained control of themselves, Max said, 'What now?'

'We have now paved the way very nicely for the last act of this comedy,' said Alistair. 'After the porter has brought your baggage upstairs, I will go down with a despondent air, and say that I have been dismissed. Arrangements have been made to get me to Harwich, so I'll make my way to the appointed rendezvous. In the meantime, you can be as obnoxious as you like, declaring how useless I was, and that you cannot possibly stir another step without a valet.

'Barnes has instructions to appear tomorrow morning at about nine o'clock. He will have a tale to tell of a master who has recently died. He will say that he is on his way to London to find a new situation. No doubt someone will remember that you are in need of a valet.'

'And if not?'

'Improvise.'

'No one with any sense would want to work for me after the way I have been behaving,' Max pointed out.

'Barnes is as used to playing a part as am I,' said Alistair. 'He won't take any of your theatricals to heart, you may be sure.'

Max nodded. 'I'll not deny I've enjoyed playing the role, although it does go against the grain with me.'

The baggage duly arrived and Max eyed it scathingly, pretending to detect that the wrong luggage had been used, Field having foolishly left behind the new receptacles, pale blue, and printed with His Grace's crest, and used the old maroon instead. 'That should do it,' Alistair grinned. 'Max, I must be going.'

'Alistair,' Max replied, his voice holding sudden recognition that now the whole business, which had seemed for a time like a carefree schoolboy jape, had a deadly purpose. 'Be careful, won't you?'

'It's how I survive,' his cousin replied.

'By the way, what do I do if anyone seems to be acting suspiciously, or questions my identity too closely?'

'Kill them,' was the tranquil answer.

Max blinked. 'Godspeed, then.'

'And to you.' Briefly, the two men embraced. Then Alistair opened the door. 'Your Grace, I beg you,' he exclaimed, his voice high with panic.

'Enough!' Max replied in an arrogant tone. 'Just get out of my sight.'

As Alistair appeared in the taproom, the landlord caught his eye. 'Is His Grace comfortable?' he asked anxiously. 'Is there aught I can do?' He glanced over Alistair's shoulder to see that two ladies had entered. Since he surmised that they would certainly not outrank a duke, he decided to make sure that his more exalted guest was attended to before he turned his attention to lesser mortals.

'It's nothing to do with me,' Alistair replied, with the air of a man who is trying to be nonchalant when he feels much more like bursting into tears. 'I have been dismissed.'

'Dismissed?' exclaimed the landlord.

'After five years' service,' Alistair confirmed, lifting his handkerchief to his eyes. 'As for what I am to do now, I have no notion.'

There was an awkward silence. 'You could stay here tonight,' said the landlord grudgingly. 'If'n you have the ready—'

'If he does not, landlord, I will gladly pay for a night's lodging,' said one of the ladies at the door.

The landlord looked at them again as they stepped out of the shadows. Miss Fellowes and Miss Church had been waiting politely until the landlord should be ready to attend to them. 'That's uncommon good of you, ma'am,' he answered, directing his remark to the older lady.

'It is little enough when set against the dreadful life that this poor fellow has had to endure in the clutches of such a tyrant,' said Miss Church, revealing by her voice that it had been she who had spoken originally. She turned to the dismissed valet. 'Believe me, sir, you are well rid of him,' she went on earnestly. 'I saw you earlier at Chelmsford and was very unfavourably impressed with his manner of conducting himself. There are plenty of gentlemen in the world who know how to speak to their servants properly. Make sure that the next gentleman you work for is one of those.'

'You are very good, ma'am,' Alistair responded. 'It is just that I am used to His Grace's little ways.'

'And now you can become used to someone else's,' replied Miss Church briskly. 'I am certain that you will find someone better equipped to show off your skill. Your present master may be a duke, and dressed as fine as fivepence, but he has all the appearance of a brute and a brigand underneath.'

'You are kindness itself, ma'am,' Alistair responded earnestly, making more play with his handkerchief. 'For the immediate future I have an acquaintance living in the town. I shall find lodging with him for, to be sure, I think that staying the night here with my former master in the same inn might very well turn my stomach.'

'That's the spirit,' said Miss Church bracingly, her hazel eyes twinkling. 'Good valets are hard to come by, you know. You may very well find that he will miss you far more than you will miss him.'

'I hope it may be so, ma'am,' Alistair responded, with a little bow, before leaving the inn.

After Alistair had gone, Max stood thoughtfully, staring down at the ring on his little finger. It was Alistair's gold signet ring, worn by the Dukes of Haslingfield, and passed from one to the next only in the event of death. That he should be wearing his cousin's ring seemed ominous in the extreme.

On the next finger to the Haslingfield signet was his own ring, which was of rose gold, set with a particularly fine pearl. He had not acquired it originally with the intention that he should pass it on to an heir. Insensibly, over time, however, it had become a settled thing in his mind that that was what he would do with it.

Seized by a notion that was part superstition and all urgency, he strode to the door, then paused, his hand on the handle. How could he accomplish what he intended without putting his cousin at risk? Glancing swiftly about him, he spotted the bag which contained his own black cloak and soft felt hat. He dragged both out of the bag, threw the cloak around his shoulders and crammed the hat down low on his head, hiding his powdered hair. Then he ran swiftly down the stairs, looking neither to the right nor the left, murmuring a low-voiced but polite 'By your leave, ma'am' to a lady who stood at the entrance, before stepping out into the late dusk.

His actions had only taken minutes, and Alistair had just left the inn yard when Max caught him up. 'A moment,' he said, laying one hand on his arm.

Alistair turned abruptly. 'This isn't wise,' he said in an ominous tone.

'Is any of it?' Max asked. 'I just wanted you to have this.' He handed his cousin the rose-gold ring. 'I'll accept it back in exchange for yours.'

'And you came after me for this?'

Max coloured; fortunately, the dim light concealed the change in his complexion. 'If I have your ring, you might not come back; if *you* have *mine*, you must do so in order to return it.'

With a reluctant grin, Alistair took the ring, then gripped his cousin's hand before turning to walk away.

'Mr Field!' A woman's voice called out through the night.

'Damnation,' said Alistair. Then he turned to his cousin. 'Go, Max; go now.'

Max threw his cloak over his shoulder and merged with the shadows before slipping back into the inn, taking care not to be seen.

Constance Church had been wrestling with her conscience as the duke's misused valet had departed. There was no reason why she should feel responsible for his well-being, or, indeed, for righting the wrongs committed by his master. The fact remained, however, that she had a warm lodging and a good home at her journey's end, whereas the fate of Mr Field seemed far less certain. As she had paused in indecision at the inn door, a man of middle height, muffled up rather more than the mild evening warranted, had muttered a word of apology and swept past her into the yard. At the same time, she had become aware of a conversation taking place between the landlord and her aunt. 'If you will follow me, ladies, I have a very good room available,' he had said politely. 'You'll find it quiet up there as it's right away from the tap.'

Constance had taken one step away from the door, when she suddenly realized that this would be her last chance to help Mr Field. 'One moment,' she had said, before turning to go out into the yard. By the light of the lamps, she could see the former valet in serious talk with the man who had just passed her in the hall. She paused, reluctant to disturb a private conversation. This might be her only opportunity, however, so she ran into the yard, the valet's name on her lips. As she drew closer, the other man turned away and disappeared into the shadows.

'Ma'am?' said Alistair, touching his hat politely. He recognized her as being one of the two ladies who had expressed concern for him a little earlier.

'Mr Field, are you in some desperate trouble?' she asked impulsively.

'Trouble, ma'am?' he echoed, suddenly rather still.

'The man who was here just now; he looked as though he might be threatening you in some way.'

The valet smiled. 'No indeed, ma'am; just a fellow who thought he knew me.'

'You relieve me. Mr Field, I am persuaded that you must surely need more help than you were prepared to admit just now, so I have brought you this.' Constance held out a few coins from her reticule. 'It will enable you to pay for lodging elsewhere, should your friend not be to hand.'

'Ma'am, you are more than kind,' he protested. For all his customary *sang froid*, he was genuinely a little moved.

'No, I insist,' she answered. 'Godspeed.' So saying, she turned and hurried back into the inn.

Alistair grinned, spun one of the coins in the air, caught it, then made off for his rendezvous.

Chapter Five

Miss Fellowes and Miss Church partook of an excellent dinner before retiring. The possibility of the duke's eating in the public dining room had aroused very different emotions in the bosoms of the two ladies. Miss Church had declared herself anxious to confront him so that she could give him a piece of her mind. Hearing of this intention, Miss Fellowes had immediately begun praying that he would not make an appearance, so that an embarrassing scene might be avoided. In the event, they did not see him, so presumably he had dined in his room.

The following morning, the ladies came downstairs just before nine o'clock, intending to break their fast before continuing their journey. As the landlord had predicted, they had found their spacious bedroom very comfortable, and their rest had been undisturbed by noise of merriment from below. They were just thanking their host for his thoughtfulness and making their wishes known to him, when a quietly dressed, respectable man came in and asked if he might be served with a meal. He greeted the ladies with a polite bow, which they returned, before going back to their own conversation.

When the landlord came in with tea for the ladies and ale for his new customer, the man started to make enquiries about conveyances, and the ease of getting to London. 'The gentleman for whom I have been valet has recently passed away,' he explained, 'and I need a new situation.'

Miss Church and Miss Fellowes looked at one another and kept their lips firmly shut. Doubtless the landlord had the same thought in his head, since he said, 'I know of no one living hereabouts in need of a manservant, sir. No doubt you'll find something in London.' Miss Church looked up at him as he was leaving the room, their eyes met, and unmistakably he winked, causing her to hide a smile.

They were all just finishing their breakfast when the sound of raised voices then the slamming of a door was heard from upstairs, followed by running feet. A few moments later, a waiter came in and approached the landlord, who was asking if everyone was satisfied with their meal.

'Beg pardon, sir,' he said, 'but His Dukeship wants to get dressed. My dirty hands won't do, he says.'

'Let's see them, then,' said the landlord.

The waiter held out his hands. 'Mebbe the nails are a bit dirty,' he said doubtfully.

'Rest assured, landlord, that even if your servant's hands had been scrubbed by the Archangel Gabriel himself and dipped in holy water, they would still not be clean enough for that martinet upstairs,' said Miss Church.

The waiter turned to the landlord again. 'What shall I do? He says he won't leave until he's been shaved and dressed, and he won't let me near him.'

'Well, he can't stay here for ever,' exclaimed the landlord, provoked into unaccustomed exasperation.

'You have a gentleman upstairs in need of assistance?' asked the quietly dressed man who had just had breakfast.

'I would assist him out of the window,' said Miss Church bluntly.

'Constance!' exclaimed Miss Fellowes, for this was too much even for one used to her niece's strong views.

'The Duke of Haslingfield is upstairs,' the landlord disclosed. 'He arrived yesterday—'

'And his first action was to dismiss his valet in the most brutal way possible,' interrupted Miss Church.

'Then perhaps he may be looking for another,' said the newcomer thoughtfully.

'Believe me, sir, this will not be a happy situation for you,' said Miss Church earnestly. 'I am sure you would be much better advised to go on to London and find employment there.'

'My niece, if forthright in her views, is essentially correct,' put in Miss Fellowes. 'He was most unpleasant, both in manner and behaviour.'

The man rose to his feet. 'You may be right, ladies,' he replied. 'In the meantime, our kind host clearly needs help to speed this gentleman on his way, so I shall see what I can do.' He left the room and, presumably, ascended the stairs, since his footsteps were too soft to be heard.

Miss Church stood up. 'Shall we go and prepare for our departure?' she said to her aunt.

'Presently, my dear,' Miss Fellowes replied placidly. She smiled at the landlord. 'At my age, it is most unwise to hurry into activity after a meal, do you not agree?'

'Certainly, ma'am,' agreed the landlord, all smiles himself now it appeared that he might soon be rid of his troublesome guest. 'Pray remain for as long as you please. Shall I fetch more coffee?'

'Thank you; and perhaps just a tiny scrap more of toast?'

'What are you doing, Aunt Roberta?' Constance asked, as soon as the landlord had gone to replenish the coffee pot. 'We don't really have time to linger.' They were to travel to Diss that day and dine with friends before staying the night.

'There is no rush, my dear,' Miss Fellowes responded placidly. 'I know that the Scotts keep country hours, but even so, we will not be dining before five. There is plenty of time.' She leaned forward and continued, lowering her voice to a whisper. 'Don't pretend you don't want to hear the end of this tale,' she said, 'because I wouldn't believe you.'

'I do not have the slightest interest in what "His Dukeship" does,' Constance replied scornfully, 'except that I would hate to see this man treated as abominably as poor Mr Field.' Nevertheless she subsided back into her seat, and permitted the landlord to pour her another cup of coffee.

While he was doing so, the man who had breakfasted with them came back into the room. 'I would be obliged if you would send up some hot water so that His Grace may shave,' he said. 'In addition, I shall require somewhere to press His Grace's linen.'

After the upset of the previous day, these familiar needs were well within the landlord's power to supply, and he went immediately to see about attending to them.

There had been something about the proprietary way in which the man had spoken that had caught Constance's attention, and she said suspiciously, 'Surely you are not intending to take a permanent position with that tyrant, sir? If so, I must strongly advise you against it. He may be more pliable this morning because he is desperate for help. Remember, I have seen him at his worst.'

The man smiled slightly. 'We have agreed to see how well we shall suit,' he replied. 'Believe me, if I am not happy in my situation, I shall not stay.'

'You relieve my mind, Mr—?

'My name is Barnes, ma'am,' answered the man, bowing slightly.

'We wish you well, Mr Barnes,' said Miss Fellowes, 'and success in your new post.'

He bowed again, and went back upstairs.

'We might as well leave now,' said Constance, getting up. 'That brute will be another hour at least before Mr Barnes has got him shaved and dressed. We cannot wait as long as that.'

Miss Fellowes sighed. 'I suppose not. I do dislike not knowing the end of the story.'

The two ladies thanked the landlord and went upstairs in order to make their final preparations before setting off. It was the first time that they had stayed at this particular inn and both agreed that they would be perfectly content to do so again. 'The drama enlivened our stay, if nothing else,' said Miss Fellowes as they left their room.

'We could hardly expect the landlord to arrange such excitement for our entertainment on every visit,' Constance replied. They were just passing the door of the room in which the duke was staying, when there was a burst of laughter from inside, which ended as abruptly as it had begun.

The two ladies glanced at one another. Such laughter would never proceed from Mr Barnes, who had appeared to be a very proper valet. On the other hand, men as high in the instep as the duke had appeared to be seldom laughed either, considering such displays to be a vulgarity. 'This good humour augurs well for Mr

Barnes,' Miss Fellowes whispered, as they descended the stairs.

They settled their account with the landlord, who gave orders for their coachman to be alerted ready for their departure. It was while they were waiting for the horses to be put to that Constance suddenly realized she had forgotten to put on her locket. 'You must have placed it in your box with your other things,' said her aunt. 'Indeed, I am more than half convinced that I saw you do so.'

Constance paused in indecision. 'You may be right,' she said. 'All the same, I will just run upstairs to look. It will only take me a few minutes, and I really don't want to lose it. It was Mama's.'

She hurried back up to the chamber that they had so recently vacated, just ahead of Mr Barnes, who was obviously carrying some freshly pressed linen to his new master. A quick survey of the room yielded no sign of the locket. She looked around thoughtfully. She was perfectly certain that she would never have put it in her box as her aunt had suggested, since it was something that she wore every day.

Where had she placed it the night before? She closed her eyes in order to picture clearly how they had disposed of their things. It was not difficult. Whereas she abjured all kinds of cosmetics and skin treatments, her aunt loved pots and potions. Her dressing table at home was a jumble of jars of different sizes and colours. To stay with her on a journey was to surrender the same space for her use. In order to avoid losing her precious locket amongst the detritus, therefore, Constance had placed it on the mantelshelf.

She hurried across the room and smiled with relief as she saw it exactly where she had placed it the night before. She stood looking into the mirror over the fireplace as she fastened it around her neck; then she heard voices. She glanced about her, startled, uncertain at first as to where the speakers might be. Then she realized that the voices she was hearing must be coming from the next room where, perhaps, someone was also looking into the mirror. Obviously in some way the fireplace and chimney were conducting the sound from one room to the other.

'You're a marvel, Barnes,' one voice said. 'You even make me look like a duke.'

'As indeed you are, Your Grace,' the other voice responded.

There was another laugh, similar to the one that Constance had heard before.

Her chain fastened securely, she moved away from the fireplace and left the room, not wanting to eavesdrop further. At least, she reflected, she had something to report to her aunt.

'The duke is satisfied with his new servant's efforts,' she said as they drove out of the inn yard. She explained the circumstances in which she had chanced to overhear their conversation.

'Perhaps Mr Field and the duke simply did not suit,' Miss Fellowes suggested. 'There are people who bring out the worst in each other, are there not? Think of Mrs Wrangle.'

Mrs Wrangle had been housekeeper to Mr and Miss Fellowes for just one year, and she and her employers had never got on. Mr Fellowes had complained that she would not leave his study alone, whilst his sister, an amateur artist, had often found her paints and brushes rearranged, and things washed up which had been set aside for use later. The woman had always justified her interference with a self-satisfied smile, standing with her plump hands folded across her waist. They had all been glad when she had found a new situation where the master had no study, and the mistress had no messy pastimes. In her new employment, she was praised to the skies for her diligence and co-operation.

'Yes, that is true,' Constance agreed. Something about the short overheard conversation had unsettled her; she could not think what it might be.

Max took another look at his reflection before leaving his chamber. He had never employed a valet, since his chosen life, spent largely on board ship, was not such as to make the engagement of one necessary or even sensible. On dry land, he customarily wore clothes into which he could shrug himself without assistance. Now, donning garments that had been measured to fit him exactly, for the first time he began to see a use for one.

His hair, always inclined to be a trifle unruly, often draped his shoulders, or was sometimes held back with a kerchief for convenience, making him look rather like a pirate, as his mother was wont to complain. Today, it had been tamed, tied back in a neat queue, and powdered. By means of a hand mirror held by Barnes at a convenient angle, he could see that its wild corkscrew curls had been coaxed so that they lay back on his collar in a neat roll. His coat, of dark-green cloth, fitted without a single wrinkle, and his waistcoat, of pale-green satin with silver thread, was cut straight in the fashionable manner. His cravat was snowy white, immaculately tied and trimmed with a fringe of rich lace. The one thing that really made him pull a face was the patch placed at the corner of his mouth. On reflection, he decided that to make a fuss about it when he was enduring all the rest would be a trifle absurd.

He walked away from the mirror. The hessian boots he was wearing with his cream-coloured pantaloons met with his approval, but he did not care for the silver tassels and said so.

'They are *de rigeur,* Your Grace, I assure you,' said Barnes earnestly.

'Very well, then,' Max sighed, privately resolving to cut them off and dispose of them in Cromer, along with the patch and the hair powder. 'Am I to have breakfast, or am I too fashionably languid to eat anything?'

'Oh no, indeed, Your Grace,' Barnes assured him. 'I have given orders for you to be served with a roll and preserves.'

Max raised an eyebrow. 'A roll and preserves? Good God! Is that all Alistair has to break his fast? No wonder he looks like a willow wand.'

'No indeed, Your Grace,' Barnes repeated seriously. 'He also has chocolate, and sometimes he has two rolls.'

'Barnes, you cannot convince me that dukes never eat substantial breakfasts,' Max declared. 'Bring me ham and eggs on the double – *and* I'll have two rolls as well.'

Barnes permitted himself a small smile. 'I think that might be arranged,' he responded.

The hardest thing Max next had to contend with was to stand back and allow Barnes to make all the arrangements for their departure. He thought about the last time he had arrived in London after a long voyage. After disembarking at Legal Quays, he had walked into the city and, following a brief conversation with his man of business, had set out for Leicestershire on horseback, his belongings in a cloak bag strapped to his saddle. He had rested at an inn over-night, at which halt he had ordered his own accommodation, dined in the public room and downed a few drinks with the locals. The following morning he had risen betimes, breakfasted on home-cured bacon, paid his shot, and gone on his way after saddling his own horse. He had barely had to depend upon anyone but himself. This morning, he had nothing to do. By a strange irony, he found it far more stressful than taking everything into his own hands, and he could feel his brow creasing into impatient lines, and his fists clench-ing. Catching sight of his face in a mirror in the hall, he knew that his expression was nothing like that of a languid aristocrat.

He thought about how on one occasion, during one of his voyages, he had been obliged to enter into negotiations with a captain of another ship. Although Captain Santos had declared himself to be an honest merchant, Max had been convinced that there had been less than the width of the blade of his knife – which he kept in his boot as a precaution – between the so-called merchant and a pirate. It had taken the fellow some little time to come to a decision, and Max had known that to give away his feelings one way or the other might be fatal to the negotiations. He had kept his face calm and his body still, despite every temptation to jump up and down and demand a response. Eventually, he and Santos had come to an agreement, accepting most of his, Max's, terms. It had been a valuable lesson. He remembered that lesson now, as he willed his features to relax, then strolled past Barnes, who was settling with the landlord.

'I trust Your Grace was satisfied,' said that worthy, with a low bow.

'A very tolerable stay,' Max murmured. 'Very tolerable. I shall come again.'

'Not too soon, I hope,' muttered the waiter, as the carriage swept out of the inn yard.

'Pipe down until you see how much he left,' said the landlord, opening his hand so that the other man could see the glint of gold.

'Blimey!' exclaimed the waiter. 'If he wasn't an archbishop after all!'

Chapter Six

For the next night, the ducal party was to stay at the Scole Inn just outside Diss. As they travelled, Max tried to draw Barnes out over some of Alistair's adventures. Maddeningly, he found the man to be discretion itself, as his cousin had said. He had taken the precaution of bringing a copy of Defoe's *A Tour Through England and Wales*, intending to familiarize himself with the part of the world to which he was travelling, and had never visited before. He read about the dangers of the Norfolk coast with great interest. He had heard Cromer Bay referred to by seamen as the Devil's Throat, so this was no surprise to him. He was interested to discover that along the coast, Defoe had noted that all the barns and outbuildings seemed to be constructed from wood salvaged from wrecked ships.

He then became very absorbed in Defoe's report of a severe maritime disaster almost exactly one hundred years before, when, through a mixture of unwise decisions and unfortunate accidents, 200 vessels and over 1,000 lives were lost in the region of Happisburgh. He counted himself very fortunate never to have been shipwrecked, usually thanks to Abe Collings's admirable seamanship. Even so, he had had one or two close escapes, in which he had been made to feel very puny when confronted with the might of wind and waves. 'Poor souls,' he murmured. 'Poor souls.'

'Your Grace?' questioned Barnes, looking up from his own copy of James Bruce's *Travels to Discover the Source of the Nile*.

'Just something I was reading,' Max replied. Glancing down the page, his attention was caught by the name of the very place to which they were going. '"*Cromer is a market-town close to the shore of this dangerous coast,'* he read. *"'I know nothing it is famous for (besides its being thus the terror of the sailors) except good lobsters, which are taken on that coast in great numbers."* We must have some of those, Barnes. Are you partial to fish?'

'Exceedingly partial, Your Grace,' replied Barnes, permitting himself a smile.

Max laid his book on the seat beside him. 'Barnes, you don't need to call me that when no one's around, you know,' he said, smiling impishly.

'If I call you Mr Persault when we are alone, there is a danger that I may do so when others are by,' Barnes answered seriously. 'Better to maintain the pretence between us at all times – Your Grace.'

Max nodded ruefully. 'You're wiser than I am,' he agreed. 'Alistair told me I might depend on you; so tell me if I'm doing aught to give the game away, won't you, there's a good chap?'

'You may depend upon me, Your Grace,' said the valet politely, before both men turned back to their books.

On their arrival at the Scole Inn, Max allowed Barnes to assist him from his carriage, and sauntered in, according the landlord a brief nod, before following the valet up to the magnificent room that had been allotted to the most illustrious guest that the innkeeper could remember entertaining for a very long time.

Max was also provided with a private dining room, in which he ate in splendid isolation. To give himself something to do, he brought his copy of Daniel Defoe to the table, and amused himself with flicking through the pages to try to discover which of the many Norfolk places the famous traveller had visited had most incurred his disapproval. To his great disappointment, Defoe appeared to find little in the county to criticize. He had words of praise for Norwich, calling it *'an antient, large, rich and populous city'*. His approval of the cathedral meant little to Max, who did not have very much enthusiasm for architecture in general. His interest was caught by Defoe's description of the navigability of the rivers Yare and Waveney. He would have liked to have spent some time exploring them, but concluded reluctantly that to do so might easily draw unwelcome attention. Once Alistair had returned safely, he promised himself that he would make such an exploration.

The door opened as the waiter came in with a tray, and coincidentally, there was a burst of laughter from the taproom. Max turned his head towards the sound. Oh, how infinitely preferable to be one of that laughing number instead of sitting here with only his own company for entertainment! He would have felt very much more at home in the taproom with a pint at his elbow and a hand of cards before him, than here in this solitary state. The waiter, evidently misunderstanding his expression, murmured apologetically, saying something about going to hush them up.

What would a duke do now, Max thought to himself. He waved a careless hand in the air. 'It's of no consequence,' he said. Then, in a moment of inspiration, he took some gold out of his pocket. 'For their continued enjoyment,' he said, handing it to the waiter. 'Tell them to try to keep the noise down.'

The next time the waiter came in, he brought with him the thanks of all the drinkers present; and for the rest of his meal, Max had the very entertaining experience of hearing bursts of jollity punctuated by someone saying 'Hush!' very loudly. The consequence was that those working at the Scole Inn had a very different impression from the staff at the Swan at Stanway, and spoke ever afterwards of His Grace of Haslingfield as a very open-handed gentleman.

The incident had the effect of making Max feel rather restless. As he listened to the laughter, he recalled an occasion when he had been a schoolboy at Eton. It had been only a few short days before Alistair had left school, and he and his chosen friends were planning to go into the town and celebrate their impending freedom at one of the local hostelries. By this time, the two cousins were living in the same house, Alistair having a room of his own, Max sharing with a number of other boys.

It was hardly likely that anyone in authority would concern themselves with the actions of young men so soon to be out of their sphere of influence, so the excursion had been planned without any recourse to secrecy. Max had known what was afoot. He wished his cousin well, and would miss him when he returned the following term and Alistair was no longer there; he had not expected to be included in this outing. He had been much surprised, therefore, when, as he was dropping off to sleep, a hand had touched his shoulder and a voice had whispered in his ear, 'Come on, coz; time to go.' Obediently, he had scrambled into his clothes, being careful not to arouse those with whom he shared a room.

It was by no means the first time that he had gone out without leave. He had made his escape by the simple expedient of climbing down the drainpipe, helped at the bottom by Alistair and his friends. They had spent a convivial evening at a local hostelry, and returned in the early hours of the following morning. It had been quite impossible for Max to scramble up the drainpipe, given the merry state that he was in. A solution was found by Alistair and his friends, who had crowded around him, shielding him from view, and had hustled him back into the house under the very eyes of the dame in charge, who had emerged sleepily from her chamber and warned them not to wake the younger boys who were already abed.

After a few moments' thought, Max got decisively to his feet and rang the bell. 'I have finished now,' he told the waiter. 'You may clear away.' He left the room with a slight inclination of the head to the man, who had sprung to open it for him, and walked slowly up the stairs to his room where, as he had suspected, Barnes was tidying his things, having eaten his own meal already.

'I am feeling quite fatigued,' Max said, raising his hand to his mouth as if to stifle a yawn. 'I would be glad if you would leave those things now. Just help me out of my coat, there's a good fellow. You can have the rest of the evening to yourself. I don't want to be disturbed again until morning.'

Anyone intimate with Max would have been quite suspicious at the extraordinary suggestion that he should be fatigued enough to retire at eight o'clock after a simple coach journey. Fortunately, Barnes did not know his new employer well, so he simply took the coat away to be pressed and wished Max a peaceful night.

As soon as Barnes had gone, Max grinned, and went to the trunk under the window in which some of his clothes were stored. Although most of his things had been chosen with his character of a dandy in mind, he had managed to persuade Alistair that he would need some country wear also. He had had an additional point to make. 'What of when you eventually appear?' he had asked. 'I may need to meet you or go on some errand. I must be able to escape notice, or simply slip away.' Alistair had conceded the point, and therefore, Max had succeeded in procuring for himself a coat of corbeau-coloured cloth, with a similarly dark waistcoat, a pair of buckskin breeches, and some serviceable boots. All of these he had taken good care to ensure were items which he could put on without assistance. From the very beginning, he had harboured a suspicion that at some point he might want to escape.

His clothes selected, he stripped off his shirt, poured water from the ewer into the basin, and pulled off the silk bag which enclosed his hair. He dipped his whole head into the water and washed off the mixture of starch and grease with which it had been covered. That done, he shook his wet hair back, sighing with relief. When this masquerade is over, he told himself, my hair won't feel the tiniest grain of powder again for as long as I live.

Having rubbed his hair dry with the towel provided, he donned a plainer shirt than the one he had been wearing, together with the other garments selected. That done, he took out the hat and cloak that he had worn when he had given his ring to Alistair. He also picked up a pistol, and his sword, a far more workmanlike, serviceable item than the dress sword which lay in the other trunk. He glanced in the mirror. His corkscrew curls, encouraged by the recent wetting, massed wildly about his face and shoulders. He grinned. Anyone looking less like a duke would have been hard to imagine. He put on the hat, tilting it carefully to shade his face, and threw his cloak over his shoulder.

His room lay at the front of the house, so to climb out of his own window would be far too conspicuous. A careful listen at the door, and a swift glance outside revealed that no one was in the passage. He left his room, closing and locking the door behind him, and made for the window at the end of the corridor. Thanking his stars that it opened easily, he climbed out and, with the facility of one who had been climbing the rigging for much of his adult life, scrambled down the drainpipe to the ground.

*

The house in which Mr and Mrs Scott resided was situated in the middle of Diss, just off the marketplace. Its owner was often heard to remark ironically that all their friends used his home as a staging post, which meant that he was never obliged to exert himself in order to visit anybody else. In truth, he and his wife were delighted to welcome guests, and since Mrs Scott and Miss Fellowes were childhood friends, they soon had their heads together. Mr Scott glanced over at the two plump, grey-haired ladies who were deep in conversation.

'It never fails to amaze me how much they find to talk about,' he said to Constance, as they stood looking out of the window, watching all the comings and goings. Mr Scott was a short, spare man with a rather long, gaunt face which was redeemed by a mobile, humorous mouth. 'They write every week, so I would be surprised if there were any news to tell.'

'Ah, but Aunt Roberta has all the excitement of the journey to recount,' she replied. 'Such adventures as we have had.' She told her host about the objectionable duke, his unfortunate employee, and the foolhardy man who had offered to become his valet.

'Haslingfield,' said Mr Scott thoughtfully. 'I have heard something of the man, and none of it to his credit.'

'Indeed,' murmured Constance, trying not to sound pleased at having her opinion supported.

'By all accounts he's a dandy, a gambler and a wastrel,' Scott continued. 'I wonder what brought him into the wilds of Norfolk?'

'His carriage looked new, and he was attended by a number of servants,' said Constance thoughtfully. 'Perhaps he is making a grand tour of his property.'

'Is that what *you* would do?' asked Mr Scott quizzically, before responding to a remark from his wife.

Suddenly, Constance realized what had struck her as odd about the overheard conversation between the duke and his valet. 'You even make *me* look like a duke,' the nobleman had said, emphasizing the fourth word. Why would he do that?

The family dined at five, and by eight o'clock, they were back in the drawing room with the excellent view onto the street. Constance was fascinated by it, and after tea had been served and drunk, she wandered again to the window to look outside. Although it was getting late, the evenings had drawn out, and she could see very clearly what was going on. There had been a market that day, and even though all the wares had long been cleared away, there were still extra people in the town, catching up on news, or perhaps celebrating a good day's sale.

'When we first came to live here, I could not keep away from the window either,' Mrs Scott confessed. 'There is always something to see.'

'It would be the perfect place to sit if one were not well enough to go out,' Constance responded, turning back briefly to the others in the room.

'That is so,' Mrs Scott agreed. 'I remember last year being confined to the house with a stubborn cold which would not go away, and I scarcely moved away from that window.'

'One could also paint or sketch from here,' put in Miss Fellowes. 'The light is good.' Her relations were wont to say teasingly that she looked far too well-fed and contented to be an artist. The truth was that Miss Fellowes was quite gifted with pens and brush, so much so that she was often asked to give private lessons.

Constance smiled as she turned back to the window. It certainly was a fascinating scene, full of activity and colour. As she stood there, her eye was caught by a fragment of spider's web which must have been missed when the room had been cleaned, and she reached a hand up to brush it away.

As she did so, all at once she became conscious of being watched and, glancing down, she saw a man on horseback looking directly up at her. He was dressed in a dark cloak and a broad-brimmed hat, worn atop a mass of very dark curly hair which tangled wildly about his shoulders. He held the reins of his horse in his left hand, whilst his right, ungloved like the other, rested lightly on his hip. Her attention caught, she remained in the same position, her hand extended towards the top of the lower panel of the window. For a long moment, their eyes locked; then to her astonishment, he raised his right hand to his lips and blew her an extravagant kiss.

She gasped and stepped back from the window, her hand

involuntarily going to her breast in shock. Fortunately, at that moment, the rest of the occupants of the room were occupied and did not notice. When she stepped back cautiously, she found that the impertinent man had gone.

She thought about the incident when she was in bed that night, trying in vain to fall asleep for what seemed like hours. She was a good-looking woman, with light-brown hair, warm hazel eyes set in an oval face, a determined chin and a well-shaped mouth, and she was accustomed to hear herself described as handsome rather than pretty. Her firm, no-nonsense manner had deterred more men than it had attracted, and she had never been the kind of female with whom anyone had ever thought that it would be wise to take a liberty. Gestures such as the man in the square had made that evening, therefore, were something of a novelty. 'Shocking insolence!' she exclaimed out loud. It then occurred to her that the movement of her hand might have been misinterpreted and that he might – shameful thought – have supposed that she was waving to him! This was such a mortifying notion that it effectively banished any idea of going to sleep. She lit her candle and took up her book, intending to tire herself out so thoroughly that she would then simply drop off.

Her efforts met with little success. Her thoughts had been so disturbing that she found that she had turned over two whole pages and then did not have the slightest idea what she had read.

Finally conceding defeat, she concluded that by attempting to go to sleep, she would at least be resting her eyes. She blew out the candle, therefore, and tried to send herself off by remembering the different varieties of flowers cultivated in her uncle's garden at West Runton.

She must have drifted off eventually, for she found herself dreaming of Cambridge. In her dream, she was standing in her father's study overlooking the quadrangle of Trinity College. Some students were making their way through, celebrating noisily, and she heard her father's voice saying that he must go and disperse them.

She was aroused from sleep by a noise outside. For a moment or two, she was not sure whether the noise she had heard was real, or simply a part of her dream. Now used to country living, the night sounds to which she had become accustomed were the cries of owls, foxes and other occasional night creatures. By way of contrast, Cambridge nights were indeed occasionally disturbed by the sound of unruly students going back to college after an evening's roistering. Momentarily, she imagined herself back in the ancient university town. Then, as she returned to full wakefulness, she remembered where she was, and at the same time realized that some kind of altercation was going on outside. She rose from her bed, and, going to the window, lifted up the corner of the curtain to see what was happening.

It was a moonlit night, so the scene that was being played out in the street beneath could be seen quite clearly. There appeared to be an argument of some sort taking place between four men. As she watched, two things became clear to her. The first was that the disagreement was between one of the men and the remaining three. The second, which caused her to gasp out loud, was that the man on his own was the same rogue who had blown her a kiss earlier that evening.

It was not long before what had appeared to be just a verbal altercation became more physical. One of the group of three aimed a blow at the lone man which he parried easily, blocking it with his right arm raised, whilst with his left fist he jabbed at one of the other men. What followed after that happened so quickly, that Constance blinked in surprise; for in less time than she could have imagined was possible, two of the assailants were on the floor and the other was fleeing, hurried on his way by a threatening gesture from the buccaneer. She was still looking down at the scene when he turned his head and looked up in her direction, his cloak swirling about him. Swiftly, she dropped the curtain. It would never do for him to suppose that she was looking at him!

For some time after the noise outside had ceased, Constance stood beside the window, lost in thought. What would have happened had she been the kind of light woman whom he had obviously supposed her to be earlier? Would they have enjoyed a desperate flirtation, with perhaps a kiss or two? Would she have run down even now to congratulate him on his escape from harm, and reward him with another embrace?

She blushed in the darkness. What was she thinking, indulging in such improper fantasies over a passing stranger, never to be seen again? Severely quelling an unaccountable and quite illogical twinge of regret, she climbed back into bed and this time was soon fast asleep.

Chapter Seven

The following morning, Barnes greeted Max with a cup of chocolate and a reproachful stare. 'Your Grace,' he murmured in carefully neutral tones.

For response, Max yawned and stretched luxuriously. 'My thanks, Barnes. There can surely be no sweeter smell than that of one's morning chocolate.'

'Indeed, Your Grace?' Barnes responded, hovering as Max pulled himself up into a sitting position.

He had had a splendid time the previous evening. He had hired a horse with the greatest of ease. The groom with whom he had spoken had plainly made no connection between the aristocrat who had entered the inn earlier, and the devil-may-care fellow in search of a mount for the evening.

He had ridden the few miles into Diss, and had set about finding some entertainment. The evening had begun promisingly with that delightful exchange with the rather attractive-looking young woman in the window of a town house. It had continued with a convivial drink at the White Horse, and a few games of cards, from which he had risen a modest winner. Some of those from whom he had won money had resented the fact, and they had thought to ambush him as he prepared to leave Diss. They wouldn't be trying that again in a hurry, he thought to himself, rubbing his knuckles, which were slightly grazed. Then, just as he had chased the last rogue away, he had glanced up, and he could have sworn that he had caught another glimpse of the intriguing watcher whom he had seen earlier.

Who was she? he asked himself. Perhaps the daughter of some well-to-do merchant or attorney, well guarded and protected, and no doubt longing for a bit of excitement. A pity that circumstances had not permitted him to oblige her! Fleetingly, she had reminded him of someone; even now, he could not think of whom.

Now, as he sat up to drink his chocolate, he could see the havoc that he had wrought the previous evening. The clothes that he had been wearing when Barnes had left him were thrown carelessly onto a chair, all higgledy-piggledy. Those that he had put on for his outing he had laid down on another, from which half of them had fallen onto the floor. His hat was lying in the same corner into which he had tossed it in the early hours of the morning. Various others of his possessions were strewn about the room. Max looked around guiltily. 'Lord, I appear to have made rather a mess in here, Barnes. My apologies.'

'It is soon remedied, Your Grace,' Barnes replied. 'However, had I known Your Grace wanted to change, or needed anything further, I could easily have given assistance.' As he picked up the neckerchief which Max had knotted loosely about his neck the previous evening, he looked straight at the man sitting up in bed. Suddenly, Max was convinced that the valet had a fairly good idea of what he had been up to.

'Barnes, I had to escape,' he pleaded. 'This prim and proper existence will drive me mad if I can't ever get away.'

Barnes paused in his tidying activities. 'The whole purpose of this masquerade is to give the illusion that the Duke of Haslingfield is travelling to Cromer,' he said. 'Forgive me if I venture to say that there is very little point in constructing a story if you act in such a way as to destroy it.'

'Barnes, I'm not a fool,' Max answered. 'My life has had its share of adventure, and its moments when secrecy has been vital. Believe me, I was very careful. I rinsed off my powder, and wore my plainest clothes.'

'And how did you leave the inn, Your Grace?'

'Out of the window at the end of the passage and down the drainpipe.'

Barnes looked even more disapproving, had that been possible. 'It is a blessing you did not miss your footing, Your Grace.'

'I have climbed the rigging of a three-master just ahead of a howling gale, in order to furl the sails,' Max said calmly. 'If I couldn't scramble down a drainpipe from a first-floor window, I should be very ashamed of myself.'

Barnes permitted himself a small smile. 'You have vast experience that is unknown to me,' he replied. 'However, I have the interests of my master very much at heart. You must forgive me if this leads me to be more cautious than perhaps you feel to be necessary.'

'You cannot possibly be more concerned for Alistair's safety than am I,' Max told him. He leaned back against his pillows. 'By God, I feel rested,' he declared. 'Don't worry; I shall behave myself today. What's the weather like?'

'The day is fine and bright – a good day for travelling, Your Grace.'

From Diss, the plan was to skirt Norwich, and spend the night at a less frequented inn just outside the city. Max would have liked to push on to Cromer, but was advised against it by the coachman. 'There's no turnpike, Your Grace,' he said regretfully. 'We'll not be making such swift progress, I fear.'

His fears proved to be justified. After they had left Norwich behind, the roads deteriorated considerably, and at times, they were obliged to slow to a walking pace, in order to negotiate the potholes in the road. Max, becoming bored with this mode of travel, closed his eyes. To his great surprise, and despite the jerking of the carriage, he fell asleep, and found himself dreaming that he was obliged to go to court for some important function. Barnes, who had apparently grown a huge mane of bright-orange hair, was dressing him in garments of pale-green satin which, although they had been measured for him, did not seem to fit. The shirt in particular caused problems, as although it had sleeves, which were far too long, there was no aperture through which to put his head. He appeared to be the only one who found this to be a problem, however, as Barnes was urging him to dress with all expediency, since the king was expected. Then, as he was struggling to find a way out of the shirt, there was a knock at the door and the king himself came in, bearing a marked resemblance to the landlord of the Swan – although how Max could know it when he was still trapped inside the shirt was impossible to say.

'You, sir, are a disgrace,' said the king, shaking his arm. 'A disgrace! Disgrace grace ... grace....'

'Your Grace! Your Grace! Pray, wake up, sir!'

Max opened his eyes to find that Barnes was leaning over him, looking anxious. 'Was I making a commotion, Barnes?' he asked.

'You were becoming a little agitated, Your Grace. I was afraid that you might fall off the seat.' As if to corroborate his fears, the carriage lurched violently, before moving on again at a snail's pace.

'How far have we travelled since I fell asleep?' Max asked suspiciously.

'Two or three miles,' the valet answered.

'Two or three? God almighty, this is intolerable!' Max exclaimed wrathfully. 'I could walk to Cromer more quickly.'

A few moments later, there was another lurch, and the carriage halted. After a brief wait, Max opened the door and sprang down lightly, regardless of Barnes's protests. 'What's to do?' he asked the coachman, who had got down from his seat in order to investigate the problem.

As he was speaking, he heard the sound of a horse's hoofs, and looked up to see an African approaching on horseback, his straight-backed carriage one of dignified grace. He wore his own hair unpowdered and was dressed in a squirrel-brown coat and breeches, with a darker-coloured waistcoat and a beaver hat. As he came closer, he grinned broadly. 'Your Grace,' he said, his voice deep and rich. He inclined his head in a dignified bow before dismounting, and passing the reins over his mount's head so it could graze.

'Okoro,' said Max, only just repressing an answering grin. 'In a good hour. You see us in some difficulty.'

'Indeed, Your Grace?'

'Indeed. In fact, this journey has been one problem after another. I have been obliged to turn off that useless valet, Field, and feared for a time that I might be stranded at Colchester with no one to dress me. Fortunately, my new man is a marvel.' He led Okoro over to the coach, where Barnes was still seated. 'Okoro, this is Barnes, my new valet. Barnes, this is Abdas Okoro, my secretary.' He paused as the two men acknowledged one another. 'Barnes, I believe you said that your former master trusted you implicitly. I trust Okoro to the same degree. You may be similarly confident in him.'

The African inclined his head again. 'And I in Mr Barnes, I'm sure,' he said. 'With your permission, I'll help with the horses, Your Grace.' Max, resisting the temptation to join him, nodded carelessly and watched him approach the groom, who was releasing the carriage horses from their harness.

Abdas Okoro carried himself like royalty, but he had never told Max precisely how exalted was his lineage. Along with others from his village, he had been seized and sold into slavery. The ship on which he had been imprisoned had been attacked by pirates and sunk in a sea skirmish. The *Lady Marion* had arrived on the scene in time to pick up survivors, of which Abdas had been one of only a handful. None of his family members had survived the disaster. Perhaps this might have been the reason why, given the choice as to his fate, he had elected to remain with the *Lady Marion*, learning the various tasks on board ship as Max had done, showing his keen intelligence by his attitude and his initiative.

That had been five years before. In the intervening time, Okoro had learned to speak English, as well as to read and write. Accompanying Max on many voyages, he had proved his worth over and over again.

On one occasion, early on in their association, Max had gone ashore in a foreign port in search of a certain merchant, and due to an error of judgement, had found himself in a highly insalubrious spot, under attack by four villainous ruffians. He was preparing to acquit himself as well as possible, determined not to go down without putting up a fight. All at once, the attitude of the men had changed as the athletic-looking African had appeared from nowhere and had crouched back to back with Max, sword in hand. The two of them must have looked far too formidable to tackle, and the four ruffians had fled.

'My thanks,' Max had said, turning to Okoro. 'I didn't realize you had learned to use a sword.'

Okoro had grinned, his teeth shining white in his ebony face. He had held up the sword. 'This is the end I hold, right?' he had said, pointing to the hilt with the other hand.

Max had burst out laughing, and clapped him on the back. From that point on, he had attended to the other man's fencing tuition personally. The next time they had been in a similar situation, Okoro had disarmed his opponent with ease.

Since that time, the African had become Max's right-hand man. At first paid a wage commensurate with his responsibilities, he was now the master of a comfortable independence by dint of certain wise investments, mostly made through Boughton, and a ship owner in his own right.

Max turned to the coachman, who was still examining the front wheel furthest from the bank. The man straightened, and touched his forelock. 'A cracked felloe, Your Grace,' he said apologetically.

Max's heavy brows drew together. 'The devil, you say,' he said, joining the man and bending down to examine the problem. There was indeed a deep crack running along the wooden framework of the wheel. It looked as if it might widen with every possible jolt. 'This is a new carriage!' Max exclaimed wrathfully, as he drew himself up to his full height, and stared at the coachman.

'I'm ... I'm very sorry, Your Grace,' said the coachman anxiously, taking a short step backwards. He had heard how this haughty nobleman had dismissed his previous valet, and did not want to suffer the same fate.

'I'm sure you are,' Max replied, briefly forgetting his role and speaking as one exasperated man to another. 'Damned inconvenient for both of us. Can this take us as far as the next town, do you think?'

Relieved at not being blamed for this mischance, the coachman bent down to have another look. 'I wouldn't advise it, Your Grace,' he said. 'Not laden, anywise. You see this crack? I reckon it's owing to a fault in the wood.'

'Then what do you suggest we do?' Max asked him.

'I could walk to the nearest town, and bring another carriage back to transport Your Grace and Mr Barnes and the luggage,' the coachman ventured. 'Your own carriage would probably get there unladen, where we could find a wheelwright and have the wheel mended or replaced.'

'Okoro could ride into town and save you walking,' Max pointed out. He glanced round to see the African and the groom leading the horses to a nearby stream where they could take refreshment.

'I'd as soon make the arrangements for the repair myself, if Your Grace is agreeable,' the coachman answered. 'And I don't want anyone but me driving this carriage – not in the condition it's in.'

Given the freedom to consult only his own wishes, Max would probably have chosen to walk with the coachman. Unfortunately, he had Barnes and his disguise to consider. He sighed. 'Let it be so,' he said, waving a hand resignedly. At least, he reflected, the longer they spent on the road, the less time he would have to pass himself off as lord of the manor.

Chapter Eight

Constance and her aunt had spent the night at Norwich. They had made an early start in order to get to Marsham in good time and return Mrs Brewer's post chaise. There they had accepted her offer of cakes and wine, before collecting Patch and the gig from her stable.

They had refused her invitation to stay for the night, pleading the need to get to Cromer. In fact, they intended to stop off in Aylsham and do some shopping before spending the night at the Black Boys. 'I can't help feeling guilty because I know she is so lonely,' said Miss Fellowes, as they waved goodbye to their tearful-looking hostess.

'We can invite her to dine with us instead,' said Constance, as she took up the reins and pointed Patch in the direction of home. 'I cannot and will not sleep in her house again. Her beds are lumpy; and as for what I saw that night, it was far too big to be a mouse!'

She was still speaking when they rounded the bend and saw a carriage standing at the side of the road. As luck would have it, they witnessed the very moment when the coachman took an involuntary step backwards, fearing his employer's possible anger. 'Devil take him!' Miss Church exclaimed wrathfully. 'It's a wonder anyone remains with him for more than five minutes! I declare, under his fine clothes he's nothing but a common bully.'

'I wonder how poor Mr Barnes has fared,' said Miss Fellowes. Then, seeing that her niece was bringing Patch to a halt, she added quickly, 'Oh pray, Connie, don't interfere!'

'Interfere? They are plainly in distress. I must offer assistance to fellow travellers,' she answered, reining in the horse as she called out, 'Can we help in any way?'

Max looked up at the two ladies in the gig. At the inns where they had stopped, he had been preoccupied, first with the need to get Alistair off safely, and then by the requirement to play the part allotted to him. Consequently, although Miss Church and Miss Fellowes recognized him at once, he had only a vague idea of having seen them somewhere before.

'You are very good, madam,' he said, bowing with his best ducal flourish, whilst maintaining an air of hauteur. 'As you see, we have come to grief.'

'Yes, I do see,' Miss Church replied. 'I also noticed that you were in the process of blaming your coachman for the difficulty.'

'Blaming him?' Max echoed, rather taken aback, because he had not been doing any such thing. 'Indeed, madam—'

'Please do not try to pretend that you were not,' Constance replied, enjoying this pleasant feeling of superiority which sprang partly from his mishap and partly from the fact that he was obliged to look up at her. 'I saw the poor fellow flinch as if he expected to be struck! And no wonder, if he witnessed the heartless way in which you dismissed your poor valet!'

Max stared at her. In spite of everything that Alistair had said, he had really not expected their movements to arouse any interest. He now perceived how mistaken he had been. In a rural area such as this, any stranger might be noticed. He could not afford to allow any attention to turn to suspicion, especially when Alistair's safety was at stake. He raised his brows. 'My good woman, you are speaking of matters of which you know nothing.'

'Nothing?' she retorted. 'When I witnessed your inhumanity for myself? That poor dismissed valet was as much one of God's creatures as you are, and with as much right to decent treatment.'

One consequence of the training to which Max had subjected himself under Abe Collings had been a real appreciation of the difficulties experienced by ordinary sailors. Collings was firm but humane in his approach, and severe punishments were reserved for those who endangered the safety of the ship and its crew by their actions. Life aboard ship as a working seaman was very hard work, as Max well knew. To exclaim 'Hear hear' in response to the young lady's words as his instincts demanded, however, could well involve him in exactly the kind of exchange of views which he was anxious to avoid. He therefore put his head back and said nothing, staring down his nose at her.

She sighed in exasperation and shook her head. 'I do not know why I am troubling myself to address you when it is patently obvious that you do not have the smallest understanding of what I am saying.' She turned her attention away from Max, and looked at the coachman. '*You*, on the other hand, look like a sensible man,' she said. 'May I be of any assistance to *you*?'

The coachman looked nervously from Max to Miss Church and back again. Max said nothing, making a dismissive gesture as if the whole matter was beneath his notice, and began to study his fingernails. The man glanced at him again, then said hesitantly, 'Well, ma'am, I … I would be glad of a ride to the next town, so I can get help for His Grace.'

'You are very welcome, although personally I would make *His Grace* walk,' said Miss Church, moving over to make space for the coachman, and tactfully handing him the reins. '*And*, if you were to decide that you did not want to remain in the employ of so unpleasant a person, I would make it my business to find you another situation.'

They were about to pull off when Max bethought him of something. 'Dickinson,' he called. The coachman brought Patch back to a halt. Miss Church looked round and witnessed the astonishing sight of the duke approaching them with two or three running steps. 'You may need some money,' he said, throwing a purse up to the man.

'Thank you, Your Grace,' said Dickinson, pocketing the purse, before setting Patch moving as before.

Relieved of the responsibility of controlling the horse, Constance found herself staring down at the duke. His running steps from the carriage to the gig had given her pause for thought. This, together with the angle at which she was seeing him, his face upturned towards hers, amounted to an unsettling and quite illogical feeling that she had seen him somewhere before, in different circumstances.

For his part, Max stood watching the gig until it turned a corner and disappeared from sight. When he got back into the carriage, he was laughing; but when Barnes asked him what had so amused him, he simply replied that it was one of those jests that did not bear repeating. He urged the valet to go back to his book, leaving him free to sit back, close his eyes and think again about the recent encounter.

Max had spent as little time in the company of simpering debutantes as he could possibly manage. His mother's notion of suitable young ladies for him to meet seldom chimed with his own. He much preferred women who knew their own minds, and were able to express their opinions; in fact, very like the forthright young woman who had raked him down so thoroughly.

He allowed his mind to dwell on the moment when he had looked up at her, and their eyes had met. There had been an odd moment of connection, coupled with a sense of recognition which, like Miss Church, he had dismissed at first as being impossible. Then he recalled looking up at a window in Diss and seeing a young lady look down at him – a young lady to whom he had kissed his fingers. It was the same girl; he could swear it! She could easily have been in Diss. Her knowledge of Field's dismissal confirmed that she had been following the same route. His grin grew broader. How annoyed she would be did she but realize! It was an entertaining thought to savour.

He could have sworn that she had waved at him that evening. Were there two sides to the lady: the prim and proper one that the world saw, and the wilder, more adventurous one that waved to rogues and scoundrels? He found himself feeling quite regretful that he would never have the opportunity to put this to the test. They were most unlikely to meet again, and even if they did, he could not taunt her with that spontaneous moonlit encounter without endangering his very purpose for being here.

It was well over an hour before Dickinson got back to them with a hired coach driven by a groom. He explained that there was a wheelwright in Aylsham who would examine the wheel and repair it if possible, or replace it with a new one if necessary. In either case, the work would be done by the following day.

'Did I do right, Your Grace?' Dickinson asked anxiously.

'I cannot see that you could have done any other,' Max replied. 'Did you deliver the ladies safely?'

'Yes, Your Grace,' Dickinson answered. 'They're stopping over-night at the Black Boys inn, where I hired the carriage from.'

'The Black Boys? Is that a good establishment?'

'It looks like the best, Your Grace.'

Following this brief conversation, the next task was to transfer the luggage to the hired coach, in order to lighten the damaged vehicle so as to put the smallest possible strain on the wheel.

The horses were now put to again, and not for the first time, Max was torn by frustration. He did not enjoy periods of inactivity, and longed to be helping the men with some of the physical work. The only way that he could restrain himself from leaping up onto the roof and unfastening the straps that held the luggage in place was by climbing indolently from one coach to the other, and pretending to lose interest in the whole proceedings. As he did so, he caught Abdas's eye, and the other man grinned sympathetically.

They were soon underway again, but the road continued to be as bad and by the time they were approaching the outskirts of Aylsham, another hour had passed. 'We'll stay the night at the Black Boys,' Max told Barnes.

'Is that wise, Your Grace?' Barnes asked anxiously. 'Surely somewhere outside town as before—'

'Barnes,' Max interrupted politely, 'which of us is the duke?'

'Very good, Your Grace,' said Barnes after a tiny pause. 'Pray exercise some caution this time. No climbing out of windows, I beg of you.'

Max grinned. Perhaps it wasn't wise, as Barnes had said. Perhaps he ought to avoid the young lady, but he didn't want to. In any case, if this inn was the best in town, then it was logical for him to stay there. If he happened to bump into her, well it would be down to Dame Fortune. 'I shall be the model aristocrat,' he promised, as they pulled into the yard of the Black Boys inn.

His resolve lasted for perhaps half an hour. It was not late, and rather than sitting in his rooms, Max announced his intention of strolling about the town before dinner. 'Have a care, Your Grace,' murmured Barnes.

'I'm not made of glass, man,' Max replied, trying not to sound irritated, before sallying forth with Abdas in attendance.

It was not the kind of sight that was very common in Aylsham. Max was in a coat of fine blue broadcloth with buckskin breeches, and glossy hessian boots. His waistcoat was of pale-blue silk with a fine gold stripe, and his cravat was edged with lace. Abdas, at his shoulder, was a little taller than Max, and he cut an athletic figure. More than one head turned at the sight of the aristocratic nobleman and his companion.

They paused on the threshold of the Black Boys Inn, surveying the market square on which it stood. The square, known as such from its function rather than from its shape, which was not exact, sloped slightly, with the inn occupying one of its upper corners. They walked slowly around the square, pausing at the corner diagonally opposite to the inn. In front of them was a fine shop, well appointed and of a good size, displaying all kinds of haberdashery goods in the window.

Max turned to Abdas. 'This part of the world is famous for its cloth, or so I'm told,' he said. 'What say we take a look?'

'And here was I thinking that you'd got enough coats,' murmured Abdas.

'Not nearly,' Max retorted. 'Why, I'll wager I might have to wear one of them twice before Christmas!' Then he went on more seriously, 'I'm just wondering how they get their fabrics away from here and onto the market. It can't be more than ten miles to the coast, compared to a long, tedious journey to London by road. There might be a new venture for both of us.'

The shop was already busy with customers. A stout man was just concluding his purchase, whilst an elderly lady was waiting for a young assistant to bring some lace from a top shelf by means of a ladder. Two other ladies were admiring a length of stuff which was being displayed to them by a well-dressed man standing behind the counter, on which a large quantity of material was laid out.

'And I think, ladies, that you will find that this will be admirably suited to your purpose, although this also—' At that moment, he looked up and took in the exalted nature of the customer who had just entered. Breaking off his sentence with a cursory 'Excuse me', he beckoned a young assistant over to attend to the ladies, and came around the counter, bowing. 'Welcome to my establishment,' he said obsequiously. 'In what way might I serve you?'

Max's response was utterly instinctive. 'By finishing your trans-action with these ladies,' he said promptly, bowing slightly in their direction as they turned. His words were courteous, and no less than would be expected of any gentleman.

Miss Church had realized the exact moment when a customer whom the proprietor perceived as being more significant than themselves had come into the shop. Mr Planter, who had until that moment been almost overpoweringly polite, was suddenly address-ing his remarks over her shoulder in the direction of the door. Moments later, he had bustled away importantly, leaving the poor assistant whom he had summoned quite at a loss as to what he was expected to be doing.

She turned to protest, and indeed, already had her mouth open to do so, when Max spoke, taking the wind completely out of her sails. He stood at his ease, looking as much the man of fashion as he had appeared on previous occasions.

The last time she had seen him, as she had looked down at him from the gig, she had felt a strange frisson run all the way down her spine, and sensed that perhaps there might be more to him than could be seen on the surface. Now, she was conscious of something similar happening.

She looked at his hand, once again ungloved, gripping his cane not tightly, rather testing its balance; as though it could take on the function of a sword at any moment should its owner so desire. She moved her gaze to his face. There was something in the look in his eyes that said he was not to be trifled with.

Clearly Planter felt the same way. His rather sycophantic step was halted immediately. Constance could see the tension in his broad back, and hear it in his voice, as he said, 'Of course, of course.' He turned to help the ladies finish their transaction, shooing away the assistant whom he had beckoned over just moments before. 'Fetch a chair for the gentleman, you idiot,' he muttered, before painting a false smile on his rounded features, and turning back to Miss Fellowes and Miss Church. 'Now, ladies, have you made a deci-sion?' he asked them, for all the world as if it had been they who had caused the delay by their feminine vacillations.

'Certainly I have,' said Miss Fellowes coolly. 'We have been to your shop before, Mr Planter, and have always considered ourselves valued customers. We have not been treated as such today. I find that the experience has so unsettled me that I must give my purchase further thought. Good day to you.'

Constance was used to being the more forthright of the two of them, and was surprised as well as amused to witness her aunt turning on her heel and stalking towards the door, leaving Mr Planter opening and closing his mouth like a landed trout on a riverbank. 'Good day, Mr Planter,' she murmured. 'I must attend my aunt, who is understandably very upset.'

The dandy brute, she noticed, was sitting on a chair and watching the proceedings, much amused. He rose to his feet as they passed, and bowed slightly, his hand on his heart.

'We are indebted to you for your courtesy, Your Grace,' said Miss Fellowes. 'Are we not, Constance?'

Feeling a little like a sulky schoolgirl and wanting to shout, 'I don't want to say thank you,' Constance bobbed the smallest possible curtsy. 'Indeed,' she said. 'Thank you, sir.'

'Not at all,' Max replied, bowing again. 'It gives me the opportunity to repay your kindness to me on the road.' To her great astonishment, he moved as if to open the door with his own hands. Before he could do so, another man, who had been standing in the shadows, stepped forward.

'Allow me, Your Grace,' he said. 'Ladies.'

Constance looked up and saw a dignified African in squirrel brown, with a face almost as dark as coal. At that moment, she was too astonished to do other than nod her thanks as he opened the door and walk out of the shop. Once in the street, however, she turned to her aunt, with an expression upon her face that was half horror, half disgust. 'A slave,' she breathed. 'He keeps a slave!' As she half turned to go back into the shop, her aunt caught hold of her arm.

'You don't know that,' Miss Fellowes said placidly. 'The man might easily be a freed slave who is working in the duke's household. You know that there are many such.'

'That is just quibbling,' Constance responded. 'That so-called duke probably has huge plantations to his name, all built on the backs of people's misery. What right does he have to stalk around as though he owned the place, whilst that other, equally a man in God's eyes, has to do his bidding, probably spurred on by a whipping or two?'

'I still say that you are being unfair,' Miss Fellowes replied, as they strolled around the market square, making their way back to the inn the long way round. 'What do you know about the man? Next to nothing; and you must agree that he was all that was courteous just now.'

'His conduct was no more than I would have expected from any gentleman,' Constance replied, sounding very unimpressed. 'Anyway, because of his appearance in the shop, we were obliged to walk away without making our purchase, and you know that we really wanted that material to take to Mrs Pargeter so that she could make us new gowns.'

Miss Fellowes chuckled. 'I doubt very much whether we shall have to do without the material,' she said. 'Unless I mistake my man, a parcel will be delivered to the Black Boys free of charge with Mr Planter's compliments, and his apologies for having caused us any distress.'

Miss Church stopped in her tracks and stared at the other lady. 'My dear aunt, you are positively Machiavellian,' she declared.

'Oh, I do hope so,' her aunt replied.

Chapter Nine

The ladies were just walking into the inn when they heard themselves addressed. Turning, they saw a stocky, well-looking man of medium height, with a tanned complexion. He was dressed in serviceable brown coat and breeches and wore his own light-brown hair tied back in a neat queue.

'Mr Snelson,' said Miss Fellowes delightedly, recognizing the bailiff from Beacon Tower. 'This is an unexpected pleasure.'

'And for me also, ma'am,' Snelson replied, bowing. 'Good day, ladies.' His admiring gaze fixed on Constance's face betrayed the nature of his interest.

'Mr Snelson,' Constance acknowledged politely.

'We are on our way back to Cromer and will be setting off in the morning,' said Miss Fellowes. 'Might we count on the pleasure of your company at dinner?'

Snelson refused with regret. 'I am going to Cambridge to pay an overdue visit to relatives, and am expected at a friend's house tonight, so must not delay,' he explained.

Miss Fellowes smiled benevolently. The young man was of good if impoverished family, and lived in a snug house provided by the Beacon Tower Estate. He was a little older than Constance, just a few months short of his thirtieth birthday, and had been showing an interest in her ever since her arrival in the area two years before. Miss Fellowes was fond of her niece and often thought how agreeable it would be to have her living nearby.

Had they been sitting at table, Miss Church would have been at pains to kick her aunt underneath it. She knew of Miss Fellowes's hopes, and part of her recognized that it would be a convenient match. Snelson had already proposed just before their visit to Chelmsford and she had refused him. He had chosen to believe that she needed more time to make up her mind, and had promised to ask her again on her return. She hoped that he would not do so. His departure provided another delay, for which she was thankful. She found the young man rather self-important for one of his years and position. Nevertheless, despite her own misgivings, she feared that he might eventually wear her down. She loved her uncle and aunt, but there was no reason why they should house her for ever. Marriage to Snelson would be a solution of sorts.

In the meantime, Miss Fellowes was making regretful noises at Snelson's refusal. 'You must dine with us when you return, Mr Snelson, must he not, Connie?'

Constance was trying to think of something to say that would be courteous whilst at the same time not encouraging, when the dandy-brute duke and his attendant approached the inn having finished their own perambulation. Suddenly, it became necessary to demonstrate to this posturing bully that she was sought after. Instead of saying something neutral about her uncle being pleased to have another man to talk to, therefore, she smiled a more welcoming smile than Snelson had received from her in a twelvemonth and said, 'Yes indeed. We shall be delighted to entertain you.'

Snelson smiled back, then bowed and took his leave. The duke and his servant were about to enter the inn, and Constance threw the aristocrat a challenging glance before entering just in front of him.

If Miss Church had hoped to give His Grace of Haslingfield any further food for thought, she was to be sorely disappointed, for they did not meet again that evening. The duke dined in a private parlour 'attended by his slave, no doubt', Constance speculated scornfully, whilst the two ladies were served in the dining room, where a family with two older children, two clergymen, and an elderly woman and her middle-aged son were also having their meal.

Before they had gone down to take their places at the table reserved for them, an inn servant had come to the door of their chamber with a parcel, saying that it had been delivered 'with Mr Planter's compliments'. The note enclosed with the parcel had contained much the same protestations that Miss Fellowes had predicted. It was not that Mr Planter had thought the gentleman to be more worthy of his attention. It was simply that the man was a stranger, unaccustomed to the ways of the town. ('Fustian!' Miss Church had exclaimed scornfully.) What was more, the gentleman had had an 'exotic' servant with him, which had led Mr Planter to believe that perhaps he might be foreign, and therefore unfamiliar with how shops in Britain conducted their business. ('Foreign places do not have shops, then,' Miss Church interjected in the same tone.) He had feared to entrust such a foreigner to one of his assistants, as they might not know how to cope if he had spoken to them in another language. ('And Planter would presumably have understood every word,' added Miss Church.) He begged them to accept this fabric as a token of his esteem and to assure them of his continued desire to serve such valued customers.

'Loathsome man,' Miss Church had declared, having put the letter down. 'And as for that slave-owning dandy-brute bully-boy...!'

'Take care,' Miss Fellowes had said mildly as she examined the contents of the package. 'Give the gentleman any more epithets, and you will find it quite impossible to remember them.'

'I can remember those,' Miss Church had murmured darkly.

'I'm sure, dear,' her aunt had answered in the same calm tone. 'Do come and look at these silks. I think that they are the more expensive of the ones that we examined.'

'We'll have to walk out of Planter's shop in dudgeon again, if that is the result,' Miss Church had said with a laugh, dismissing the duke from her mind.

They did not meet either him or any of his entourage on the following day, and for a most unwelcome reason. Constance woke up with an intense headache, quite unable even to travel, let alone drive. Miss Fellowes, a practical woman, resigned herself to the fact that she might not get to her sketching group, for experience told her that Constance would be very unwise to attempt the journey that day. She dressed with the minimum of fuss in order to leave her niece alone as soon as possible and made sure that the curtains were tightly shut and some water was available on the bedside table.

Having ensured her niece's comfort with every measure that was in her power, she went down to breakfast in the dining room.

Knowing that Constance would expect a report on the duke's activities when she was well enough, she kept her eyes and ears open, and soon learned that His Grace had broken his own fast in his room, and was at that moment climbing into his carriage, preparatory for departure.

'Thank goodness for that,' Miss Fellowes murmured to herself, as she prepared to pour a second cup from the teapot in front of her. She had no desire to witness Constance ringing another peal over him. She suspected, however, that Constance might be a little disappointed to be denied this opportunity.

Miss Fellowes filled the day, first by visiting a number of shops, including that of Mr Planter, where she was treated with gratifying obsequiousness, and one which catered to the needs of artists like herself. She spent a happy hour browsing through brushes, paper and pigment before sharing a light nuncheon with the vicar's wife.

On returning to the Black Boys in the middle of the afternoon, she found Constance sitting up in bed, and looking very much better. 'Your colour has come back,' the older lady observed, as she rang the bell to order some tea and toast, the first thing which her niece usually fancied after a headache. 'You were as white as your fichu this morning.'

'I do feel better, I must say,' Miss Church replied. 'I shall get up after my tea.' She was guiltily aware that she might have been partly responsible for her own discomfort. She had berated herself half the night for having given Mr Snelson the kind of encouragement that would get his hopes up to no purpose.

She knew why, of course: she had wanted to display to the dandy-brute duke the fact that she was sought after. Why had his opinion mattered to her in any way? In her mind's eye, she pictured them standing side by side. There was not a great deal of difference in height and build between the bailiff and the duke. Yet there was a stolidity about the bailiff's figure and bearing which had been thrown into sharp relief by the athleticism of the nobleman whom she so despised. 'Foolishness! Sheer foolishness!' she had muttered under her breath, punching her pillow and turning it over. Finally, in the early hours of the morning, she had managed to drop off, and had slept very heavily, hence the headache.

Her aunt half expected her to make some enquiry about the duke's activities. Thanks to the poor night that her niece had had, partly on his account, such an enquiry was not forthcoming, and the subject of the objectionable aristocrat did not arise.

The objectionable aristocrat in question made better time on the last part of the journey than might have been expected, and arrived at the most remote of Alistair's estates shortly before midday. Set near the summit of Beacon Hill, Beacon Tower was a medieval manor house, originally comprising a great hall, with a great chamber above, a few ancillary rooms, and a substantial kitchen. It had been enlarged in Elizabethan times, in order to add a book room, two drawing rooms and a dining room downstairs. Above these new rooms were a long gallery, which also served as a library and music room, and some further bedchambers. The tower after which the establishment was named had originally been separate from the house. The Elizabethan occupant had had some cloisters built to connect the two buildings, so that it was possible to walk from one to the other undercover.

The property had been built by one Sir Gervase Markyate, whose descendant had been granted the Barony of Runton by Queen Elizabeth, in grateful thanks for the part that he had played in helping to discover the Babbington plot. It had been with the money that had come with this honour that he had made the improvements to his family home.

The family name of Markyate had died out some years before. The Barony had continued, although it was now a minor holding possessed by the Most Noble the Duke of Haslingfield, Earl of Bury St Edmunds and Upchurch, Viscount Clifton, and Baron Runton.

Max had had no idea what to expect when he arrived in Norfolk. Other than the fact that this was a small property, not visited by the previous duke or possibly the one before that, he had been told virtually nothing about it. As he stepped down from his carriage, he looked up at the ancient building, its stone weathered by the Norfolk climate, and had a sudden and most unaccountable sensation of coming home. Alistair's a lucky man, he thought to himself; and he's never even seen it.

He turned to the coachman. 'Dickinson, have the men unload

the luggage, then take the carriage and horses to the stables. Come and find me immediately you have done so, and tell me what state of affairs you find there. We'll need to make sure the accommodation is prepared for the other carriage and horses before they arrive tomorrow'.

'Ay, Your Grace,' Dickinson replied, knuckling his forehead. The other men glanced briefly at Max with new respect. Without being aware of it, he had spoken his orders in something approaching the clear, commanding style that he generally used aboard ship when men jumped to it.

'Well, well,' he said to Barnes and Okoro. 'Let us go in and throw our weight about. So no one has received my letter, have they? I am outraged!'

While he was still speaking, Barnes approached the great oak door and lifted the knocker. It took some time for anyone to come, but just as Barnes was about to knock again, the door opened, and a diminutive girl, who could not have been much more than eight or nine, stood on the doorstep. Her eyes grew very round, as she looked first at Barnes, then at Max in all his ducal glory, and finally at Abdas.

'Co ter heck!' she breathed, before running back inside, leaving the door half open.

Max looked from one man to the other, an expression of amusement on his face. 'Was that the bailiff or the caretaker, do you think?' he asked, pushing the door open with one hand and walking through. They found themselves standing on stone flags in a large oak-panelled room, with a huge stone fireplace at one end. Between them and the fireplace was an oak table, with proportions suited to the room.

They waited briefly in silence, until the sound of running footsteps warned them of someone's approach. Moments later, a bandy-legged man of indeterminate age entered, hastily buttoning his coat and looking much surprised. 'Begging your pardon, sir, we wasn't expecting no one,' he said. 'Can I help you in some way?' His manners, although courteous enough, were not those of an indoor servant. Clearly he had no idea of the exalted nature of his visitor. 'Was you after d'rections?' His face split into a grin. 'Not but what you'd be proper lost an' no mistake if you was axing d'rections from here. A'nt nowhere to go – 'cept into the sea.' So saying, he chuckled rustily.

Barnes opened his mouth to speak, but Max silenced him with a gesture. 'You may help by fetching the bailiff, if you please,' he said pleasantly. 'He was certainly apprised of my visit.'

The man looked nonplussed. 'I don't rightly know as I can do that, seeing as he ain't here,' he replied.

Max could feel Barnes beginning to fume just behind his left shoulder. Slightly to his right, he could see Abdas out of the corner of his eye. The man was standing in the dignified, calm, self-contained way that was so much a part of him. Max smiled slightly. The irony of the fact that it was when things started to go slightly wrong that he felt more at ease did not escape him.

'Then perhaps you will tell me first who you are, and secondly how it comes to pass that although my man of business told me that there was a bailiff, he has absented himself.'

The man looked at him through narrowed eyes. 'Mayhap I will, if'n you'll tell me by what right you're axin' me these questions,' he responded, in a reasonable tone.

Max had walked up to the door, prepared to act the part of haughty aristocrat to whoever had admitted him. His unconventional welcome had completely taken the wind out of his sails and he could feel his ready sense of humour rising to the surface. It was all that he could do to stop himself from erupting into gales of laughter in front of them all, and he was obliged to turn away to hide his expression.

'My good man—' Barnes began, in outraged tones.

Max silenced him with a gesture, without turning round. 'Leave be,' he said. 'It's a fair enough question. I might be anybody; I happen to be Haslingfield.'

The man's eyes widened. 'Him what owns this place?'

'The same,' Max answered, turning, the ghost of a smile remaining on his lips. 'And who would I be addressing?'

'Davis, sir,' said the man, belatedly knuckling his forehead.

'Then, Davis, perhaps you might tell me who there is available to attend Barnes and see to the disposal of my luggage,' said Max, indicating the various trunks and boxes just inside the door.

'Just me, Y'r Honour. And little Jilly.'

'The one who shrieked and then ran off?

'Ay, that's her.'

'What is her role here?'

'I'm her granfer. I keep an eye on her for her mother.'

'And I take it that you are the caretaker?' Max asked, fascinated.

'I was the odd-job man. After the last owner died, all the indoor staff was laid off. Mr Snelson stayed on to look after the estate and Mr Kilver tends the horses.'

'And Mr Snelson is.?'

'The bailiff, sir. Kilver's the head groom.'

'Barnes, take a look upstairs and assign us some quarters. Davis, you can show us into one of the downstairs rooms. We've stood about in the hall for quite long enough.'

'You'd best come this way then, sir.' Davis led Max and Abdas into a drawing room, which, by its higher ceiling and plastered walls, was clearly of a later date than the hall that they had just left. The furniture was covered with dust sheets, and the curtains and carpet showed signs of wear.

None of these things concerned Max, however, for from the window he caught a glimpse of a most welcome sight. 'Look, Abdas,' he exclaimed, forgetting his role as he hurried to the window. 'The sea!'

'Ay, well that's natural at the coast,' remarked Davis laconically.

Max opened his mouth to declare that for a sailor like himself, the view from the window was indeed a sight for sore eyes, when he remembered the part that he was supposed to be playing.

'Doubtless,' he murmured, turning his back on the view, and taking his place by the mantelpiece, with one foot on the fender. 'Now tell me about the bailiff.'

'Bailiff ain't here, sir.'

'Yes, so you've already told me,' said Max, rapidly becoming exasperated. 'Where is he, man?'

'Gone to visit his relations, sir. "I've put everything in order on the estate and the farm," says he. "Ain't nobody expected."'

Max turned to look at Abdas. 'So no letter was received from London,' he remarked, with perfect truth. He turned back to Davis.

'I'll need you to show us round the house presently. For now, go and give Barnes what assistance you can.'

After Davis had gone, Max said to Abdas, 'The skeleton staff which we were promised in London seems to be even more skeletal than I had anticipated. It seems like you're going to be very busy, my friend. What job do you fancy? Housekeeper? Cook? Remind me to keep a careful tally of my expenditure, so that I can present Alistair with a bill!'

'I'll take a look at the kitchens,' said Abdas, grinning, as he crossed to the door. 'None of us can live if we don't eat.'

'Send Davis to procure eggs, milk and bread from a local farm. For now, we can take most of our meals at a nearby inn.'

Left alone, Max walked over to the window again, and looked out towards the sea. He heaved a sigh. The sun was shining, and the water looked blue and inviting, although he knew that the North Sea would be exceedingly cold, even in summer. What he wouldn't give to take a boat out on the sea today, and leave all this imbroglio behind! At least he had ample funds to draw upon to provide the service that he required for the present. Promising himself a trip out on the water as soon as he could manage it, he wandered out to the hall, to encounter his valet coming down the stairs.

'Well, Barnes, there's no bailiff, and no indoor servants to speak of, save an elderly man and a small child who has yet to say a comprehensible word. We're on our own.'

'It's not what we expected, Your Grace,' was the reply.

'We've both coped with worse – haven't we?' Max responded, raising a quizzical eyebrow as he looked at the servant.

Barnes permitted himself a small smile. 'Perhaps. I am exceedingly perturbed at the way things have turned out. Plans have been made very carelessly, in my opinion.'

'Look at it this way: the less people around, the less people there are to see.'

'There is that, Your Grace.'

'Come on then, Barnesy,' said Max, clapping the manservant on the back, and making him wince as much from the inappropriateness of the words and gesture as from any discomfort caused. 'Show me where I am to sleep.'

Chapter Ten

M r Fellowes's great love, apart from his books, was his garden. As the day was fine, the ladies were not at all surprised on their return to find him outside, tending his roses. He looked up at the sound of the gig, and smiled broadly from under the wide brim of his country hat. 'I thought you were intending to come home yesterday,' he remarked, straightening, and wiping his hands on his coarse apron.

Miss Fellowes explained about Constance's headache. 'I hope you weren't worried,' she said. 'There was no way of letting you know.'

'As long as she's well now,' he replied, looking up at his niece from beneath a pair of shaggy grey brows.

'Very well, thank you, Uncle,' Miss Church answered with a twinkle.

'I'm glad you're better. How was the visit?'

'It was delightful,' Miss Fellowes answered him. 'No, pray don't help me down with those grimy hands. I shall manage very well on my own.'

'Why don't you both get down?' he suggested. 'I'll take the gig round to Beacon Tower.' The house in which they lived was about fifty years old. Named The Brambles after the prolific blackberry bushes which bordered part of the orchard, it nestled comfortably in a hollow just above the village of West Runton. It was known locally as a cottage, even though it had a book room, two dining rooms of different sizes, three parlours and a spacious kitchen, with plenty of bedrooms for the family as well as guests. A lack of stables was its weakness, so as a consequence, Mr Fellowes had an arrange-ment with the head groom at Beacon Tower, to stable his gig and his horse there. Apart from Mr Snelson's mount, Kilver only had the horses from the home farm to tend, and he was more than happy to keep an eye on Patch.

'Certainly not,' said Miss Fellowes indignantly. 'I will not have you going out in public in all your dirt. You look like a vagrant. Constance will not mind driving that little extra way, will you, my dear?'

'Not at all,' Constance answered cheerfully, as her uncle lifted their baggage down from the back of the gig. 'I shall be glad of the walk back.'

She tooled the gig the short distance to Beacon Tower, allowing Patch to set his own pace, since they were travelling uphill. He hardly needed directing. 'Glad to be going back to your stable, old fellow?' she said affectionately. Patch nodded, snorting gently as if in agreement.

Constance much preferred this version of the journey: driving up the hill and walking down it. It was not that she was lazy, or disliked the walk, it was simply that on the return journey, she would have the benefit of the sea view.

Although she had not grown up close to the sea, she would have been the first to admit that she would now find it a wrench to live away from it. She looked up at Beacon Tower. On one occasion, she had been privileged to climb the structure which gave the house its name. The window in the room at the top offered a fine view of the sea. She could well imagine that if she were a child, she would be up there playing games of being on board ship, and keeping watch from the crow's nest. She smiled. It had been some years since it had been a family home, from all she had heard.

She guided Patch around to the stables, and was surprised to find it much busier than she had ever known it to be. A number of the stalls that had previously been empty were now occupied. There was more equipment about, and the whole area gave the unmistakable impression of being more populated. Naturally there was no sign of Colin Snelson's horse; she knew him to be on his way to Cambridge, and was conscious of a feeling of relief. Perhaps he would have forgotten that stupid piece of encouragement that she had given him by the time he returned.

At the sound of her arrival, a man of late middle years with a compact build and grizzled hair came out of one of the buildings. 'I thought that was the sound of your gig, Miss Church,' he said, going to Patch's head.

'Good day, Kilver,' said Constance, climbing down. 'You are busier than usual, I see. Would you rather I drove on to the New Inn?' This hostelry was in Cromer. It was from there that Mr Fellowes had sometimes hired a travelling carriage.

'No need of that, miss,' Kilver responded. 'There's room enough for Patch and your little gig.'

'Thank you. What's the cause of all this unexpected activity? To whom does all this' – she waved her hand in the direction of the additional livestock – 'belong?'

'The owner, miss.'

'Baron Runton? So someone has inherited?'

'Aye, miss; and turned up here and thrown everything into sixes and sevens.'

Constance looked around her. 'Everything seems organized to your usually high standard,' she remarked truthfully.

'Aye, we're all right over here,' he agreed. 'I meant up at the house. Nobody had any notice of his arrival, see, although apparently some was sent. And what with Mr Snelson going off to see his relatives, there's no one to see to his requirements, 'cept old Davis.'

'When did the baron arrive?'

'Just yesterday, miss, with his few servants, and two carriages and more horses arrived this morning. I don't think he's a baron, though.'

'No, I don't think he is, either,' her uncle agreed, after she told him about her conversation with Beacon Tower's head groom.

'Probably he didn't inherit in the direct line,' she surmised.

Fellowes nodded. 'Although I seem to recall that he does have a title. I'll go and pay him a visit.'

'As tomorrow's Sunday, we may well see him at church,' his niece replied.

The fine weather which had favoured Miss Church and Miss Fellowes on their journey broke overnight, and they were obliged to don all-enveloping cloaks, calash bonnets and stout shoes to protect themselves as they walked to church the next day. Not for the first time, Miss Fellowes bemoaned the fact that they did not keep a closed carriage at home. 'For,' she said, 'we would be protected from this tiresome rain.'

'And be put to the expense of maintaining a stable, which for the majority of the time we do not need at all,' answered her brother from beneath the broad brim of his hat.

The rain was steady but light and, as they were all seasoned walkers, they accomplished the short journey to Runton parish church within a very short space of time. A regrettable delay occurred at the church gate where a carriage was setting down its passenger, over whom a servant was carefully holding an umbrella. Other than barging past, there was no alternative but to wait whilst this party made a stately progress down the church path. Fortunately, the delay was slight, and they were soon inside being relieved of their cloaks and calashes by the sidesman, who hung them up to dry. By then, the individuals who had delayed them had taken their places.

Mr and Miss Fellowes and their niece were well known in the neighbourhood, and they acknowledged a number of polite incli-nations of the head as they walked to their places. Although they did not rent a pew of their own, they were accustomed to sitting in much the same place each week, towards the front on the right, just behind the seats occupied by the vicarage party.

Hearing their footsteps, Miss Matilda Mawsby, the vicar's daughter, turned her head to greet Miss Church. The two ladies were much of an age, and were sometimes thrust into one another's company, although Constance sometimes found Matilda to be a little narrow-minded, and rather inclined to gossip.

They only had time to exchange a few words before Mr Mawsby made his entrance, and the service began. It was not until after the opening responses and prayers had been concluded, therefore, that Constance realized that the pew which belonged to the master of Beacon Tower was now occupied by two gentlemen. Unfortunately, that was as much as she could detect, the position of the seat that she occupied ensuring that she could not get a proper look at the new-comer without craning her neck in a vulgar and unbecoming manner.

The service proceeded along the usual lines, Mr Mawsby delivering a sermon which did not hold much of Constance's attention since she could remember having heard it at least twice before. Instead, she went over in her mind the journey so recently undertaken, and the different events that had punctuated it. She found herself thinking about the moment when she had stood at the window of their friend's house in Diss, and caught a glimpse of the swarthy buccaneer with flowing dark curls, who had blown her a kiss. Was it just her imagination that painted him as being rather handsome? Pretty pink and white china misses were probably greeted in such a way every day of the week. No doubt it was because such experiences seldom came her way that she was dwelling upon it in this manner. In church, too! Such inappropriate behaviour, she scolded herself crossly. This was not the first time that she had reproved herself over this matter. Why could she not get him out of her mind? She turned her thoughts back to the service, only to discover that it was nearly over.

Mr Mawsby delivered the blessing, and walked down the aisle in order to say a word of greeting to each member of the congregation as they left. In keeping with accepted practice, the occupants of the Beacon Tower pew left first, whilst the congregation took the opportunity to have a closer look.

Constance was unable to see them properly until they were almost upon her. Then she gasped involuntarily, for the man in front was one whom she recognized immediately, and had hoped never to see again. He was walking down the aisle with a measured tread, his carriage athletic rather than graceful, his gaze fixed straight ahead of him. He was even wearing the same violet striped silk coat that he had had on when she had first seen him. Almost as if he had heard her swift intake of breath, his eyes flickered briefly towards her as he walked past. Even so, he neither acknowledged her presence nor checked his pace. Just behind him walked his black servant, dressed in a dark-green coat and tan breeches, with a snowy white wig on his head.

For perhaps five seconds, she managed to resist turning round. Then, as she looked back, she caught a glimpse of his servant helping him on with his coat.

Swiftly she turned to her aunt, who had been sitting furthest from the aisle. 'Did you see him?' she asked 'The dandy-brute duke!'

'Hush,' answered her aunt, glancing about her to see if anyone had overheard. 'No, I did not. Was it indeed he?'

'Yes it was; and looking just as arrogant as usual. *And* he had his slave dancing attendance upon him.'

'Forgive me for interrupting,' said Miss Mawsby in rather sharp, inquisitive tones. 'Are you speaking of the new owner of Beacon Tower? I could not help overhearing. I didn't mean to eavesdrop.'

'Of course not,' Miss Fellowes answered, directing another accusatory glance at Constance, with whom she had had cause to remonstrate upon more than one occasion for her forthright remarks. 'We did meet the gentleman as we travelled back from visiting our friends recently.'

Constance snorted. 'Gentleman!' she exclaimed scornfully, as her aunt turned to speak to someone who had attracted her attention from the pew behind. 'He is one of the most arrogant men whom I have ever met. I am sorry that he is living so close for I have no desire to resume my acquaintance with him.'

'Oh dear, that is very unfortunate,' said Miss Mawsby, the gleam in her eye at variance with the sentiment that she was expressing. 'He is intending to consult Papa about employing servants from the village.'

Constance made a face. 'They had better be thick-skinned,' she said frankly. 'From what I have seen, he is an unreasonable employer, and I'm afraid that he even keeps a slave.'

The vicar's wife had been exchanging remarks with a parishioner; now, she joined her daughter and Constance. 'Who keeps a slave?' she asked.

'The new owner of Beacon Tower, Mama,' said Miss Mawsby.

Mrs Mawsby's face grew rigid with disapproval. 'I must inform Peter,' she said. 'He will not want to recommend anyone to work for such a person.'

After this, the vicar's wife's attention was claimed by someone else. Constance and her aunt were eagerly greeted by other members of the congregation who had missed them during their absence, and it took them long enough to reach the door. By the time they had done so, the duke had left.

The rain had exhausted itself during the church service, and a rather weak sun was now struggling to shine between the clouds, so the congregation was glad to stand and chat for a little. Constance glanced towards the church door, and observed Miss Mawsby talking earnestly to one or two ladies. The tale of the duke's brutality and his slave-owning propensities would no doubt soon be bruited about the village. For a brief moment she felt guilty, until she recalled the haughty aristocrat's behaviour. Serve him right, she said to herself stoutly, before tucking her hand into her uncle's left arm, whilst her aunt took his right.

As they walked back home, Mr and Miss Fellowes chatted idly of the people they had seen at the service, whilst Constance allowed her mind to wander. The conversation about the duke had brought back memories of some of the talk that she had heard in Cambridge when her father was alive. There, in his study, men were respected for their achievements and not for the rank to which they had been born. In that academic forum, revolution in England was often spoken of as desirable. At the time, it seemed to be the only way in which necessary change could come about, meaningless titles could be abolished and a fairer system of government established.

Since the time of these conversations, the French Revolution had begun in earnest, and Constance had started to believe that more measured reform would be a better way of proceeding. With her observation of a man behaving with the dandy-brute duke's arrogance, however, her revolutionary preferences had returned. A ride in a tumbril would do him a power of good, she decided. What right had he to look down on others? What right had he to own a slave? He deserved to be shaken out of his complacency. Would that she could be the one to do the shaking!

'Such shocking news,' Miss Fellowes said, breaking into her thoughts. 'Mrs Reynolds told me that Miss Grayleigh has broken her arm in a fall from her horse.'

'Oh no, poor Melinda,' Constance exclaimed, concern for her friend putting the duke to the back of her mind. 'I shall visit her this week.'

Chapter Eleven

The rain, which had ceased when they left church, came down again in torrents on the following day. It was plainly not a sensible idea to drive even such a small distance as three or four miles to Upper Sheringham, where Miss Grayleigh lived with her parents. Instead, Constance spent the day helping her aunt to assemble and wash the jars that they would be using to store preserves when the fruit ripened. This task could not take up the whole day, however, and as soon as they had finished, Miss Fellowes set about sorting out her paints and brushes, whilst Constance turned her attention to her correspondence. She had the book room to herself. Despite the inclement weather, Mr Fellowes could not keep away from his garden, and was even now engaged upon some horticultural activity in his potting shed.

A number of letters had arrived for Constance whilst she had been away. One was from a Mrs Horwich, who had been a neighbour and a friend of her mother in the village where they had lived in her early years. After the departure of Mr Church and his daughter for Cambridge, Mrs Horwich had begun to correspond with Constance.

Her letters were always crossed and crossed again at least twice, and Constance was guiltily aware that she seldom gave those detailed letters the time and attention that had gone into their construction. The life that she had lived then had been left behind long since, and most of the people about whom Mrs Horwich wrote, Constance was ashamed to admit, she regarded with tepid interest at best. Knowing that her aunt would enjoy hearing the letter read out loud – for although she knew none of the people, the events of village life were always of interest to her – she put it on one side, and picked up the others.

One of these was from another childhood acquaintance, now living in London, and enjoying her first season as a married lady. It was brief, and gave the impression of a very busy person, only just managing to snatch half an hour from an extremely active life.

Constance put the letter down and stared into space. Nobody had ever suggested that *she* should have a London season. Her mother had died before such a thing had been discussed, and it would never have occurred to her father to even think about such a matter. There had been no female relatives on hand to prompt him to do so. Even if someone had suggested it, it would have been difficult to know where the money would have come from. Theirs had not been a wealthy household. Mr Church had been a younger son, whilst his wife's family had only been able to provide her with a modest income during her lifetime. Most of Mr Church's spare money had been spent on acquiring books, some of them quite valuable, and Constance had never questioned this expenditure. There was certainly not sufficient left over for ball gowns, even supposing she had ever learned to dance! It had only been since living with her aunt and uncle that she had had the opportunity to acquire such accomplishments.

The third letter was from a gentleman who had been part of the intellectual circle that had met at her father's house. He had spoken approvingly when she had made an intelligent contribution to a discussion on one occasion, and later had sent her a copy of *The Rights of Man* by Thomas Paine. In itself, this was a controversial choice. The author was now in France, having been obliged to leave England after which he had been found guilty of seditious libel in his absence. She had read the book more than once, finding his writing to be clear and comprehensible. Wisely, she had been cautious about those with whom she shared this particular opinion.

Briefly, this last letter transported her back to the days that she had spent in Cambridge, often acting as her father's amanuensis, and she was conscious of a longing for that kind of mental stimulation. Her uncle and aunt had their own interests. There was no one with whom she could discuss the political matters for which her appetite had been whetted by those years in academia.

She laid down her letters, and got up in order to take from the shelf her copy of *The Rights of Man*. It was well thumbed, and had comments of her own written in the margins. Knowing what she was looking for, she opened it and soon found the passage that she had in mind.

The aristocracy are not the farmers who work the land, and raise the produce, but are the mere consumers of the rent, and when compared with the active world, are the drones, a seraglio of males, who neither collect the honey nor form the hive, but exist only for lazy enjoyment.

'Exactly so!' she declared out loud, smiling. 'He is a drone!' Her mood of melancholy dispelled, she laid aside her book, and picked up her pen in order to finish her letters.

The next day was fine, but as it was Tuesday, which was Miss Fellowes's regular day for receiving visitors, Constance stayed at home. Mrs and Miss Mawsby both came, eager to share their own news, and to hear whatever Miss Fellowes and her niece had to impart. It soon became apparent that Miss Mawsby was far more curious about Constance's encounters with the new neighbour, than about her visit to people whom the vicar's daughter had never met.

Constance obliged readily enough, describing the various incidents in a lively fashion, which kept the other young woman very well entertained. If she was briefly conscious of a twinge of guilt as she vilified the duke, she firmly suppressed it. Why should he be able to get away with such behaviour just because of his high rank? Had he never heard of *noblesse oblige*?

'I have told Mama what you said about the Duke of Haslingfield,' said Miss Mawsby, after Constance had finished her account. 'She was very much shocked, and has already begun to warn the local people against accepting employment with him.'

'Serve him right,' said Constance forthrightly. 'I should hate to see any local person treated in the way that he treated his poor valet.'

Soon after this, Mrs Mawsby and her daughter took their leave.

The following day, Constance decided to pay the promised visit to Melinda Grayleigh. Normally, she would simply wander up to Beacon Tower and wait whilst the gig was harnessed for her. On rare occasions, if she was pressed for time, she would send the odd-job boy on ahead to ask for this to be done in order to save herself a wait. Today, as she watched young Ben run up the path with her message for the groom, she told herself that it was a perfectly reasonable thing to do. The stables would be busier now with Haslingfield's horses and carriage to be cared for, and Kilver would appreciate some notice. It had absolutely nothing to do with the fact that she did not want to encounter the Beacon Tower's newest owner.

Just in case she did encounter such an obnoxious person, she decided to take particular care with her appearance. After all, it would never do for him to look down upon country folk as dowdy. She put on a carriage dress of sage green which she had worn only once, and a bonnet neatly trimmed with green and gold ribbons. That would certainly make Beacon Tower's new owner think again, should she chance to meet him. She was spared the annoyance of such an encounter, and telling herself that she was far from being disappointed – quite the reverse! – she thanked the groom, and set off in the direction of Sheringham at as smart a trot as the road permitted.

Melinda was very pleased to have a visitor, and sent for refreshments immediately, so that soon the two ladies were sharing their news over a cup of coffee. Contrary to local rumour, it transpired that she had sprained her ankle rather than broken her arm.

'Such is the nature of country gossip,' she said, as she explained her reasons for remaining on her day bed instead of rising to greet her visitor. 'In fact, I am very much better, and will be back on my feet in a couple of days.'

'Then you will all be able to come and dine with us on Thursday. Aunt asked me to invite you.'

The two young women had met at church when Constance had attended with her aunt and uncle for the first time after her arrival in the district. Melinda had been paying a visit to a relative who lived just outside West Runton, and she had been very friendly and welcoming towards one whom she recognized as a newcomer. Since then, they had often called upon one another, and had become close friends. Although Melinda was of a gentler disposition than Constance, she was not afraid of sharing her views. Like Miss Mawsby, she had not often travelled away from Norfolk; unlike the vicar's daughter, she was well informed about current events, and open to new ideas.

'Papa told me that Beacon Tower is now occupied,' she said. 'He means to call upon the new owner as soon as he can.'

'I doubt he would be very welcome,' Constance responded. 'The man is very cold and haughty. I don't think that people in the village will take to him.'

Melinda eyed her thoughtfully. 'I hope that they will give him a fair chance,' she answered. 'To be a stranger in a new place is not easy, as you must know from your own experience. It would be too bad if people were to be hostile towards him for no good reason.'

Constance directed her attention to her empty coffee cup, tracing the delicate pattern on it with her finger. 'There is a good reason,' she answered. 'He keeps a slave.'

'Oh, surely not,' Melinda protested. 'It is not legal to have slaves in England since the Somersett case, is it?'

Constance nodded. She and Melinda had spoken about the slave trade before. She was well aware of the judgement made by Lord Mansfield in 1772 which stated that a person could not be a slave in England since English law made no acknowledgement of slavery. 'Yes, I know,' she replied. 'The thing is, does the Almighty Duke think that such laws apply to him? And what about the poor man in his employ? Has anyone told him that he is not a slave? Melinda, we all know that a servant can be kept in such vile subjection that he might as well be a slave.'

'You are right, of course,' Melinda agreed. 'But I know how quick you can be in your judgements. You cannot really claim to know what the man is like on such slight acquaintance. Remember, too, that he has only just come into this high position. He is probably unused to his situation and does not yet know how to comport himself.'

'Melinda if you had seen him; heard him,' Constance protested.

'I am not saying that you are wrong about him,' her friend replied. 'All I am saying is that it would be as well to reserve judgement. How foolish you would feel if you turned out to be mistaken; especially if you had told others your views.'

Constance fiddled with her cup, not meeting her friend's eye. 'Very true,' she said. 'Let's forget about him and talk about something else. Have you heard from Stephen? Is he enjoying his work?'

This diversion proved to be a good one, since Melinda's beloved twin brother had gone to work in the North of England as a junior estate manager. The topic of Haslingfield was not raised again until the midday meal was served, when Mrs Grayleigh asked their guest if she had met the newest arrival to the district. Mindful of Melinda's warning, Constance simply made a neutral remark about having seen him at church.

'He will have all the match-making mamas buzzing around him, no doubt,' said Mrs Grayleigh placidly.

'It is to be hoped, then, that he has not come to this part of the world in order to escape all of that,' put in her husband in an educated light Norfolk accent. A squire to his fingertips, he had been tending to some livestock that morning, and had changed so as not to sit down at the table in all his dirt.

'I hope he will entertain a little,' replied Mrs Grayleigh. 'It would be too bad if a man of such distinction could not host a ball or at the very least, a garden party.' Mindful of Melinda's eye upon her, Constance carefully bit her lip.

She left the Grayleighs during the afternoon, after she had repeated Miss Fellowes's invitation to come and dine on Thursday. 'My aunt told me very strictly to ask you, if Melinda was not as severely injured as we had heard,' she said.

'Tell her we should be delighted to come.'

It was in a thoughtful frame of mind that she drove back to Beacon Tower. She knew that Melinda was good for her, even if sometimes she found the other young woman's ability to see another side of a question a little irritating. Constance often looked at things in black and white; Melinda could always see shades of grey.

Infuriating though it was, she was forced to admit that there might be two sides to the duke. What was more, two nights' sleep in her own bed had reminded her of the comforts of home – comforts which, although he might have wealth enough to command, would not be found so readily in a new place. Doubtless some – although not all – of his failings could be explained away by his unfamiliarity with his new rank and situation. Furthermore, his regrettable character traits – notably, his arrogance and his obvious approval of slavery – would never be redeemed if he were treated like a pariah. Thanks to her outspoken comments on his behaviour, he could be exactly that. She found herself wishing that she had not given such ammunition to so inveterate a gossip as Miss Mawsby.

When Constance had left the stables earlier, she had been in a hurry to get away and had not really taken notice of what was going on. On her return, she was struck once again by the contrast between their appearance today and on previous occasions. Before the duke's arrival, her own visits and her use of Patch provided Kilver and his one stable hand with their greatest excitement. Today, the atmosphere was much more reminiscent of some busy coaching inn. Previously, Patch had only had the bailiff's horse and the plough horses from the home farm for company. Today, their arrival was greeted by whinnies and stamping, as the numerous occupants of the stalls greeted Patch. She caught a glimpse of the travelling coach which she recognized from the journey. She could also see another vehicle, which must surely be some sort of sporting carriage.

'Good afternoon, Kilver,' she said as the head groom came bustling up to assist her down from the gig. 'You have many more mounts to care for now.'

'Aye,' he agreed, grinning. 'I like it busy, miss. What good is it to be a groom, with nothing for me to be grooming, if you take my meaning?'

She laughed. 'I can see your point,' she responded. Although she would have liked to leave immediately in order to avoid any possibility of meeting the duke, courtesy dictated that she give Kilver some of her time. After all, he stabled Patch and the gig entirely free of charge, and took exemplary care of them, making sure that Patch was well brushed and fed, and the gig was kept clean and shining. Assailed by a sudden thought that he might have been supplanted, she said, 'I do trust that some smart London groom has not been brought in over your head.'

His ready smile dispelled this suspicion at once. 'Aye, I'm still in charge here, and every man knows it. His Grace could see at once that I know my work.'

She glanced over to where a glossy black head was visible, nodding over the front of one of the stalls. 'Have the duke's horses recovered from their long journey?'

'Like the thoroughbreds they are,' the groom replied.

'Does His Grace have many more horses?' she asked, strolling over to stroke the long black nose.

'There's a pair of greys over yonder,' he said, indicating with a movement of his head. 'And two or three other mounts, including His Grace's long-tailed chestnut, which he's out riding at the moment.'

As if his words had acted like some kind of a spell, they heard the sound of hoofs, and the chestnut horse came trotting into the yard with the duke on his back. He was as immaculately dressed as ever, in a dark-blue coat and tan breeches, a snowy cravat, and his boots polished to a shine. Today he wore his dark hair unpowdered and neatly tied back, giving the effect of making him look younger and altogether more vigorous. Once again, her heart skipped a beat. Inwardly, she berated herself for being so easily unsettled at his appearance.

'Miss Church, I believe,' he said, allowing Kilver to take the bridle so that he could dismount. 'Forgive me, but we have not been properly introduced. Your servant, ma'am.'

'Sir,' Constance replied, curtsying before turning back to the groom. 'I will bid you good day then, Kilver. You have much to do and I will not keep you.'

'One moment, ma'am,' said the duke. 'May I claim the privilege of escorting you home?'

'There really is no need,' she told him. 'I frequently walk to and from these stables alone, and live only five minutes away.'

'Nevertheless, I would be very pleased to do so,' he answered. 'Besides, there is a matter that I would like to discuss with you.'

'Then how can I refuse?' she said lightly, trying not to feel apprehensive. His manner was courteous enough but there was a hint of steel in his voice, reminding her that she had nicknamed him a brute.

Out of the corner of her eye, she observed that he was offering her his arm. Choosing to pretend that she had not seen, she clasped her hands behind her back. Not pressing the point, he allowed his own arms to swing by his sides.

'I hope you managed to get your carriage repaired satisfactorily,' she said.

'Yes, I thank you,' he responded. 'A wheelwright was found and a repair effected.' He paused briefly. 'I fear I may not have appeared to advantage on the road,' he went on. 'Travelling does not bring out the best in me.'

'Which means that those around you suffer too,' Constance put in swiftly.

Max raised his brows. 'I'm not aware of having caused any suffering,' he replied.

'Sir, you leave nothing but disaster in your wake, whilst you glide serenely on as though it didn't matter,' she retorted. 'What of the poor valet whom you dismissed for trivial reasons? What of the coachman whom you were blaming for something that was not his fault? What of the turmoil caused in every inn so that you should have things just your way? What of your arrogance in assuming that you must always come first in every shop or inn – even in church?'

'I perceive that I was right in my assumption,' he remarked. 'Barnes has been making some enquiries about acquiring servants, so far without success. This seemed to me a little strange until I received a visit from the vicar this morning. He had come to make enquiries into some very disquieting reports that he had heard with regard to my treatment of servants. At the time, I confess I thought of you and—'

'And what better admission could there be of your guilt?' she interrupted swiftly.

'—and immediately rebuked myself for leaping to an uncharitable conclusion,' Max went on, as if she had said nothing. 'However, since no one else in the neighbourhood had the slightest knowledge of me, I could not think who else it could be.'

Constance had the grace to blush. 'You cannot deny the truth of what I saw,' she insisted.

'On the contrary, you do not have the slightest idea of the relationship that existed between Field and myself, or of the conversation that I had with my coachman. As for the way in which people yield to me in an inn or even in church, that is an inevitable consequence of the rank of duke, I fear.'

'*The vanity and presumption of governing beyond the grave is the most ridiculous and insolent of all tyrannies,*' she said scornfully.

Max's eyes narrowed. 'You are well read, ma'am; however, to be able to quote the opinions of Thomas Paine does not guarantee that you are right. I am talking of the real world in which we live.'

'A world that needs to change.'

'I am far from contradicting you, ma'am,' he replied.

'You are?' she said, rather taken aback by his easy acquiescence.

'A gentleman should never contradict a lady,' he said calmly.

'Nonsense!' she exclaimed. 'Someone who is wrong should always be put right.'

'So if you were mistaken, it would be my responsibility to correct you.'

'Certainly it would. One would not want to hold misguided opinions; which is why I cannot allow your greatest misdemeanour to go unchallenged.'

'My greatest misdemeanour?'

'That of condoning slavery. How can you do such a thing?'

At this word, Max's brows snapped together in one line. 'Slavery?' he echoed, horrified.

'How can you say that as if you had not the slightest idea what I meant?' Constance asked him indignantly. 'That poor African who trails around after you is clearly a slave.'

'I hesitate to interrupt you in the middle of what will no doubt be a most elevating speech, but I must point out to you that slavery has been illegal in this country for some years,' he said. 'I am not a law breaker.' Although his tone was as languid as ever, she was not deceived. His eyes were as cold as ice and he was very angry.

'I know that,' she replied contemptuously. 'No doubt you describe him as a *servant* and pay him such a pitiful sum that he is bound to you for ever, unable to break free. Such service is slavery in all but name, sir; I despise you for it.'

By now they had reached the gate which led into the Fellowes's front garden. Max opened the gate for her, and stood back to allow her to go through. 'You have clearly constituted yourself as judge and jury,' he said. 'You have a strange viewpoint, Miss Church. You are fierce in your championing of one whom you perceive to be a slave, yet you deny me a fair hearing. Yours is a courtroom without the benefit of justice since I stand condemned without having had the opportunity to defend myself.'

For a long moment they stood staring at one another, and there passed between them something that was not antagonism; something that made Constance feel strangely breathless. 'I am listening now,' she said eventually, her voice coming out, to her great annoyance, with a faint tremble.

'Oh, I am sure that you could make up a far more exciting tale than anything I might have to tell you,' he answered, the anger dying out of his eyes. 'I have no hesitation in allowing you to fill in the details. Until the next occasion, Miss Church.' He sketched a bow and walked back the way he had come with powerful, athletic strides, leaving her staring after him.

He could no more have assumed Alistair's languor at this moment than he could have flown to the moon, so incensed was he at what their conversation had revealed. The lack of servants was a temporary problem. He had no doubt of his ability to convince the vicar that Miss Church had been mistaken. In the meantime, he and Abdas were more than capable of making shift for themselves. No doubt Miss Church would have been surprised to see the two of them removing the dust sheets from the furniture with their own hands.

But a slave owner! She actually thought that he might be such a repulsive creature! He recalled the circumstances in which he and Abdas had met. The *Lady Marion* had come upon the shipwreck quite by chance. He himself had taken charge of the rowing boat that had gone to the aid of some of the poor souls who had fallen victim to the ocean. There, amid the brisk green waves topped with white, he had caught a glimpse of a dark head, and a hand waving.

He had directed the oarsmen towards the figure in the water and, as they got near enough, he had leaned over and reached out to give assistance. A moment later, a dark-brown hand had locked about his wrist, and a pair of similarly dark eyes had met his gaze. Slavery had always seemed to him to be a loathsome business. He had understood why as his fingers had closed about the wrist of the other, and he had felt a powerful connection between them that was nothing more or less than simple humanity. The notion, then, that Miss Constance Church should believe him to be a slave owner seemed utterly horrific.

'Can you believe it?' he stormed to Abdas. 'How could she think such a thing?' On his return, Max had found his friend in the parlour which overlooked the sea.

'How could she think anything else, given the persona that you have sought to cultivate?' Okoro answered, offering a glass of wine which he had poured. 'Does she approve of slave owners?'

'Approve?' Max asked, frowning.

'Did she ask eagerly how many plantations you had? Or did she perhaps make enquiries as to where she could buy someone like me?'

'Certainly not,' Max answered indignantly. 'She despises me for it.'

'Then why are you upset?' Abdas asked him. 'You like the girl; she has shown herself to have principles much the same as yours. True, she's mistaken about the kind of man you are; but then you're trying to pull the wool over everyone's eyes, so you can't blame her for that.'

Ignoring the rest of the speech, Max said, 'What do you mean, I like her?'

'If you didn't, would you be so annoyed?' At that moment, the doorbell rang. 'I'll go,' said Abdas, putting down his glass.

'Heaven send it's not Miss Church,' said Max devoutly. 'No doubt she'd expect me to answer the door myself.'

Chapter Twelve

Her conversation with the duke had so disturbed her that Constance felt the need to walk in the garden before going into the house. Over and over again she told herself that she was quite right to have taken such a high tone with him. Nevertheless there had been something about his reaction that had smacked of an innocent man righteously defending himself. She felt a little guilty that she had not given him that opportunity. She could not dismiss from her mind the good impression that he seemed to have made upon Kilver.

At last, concluding that her reflections were fruitless, she went into the house to tell her aunt about her visit to the Grayleighs, and their acceptance of the invitation to dinner. That done, she went upstairs to change, trying not to think about the duke and the indignant look in his eyes. For a brief moment, he had almost looked hurt.

She thought about how the skirts of his coat had swirled about him as he had turned on his heel. His movements had been energetic at that moment, quite unlike the languid manner that he usually adopted. Strangely, she was reminded of the man who had been in conversation with Mr Field when she had given the dismissed valet a few coins. Where had he gone? Back into the inn? She did not think that she had seen him again. Of course, he would have been hard to recognize without the cloak and hat that had disguised his features. He had been much the same height as the Duke of Haslingfield. At that time, of course, the duke had been in his room.

Still pondering this interesting conundrum, she wandered downstairs, reaching the bottom of the flight just as her uncle let himself in through the front door. 'It's very pleasant out,' he declared. 'The rain has laid the dust nicely.'

'Where did you go?' his niece asked him, glad of this diversion from her own disturbing thoughts as they walked into the parlour, her hand tucked into his arm.

'Calling on our neighbours,' he told her.

'Just in time for tea,' his sister remarked, as she got up and went to ring the bell. 'Unless you've already had some.'

'As a matter of fact, I've just been drinking wine with Haslingfield.'

'Haslingfield!' Constance exclaimed. 'Not the dandy-brute duke?'

Fellowes laughed. 'Is that what you call him?' he asked, not having heard his niece use this expression before.

To her great annoyance, Constance felt her face growing hot. 'Well, sometimes,' she murmured.

'I must say, he seemed perfectly amiable to me,' Fellowes responded. 'He's still having some little difficulty in recruiting servants, and hasn't yet acquired a cook.' He paused, half expecting one of his two womenfolk to comment. When neither did so, he added, 'So I've invited him to dine with us on Thursday.'

'Thursday!' exclaimed his sister. 'The Grayleighs are coming!'

'What of it?' her brother asked mildly. 'Don't we have enough chairs?' He winked at Constance, oblivious to her consternation. 'I could always bring in that old one from the shed for his ducal posterior. You know, the one I sit on when I'm potting on my seedlings.'

'Do not use such vulgar expressions in front of Constance,' his sister admonished him severely. 'Of course we have enough chairs, and that old one comes into the house over my dead body. The question is, what am I to give him?'

'Presumably you had intended to serve the Grayleighs with something. He can eat whatever they're having.'

'My dear brother, he is a duke! Recall that we encountered him on the road. You cannot believe how exacting he can be.'

'He's a man with teeth and a stomach like any other. Our provision is perfectly good enough for the highest in the land. If he doesn't like it, he can go home again.'

'Bravo, Uncle,' Constance applauded.

Miss Fellowes threw her hands up in the air. 'Men!' she declared. 'You have no idea! Well, I had best go and have words with Cook.' She walked to the door.

'If it helps, I could walk to the coast beforehand and procure you some crabs,' he offered.

'Well, that would be something,' she said grudgingly.

'Oh, and by the way, he's bringing his secretary.'

Beyond one fulminating glance, Miss Fellowes made no response to this before leaving the room. After she had gone, Mr Fellowes said ruefully, 'She may sound anxious but she will rise to the challenge, you know.'

'Yes, I know,' Constance answered. 'Uncle—'

'Constance, my dear, I would have thought twice about asking the fellow if I had had any idea that you had taken him in such dislike,' he said. 'But it's only one meal, after all, and we ought to be hospitable to a newcomer, especially when he is struggling to find servants.'

If Constance had more than a suspicion that she was at least partly responsible for this difficulty, she did not say so. Instead, she contented herself with remarking, 'Even though I find him quite objectionable, it's only one meal, as you say. I suppose I'd better make sure that the best linen is ironed and the silver polished.'

'Heaven forbid that we should offer less than the best to the – what was it you called him? Ah yes, the dandy-brute duke. I suppose I'd better select some good wine for the same reason.'

'His secretary will probably prove to be the greater gentleman of the two,' she replied as she left the room.

The following day, when the best tablecloth was taken out, it was found to have a nasty mark on one corner. 'It's only in one place,' Constance told her aunt. 'I'll sponge it.' That done, she took the cloth outside and spread it out over a bush so that the damp corner could dry. As she was going back indoors, she saw Dickinson walking down the lane. This was the first time she had seen the duke's coachman since they had come upon the damaged carriage at the side of the road, and she wondered how he had been coping with his exacting master.

He seemed cheerful enough as he responded to her greeting, and to her surprise, instead of walking on to the village, turned aside to speak to her. 'Middling well, miss, thank you,' he replied when she asked him how he was enjoying Norfolk. 'I don't mind the change, even though it's a mite quiet for me as I'm a city lad by birth.'

'No doubt His Grace will be wanting to get back to the city before long,' Constance replied. 'I understand the coach has now been mended.'

'Oh yes, miss. The blacksmith in Aylsham knew his work, and put us onto a good wheelwright as well. His Grace was very vexed over the business.'

'We saw that he was angry,' she replied. Then, after a moment's thought she went on, 'I thought it very wrong of him to blame you.'

'Oh, he didn't, miss,' said the coachman, his expression and his tone assuring her that he was telling the truth. 'He was angry that the coach hadn't been made properly. He spoke with me man to man, like the gentleman he is, for he knew I was as vexed as he.'

'Yes. Of course,' Constance answered. In her mind, she saw again the encounter between the duke and his coachman. She had been so sure that the former had been upbraiding the latter. Now, it seemed that it had been one man inviting another to share his anger about a mutually inconvenient situation.

The coachman's voice recalled her to the present. 'It's about Patch that I've come,' he said. Then, when she looked anxious he went on, 'It's nothing too concerning, only as Patch was being led away after you had him out, His Grace noticed that he was favouring one back leg over the other. There's a bit of stiffness there, so with your permission, I'd like to try a poultice on that leg and see if it helps.'

'Yes, of course,' Constance answered. 'Kilver knows that I trust his judgement. There was no need for you to walk all this way.'

'It's only a step,' Dickinson answered. 'Besides, the poultice is a recipe of my own, and His Grace and Kilver both thought that it was best not to assume.'

Constance thanked him again. After he had gone she walked slowly inside, her mind going over the strange notion of the man whom she had termed the dandy brute, hobnobbing with his head groom and his coachman in the stable yard.

Chapter Thirteen

Fortunately, Miss Fellowes's cook was not in anyway discomposed by the news that a high-ranking aristocrat would be dining at a table of her furnishing. 'Indeed,' Miss Fellowes remarked on Thursday as they were waiting for their guests to arrive, 'I sometimes think that she would be happier in a bigger establishment which offered greater challenges to her skill.'

'Pray do not say so in front of our guests,' her brother begged her. 'I have no desire to see her going to Beacon Tower. No other cook I have ever come across has her way with a jugged hare.'

At that very moment, there was a knock at the door and a sound of murmured voices. Constance, who took a certain pride in her self-possession, was more than a little annoyed at the peculiar somersault that her heart seemed to perform at the notion that this might herald the arrival of the duke. To make matters worse, she could feel herself blushing.

In fact, the Grayleighs and the ducal party appeared to arrive all at the same time, and in some confusion, since Mrs Grayleigh entered the room on the duke's arm, her husband and Melinda nowhere to be seen. Jenkins, Mr Fellowes's valet who also acted as butler on grand occasions, had opened the door to them. Clearly a little perplexed by this circumstance, and unsure as to who should take precedence out of this ill-assorted pair, he contented himself with murmuring something inaudible before retreating to the hall.

The newcomers made a formal reverence, whereupon Mr Fellowes introduced the exalted visitor to his sister and niece. 'Although I believe you may have bumped into one another,' he added, looking at Constance with a twinkle in his eye.

'We have met informally,' she answered in carefully neutral tones.

The duke inclined his head again. 'Indeed,' he agreed, before turning to his hostess. 'It is very kind of you to take pity on us in this way,' he said, taking her hand.

'It is the country way,' Miss Fellowes responded. 'You are welcome, sir.' This evening, he was resplendent in an evening coat of silver-grey brocade, which he wore with black satin breeches and a white silk waistcoat embroidered with tiny blue flowers. Barnes had managed to persuade him to have his hair powdered, and this was confined at his neck in a black silk bag.

Constance, not wanting to be outdone, had donned a new lilac gown with a short train and elbow-length sleeves, trimmed with silver lace. She had been very well satisfied with her appearance until her aunt had remarked that she had thought that her niece would keep this for a grander occasion. Her uncle, opening his eyes very wide, had told her that she would make the rest of them look shabby. From a desire not to look countrified and dowdy in front of a sophisticated London visitor, she was then assailed by the horrible fear of looking overdressed, and would have gone upstairs to change had it not been far too late to do so. Now, confronted by the duke's splendour, she was pleased that she had made an effort, and even more so as she saw the light of appreciation in his eyes.

'This must look very odd,' remarked Mrs Grayleigh after the introductions had been made. 'We arrived at the same time as His Grace, and since I was so afraid that Melinda might trip on some unevenness and damage her ankle, which has only just healed, His Grace kindly offered to escort me, whilst his secretary carried Melinda with my husband showing the way.'

At that very moment, the door opened again and Jenkins, confident this time about his priorities, declared, 'Mr Grayleigh, Miss Grayleigh and Mr—' There was a pause and a whispered word. 'Mr Okoro.'

It was Abdas who entered first, with Melinda in his arms. Although he had carried her from the carriage and right up the path, this did not appear to have caused him any effort. Like his employer, he, too, was in evening dress, in a coat of old gold brocade. He wore his own hair unpowdered and tied back at his neck. A greater contrast to the slender, fair-haired Melinda, clad in white muslin, sprigged with tiny blue flowers, could not possibly be imagined.

Mrs Grayleigh was at once all concern over her daughter, who hastened to assure her that she was perfectly well, and quite ready to be set down on her feet if Mr Okoro would be so kind. 'I did not really need to be carried,' Melinda said to the African, her soft tones robbing the words of any offence. 'I am the only child left at home, and Mama is inclined to fuss.'

'Then I must be grateful for her concern, since it gave me the privilege of a most pleasurable duty,' Abdas replied, with a bow.

Constance happened to be standing next to the duke, and she now turned to him, her manner rather more hesitant than usual. 'Mr Okoro, I suppose, is your secretary.'

'Yes.'

'Not your slave.'

'Not my slave.' There was a brief, awkward silence, into which both spoke at the same time.

'I really must apologize—' Constance began, whilst Max started with the words 'As a matter of fact—' They both broke off.

'Miss Church, pray proceed,' Max said, with an open-handed gesture.

'I must apologize for my mistaken assumption,' she said quickly, fearing that any moment the fuss over Melinda's arrival would be over.

'Yes, I think you probably should,' he agreed gravely.

Constance now found that while it was one thing to admit a fault, it was quite another to have someone else agree. She turned towards him with every intention of telling him that if she had been mistaken over this matter, then she had certainly not been over his brutal treatment of Mr Field.

Fortunately, before either of them could say something that they would almost certainly have regretted, Jenkins came in to announce that dinner was served.

Constance had half expected that the duke would turn his nose up at every dish, and look down it at the assembled company. As she reluctantly acknowledged later, he did neither. Seated between herself and her aunt, he proved to be perfectly conversable, acquainted with country ways, and admitting to a passing interest in the sea.

'My cousin is a ship owner,' he confided, 'and has taken me on more than one voyage.'

'And you, Mr Okoro?' Miss Fellowes asked, the company being so small that it was deemed perfectly acceptable to talk across the table. 'Have you also been to sea with His Grace's cousin?'

'I have indeed,' Abdas replied with the ghost of a grin. 'I have much for which to thank Mr Persault.'

'Is that so?' asked Melinda in her soft voice. 'Pray tell us more, Mr Okoro.'

'I owe him nothing less than my freedom, my dignity, in short, my very life,' the African replied. He went on to describe how Max Persault had put his own life at risk to rescue him, and had then made it his business to educate him. 'How can one possibly repay such a debt?' he concluded. Melinda nodded, enthralled by the story.

During his description, Constance, whilst paying close attention to what he was saying, had become conscious of tension building up in the man sitting to her left. Now, as Okoro finished speaking, the duke exclaimed, 'Nonsense!' Aware that this outburst had drawn everyone's attention, Max said as casually as he could, 'Although Okoro is correct in the substance of what he says, my cousin would never want you to think in those terms.'

'Mr Persault sounds a most excellent gentleman,' offered Constance.

'And so he is, Miss Church,' Okoro replied, 'and as modest as he is gallant. Is he not, Your Grace?'

'You are better placed than I to judge,' said the duke after a short pause. Then, anxious to change the subject, he said, 'The lighthouse at Cromer looks interesting. Has it been there for long?'

'There has been a tower on Foulness for just over a hundred years,' Mr Fellowes responded. 'Before that, a fire used to be lit in the church tower.'

'Good heavens!' Mrs Grayleigh exclaimed. 'Surely that must have been very dangerous.'

'It was quite common, I believe, before towers were built specifically for the purpose,' Mr Fellowes explained. 'I cannot tell you when such towers began to be built, I'm afraid. I suspect that the one at Cromer might have been one of the first.'

'Not if it was only built around a hundred years ago,' Max put in. 'The first one built by Trinity House was at Felixstowe in 1609.'

'Indeed?' remarked Mr Grayleigh with interest. 'You seem very knowledgeable, sir.'

Max now perceived that in his haste to get away from the subject of his own virtues, he had encouraged discussion of yet another matter in which one of his station would not normally be expected to take an interest. 'It was one of those voyages with my cousin,' he answered, thinking quickly. 'Sitting in his cabin with little to do, I was driven to study his collection of books on nautical subjects.'

'It's amazing what a man will read when there's nothing else to come by,' said Fellowes. 'If you find the lighthouse interesting, you should visit it.'

'It might be' – Max paused briefly – 'amusing to compare the view to that from Beacon Tower.' He turned to Constance. 'Miss Church, you are local. Perhaps you might care to conduct me there?'

Taken by surprise by this sudden request, Constance found herself saying 'Yes; of course.' She looked around for rescue and caught her friend's eye. 'Melinda, have you ever been to the lighthouse? Would you find it interesting?'

'I am sure I should,' Melinda answered.

Max, looking across the table, was struck with a sudden thought. 'You had better come with us, Okoro. Two young ladies may be more than I can manage.'

'Of course, Your Grace,' Abdas responded with an inclination of his head and a flash of his white teeth. Melinda glanced across at him, then looked quickly away.

'If you permit, Mrs Grayleigh, Melinda could come and stay with us for a few days,' said Miss Fellowes hospitably. 'Constance will be pleased to have the company.' Mrs Grayleigh willingly gave her consent to this plan, to the delight of both young ladies.

The meal itself, which had been a source of dread to more than one person around the table, turned out to be a surprising success.

The cook had indeed put forth her best efforts, and Miss Fellowes, who had told herself that she was not really anxious, was able to breathe a sigh of relief. The guests from Beacon Tower had both proved themselves to have excellent appetites. Constance had been a little surprised to see the duke revealing himself to be such a hearty trencherman. He even went so far as to ask if the cook might be sent for in order that he might congratulate her on her expertise.

Still reluctant to think well of him, Constance was inclined to curl her lip at his playing the great man in this way. Mrs Dobbs clearly did not share her view. She appeared in a crisply clean white apron, beaming with pleasure.

'You don't have a sister who cooks, by any chance?' the duke asked her, half in jest. Mrs Dobbs was pleased to say that she did, and that her sister, who was similarly gifted, lived locally, and was looking for work. She promised to send Mrs Hays to wait upon His Grace on the morrow, and went back to the kitchen with her head held high.

'I think that went very well,' Miss Fellowes announced in satisfied tones after their guests had left. Mr and Mrs Grayleigh had offered to take the duke and his secretary up in their carriage, but the two men had declined civilly.

'Exceedingly well,' her brother answered. 'Mrs Dobbs was pleased with the compliment to her skill.'

Constance sniffed. 'Typical of the fellow to have her dragged from her kitchen so that he might play the great man,' she remarked.

'For my part, I found the duke perfectly conversable,' said Miss Fellowes. 'There was no height in his manner at all.'

'I cannot see that there is any reason why there should be,' said Constance defensively, for she had been surprised at how easily he had mixed with the company.

'He is a *duke*,' her aunt replied, 'and the first such that I have had across my threshold, what is more.'

'I thought that Mr Okoro seemed the more interesting of the two,' said Constance airily.

'I see what it is,' said Mr Fellowes astutely. 'You are determined not to give him any credit at all, my girl. You condemn him for sending for Mrs Dobbs, but if he had not done so, you would have called him ungrateful. He ate a hearty meal – for which no doubt you will say he was a glutton; but if he had picked at his food like a sparrow, you would have said that he was too proud to be satisfied. I accept that you don't like him, but it isn't like you to be so judgemental.'

'Uncle, if you had seen—' Constance began.

'Pray, preserve me from another recital of his bad behaviour on the journey,' said her uncle. 'From what I have seen of him, I could almost suppose him to have a twin brother, so unlike the man you have described have I found him to be. I wish you would lay that matter to rest, for I am heartily tired of it.'

'I beg your pardon for being so tedious,' said Constance rather stiffly.' I think I will retire now.'

'Do not go up yet,' said Miss Fellowes quickly. 'I have just rung for some more tea.'

Before Constance could respond to this speech, her uncle diverted her – as indeed, he had intended to do – by saying, 'I was talking with a fellow from further along the coast this morning. He told me that there is some notion of keeping a careful eye on the shore at Weybourne.'

His sister wrinkled her brow. 'For what purpose?' she asked.

'We have been at war with France since February,' Constance reminded her, catching his meaning. 'Weybourne is a weak spot. Big ships can get quite close in because of the deep water.'

'Then thank goodness that they are alive to the danger already,' said Miss Fellowes in a relieved tone.

'Alive to it – but prepared?' Mr Fellowes muttered as the tea tray was brought in. Constance glanced at him sharply. Perhaps fortunately, his sister did not hear.

When they had drunk their tea, Constance was the first to go upstairs. After she was out of earshot, Miss Fellowes said to her brother, 'I thought that you were a little harsh earlier. Remember she lost her father only two years ago. It is not so long really, given that they were so close.'

Fellowes sighed. 'Perhaps; she can be very decided in her opinions, and rather too quick to judge, you know. I am sure it comes from all that sitting-in on learned conversations from an early age.

It has made her rather precocious.'

'Yes, I know,' his sister agreed. 'All the same, she did have a point.'

'Please, no recitals of the duke's ill-doings from you as well,' he implored her. 'Let us not spoil the memory of a most enjoyable evening.'

Although Constance did change into her night attire, it was quite a long time before she actually got into bed. The evening had provided her with much food for thought, not least the fact that, no doubt because she had been flustered, she had actually agreed to go on an outing with their new neighbour and his secretary.

Only days ago, she would have rejected the very idea as quite impossible. Since then, she had discovered that she had been mistaken about him over a number of matters. He had not reprimanded his coachman; he did not keep a slave; he was not above being pleased in the company of ordinary folk. Whatever next?

To divert her thoughts from this disturbing man, she started thinking about her friend. There had been no denying the instant spark of attraction between Melinda and the handsome African. Constance wondered how Mr and Mrs Grayleigh would feel if her daughter fell in love with him. She would not be the first to conceive a passion for someone of another race. Literature gave a fine precedent in Othello and Desdemona, although their union had not had a happy conclusion. In real life, too, marriages between races were not unknown. Olaudah Equiano, the former slave and abolitionist, whose recent autobiography she had read, had married an English girl. Constance suspected that the welcome that Okoro might receive from the Grayleighs would very much depend upon how generous the duke was prepared to be towards his employee.

When the incident with Mr Field had been fresh in her mind, she would have warned her friend that His Grace would very likely cut his secretary off without a penny. Now, she was not so sure. For one thing, she knew nothing about the dismissed valet. Perhaps he really had been incompetent, and inclined to play for sympathy as well.

For another, Abdas Okoro was dressed, if not as richly as his master, with unmistakable style. Furthermore, whilst Okoro had addressed the duke very properly as 'Your Grace', his tone, although courteous, had lacked the obsequious deference that she would have expected the duke to demand from one who served him. In many ways, they had addressed one another as men on an equal footing.

She thought of how her uncle had thrown out the outlandish suggestion that the duke might have a twin. This was clearly absurd; yet there was no doubt that the nobleman's behaviour was markedly different from how it had appeared on the journey. Could the man be acting a part for some reason; and if so, what might it be?

Chapter Fourteen

The visit to the lighthouse had been planned to take place two days later. In order to carry out this arrangement, therefore, Melinda's father drove her to Runton in the morning. Knowing that Mr Grayleigh was a true countryman, accustomed to country hours, Constance was up betimes. She was glad that she had been so punctual when the Grayleighs' gig appeared at the gate as she was rising from the breakfast table. Trotting alongside the gig was a great shaggy handsome beast, roughly the size of a small pony.

Melinda's wolfhound, a gift from her brother, had been with her since he was a pup. Originally given the majestic name of Augustus, in keeping with his noble heritage, he soon became Gussy, and within a very short period of time, he and Melinda had become inseparable. If she spent an evening away from him, he only just found it tolerable. To be separated from his beloved mistress for more than a few hours, however, could not be borne. He would howl, refuse to eat, and bare his teeth at anyone unwise enough to attempt to lure him from the gate, where he would wait anxiously for her return. He was well acquainted with Constance, and sniffed around her amiably, wagging his tail, as she came to greet her guest.

Constance had known that Gussy would also be visiting them, as had her aunt. 'Well, he'll have to sleep in the shed,' Miss Fellowes had said hopefully, as she did every time Gussy and Melinda came to stay. Needless to say, Gussy always slept at the foot of Melinda's bed, a fact of which Miss Fellowes was well aware.

Mr Grayleigh carried his daughter's portmanteau into the house, politely declining Miss Fellowes's invitation to take some refreshment. 'I have some business at Felbrigg and must not be late,' he explained. He bade his daughter farewell, glancing about him as he stepped back outside. 'You may be well advised to postpone your visit to the lighthouse until another day,' he remarked. 'The mist has come down over the sea, and you won't see much.'

'It may clear,' Constance suggested. 'Early mists sometimes do.'

'Hmm', was the countryman's unpromising reply.

Since the exact time of Melinda's arrival had not been known, the arrangement had been that as soon as the ladies were ready, they would walk together to Beacon Tower. The duke and his secretary would then escort them to the lighthouse, which they would inspect before enjoying a picnic.

'It does look very misty,' Melinda remarked after her father had gone. 'But we must walk to Beacon Tower, or the gentlemen will wonder what has become of us.' Constance agreed.

It was not the first time that one of them had visited the other in this way. On this occasion, Constance had to wonder whether Melinda was hoping for more chances to see the handsome African. Naturally, she told herself firmly, she was not similarly anxious for another encounter with the duke. After all, their most recent meeting had been a little embarrassing.

On the morning after the dinner party, Miss Fellowes had entered the parlour with an exquisitely decorated cloisonné enamel box on the palm of her hand. 'One of the gentlemen must have left a snuff box behind,' she had said.

'It is the duke's,' Constance had replied. 'I remember his taking it out and offering it to my uncle.' He had not actually taken any himself, she recalled.

'It ought to be returned to him as soon as possible.'

'I'll take it,' Constance had said quickly.

Her aunt had looked at her in some surprise. 'Given your dislike, I would not have supposed that you would have wanted to go anywhere near him,' she had said frankly.

Constance had blushed. She had made her offer from impulse, scarcely knowing why. Searching frantically for a reason, she had found inspiration and said, 'I ought to tell him that Mr Grayleigh will be sure to bring Melinda in good time for our outing. I should hate us to find him still in bed!'

She had not quite reached the front door of Beacon Tower when she had heard the sound of voices and clashing steel proceeding from a walled garden on the left-hand side of the house. Curious to discover what this might mean, she had made her way to the narrow gateway and walked through.

She had observed two men with swords in their hands, clad in breeches and shirts, and in their stockinged feet. They had both been so absorbed by their activity that they had not noticed her at first. She had no brothers or close male kin, and had never seen men fight in this way before, so she had been unable to tell at first whether they were fighting in earnest or practising. The one facing her had been Abdas Okoro.

'Too much soft living,' the African had taunted, his teeth flashing white. 'You are out of condition.'

'I'll show you who's out of condition,' his opponent had answered, following up his words with some lightning swordplay. That was when Constance had recognized his voice as being that of the duke. She had always seen him in formal attire before. In his shirtsleeves with a mane of dark waving hair tumbling about his shoulders, a kerchief tied about his crown, he had been unrecognizable at first. It had become clear that this was a friendly bout, so she had watched with interest, waiting for a break in the fighting in order to make her presence known.

Eventually, the duke had succeeded in driving Okoro a good few steps backwards, and had finally managed to flick his sword out of his hand. 'Think twice before you say I'm out of condition,' Max had said, picking it up with the point of his own, and flicking it so that his opponent could catch it. It was at this moment that Abdas had noticed Constance, and indicated her presence to the duke with a movement of his head.

'Miss Church, you should have told us that you were here,' Max had said, as he had turned and bowed, pulling off his kerchief. 'You must forgive our undress.'

'I didn't want to spoil your sport,' Constance had replied a little breathlessly, conscious that she had not told the whole tale. In truth she had found something very compelling in the spectacle of the duke exerting himself in such a way. As he had stood before her, still a little out of breath himself, his shirt open at the neck revealing a hint of chest hair, a shiver had overtaken her from her head to her toes.

She had managed to complete her errand, passing on the snuff box and giving her message. She very much feared that she had sounded like a nitwit, so flustered had she been. The fleeting spark that she had detected in the duke's eye had seemed to indicate that, to her great annoyance, he was well aware of her state of mind.

The two young ladies set off for Beacon Tower at about eleven o'clock, accompanied by Lucy, the maid who assisted Constance and Miss Fellowes with their dressing when necessary. Miss Fellowes had been invited by the duke to join the party but given the nature of the day, she decided to send Lucy in her place for propriety's sake. 'It is not a good day for sketching,' she told her niece, looking disapprovingly at the mist. 'Another time, perhaps.' Lucy, dressed in her best and with her eyes sparkling, had no complaint to make at this unaccustomed outing.

As they walked, Gussy pranced about them, now sniffing at something of great interest amongst a clump of grass or by a gatepost, now trotting ahead, and always returning to Melinda's side at her command.

Constance had been a little concerned at Melinda's walking this distance, but her friend assured her that there would be no difficulty. 'My ankle is stronger every day,' she explained. 'Mother was exclaiming about how I had twisted it and begging me to be careful just as the duke was passing last night. Before I knew what was happening, Mr Okoro had swept me up in his arms.'

'How vexatious for you,' Constance murmured demurely, causing her friend to throw a sharp glance in her direction.

The mist obstinately refused to lift as they walked. It even obscured their view of Beacon Tower itself as they entered the gateway. A figure emerged from the obscurity and began to approach them, and the ladies soon realized that it was Abdas Okoro. Gussy, taken by surprise at the advent of this stranger, snarled and launched himself towards the newcomer, intent only upon protecting his beloved mistress from this unknown and possibly dangerous individual. 'Gussy!' Melinda exclaimed in consternation, whilst

Lucy uttered a tiny scream and hid behind her mistress. 'Stay!'

Constance had seen many reactions to Melinda's monstrous hound, from people running away, to someone actually jumping over a hedge in order to avoid him. On one occasion, they had been approached by a drunken man. He had been merry and not really troublesome. Gussy, however, had taken great exception to his attitude, and had chased him into a nearby duck pond, and it had taken considerable coaxing to persuade him to come out. On another, they had been shopping in Aylsham on market day when a lad had cut the strings of Melinda's reticule and attempted to run off with it. At her command, Gussy had given chase, brought the thief down, and stood over him, paws astride, fur bristling.

By way of contrast, Abdas neither ran away nor attempted to defend himself. Instead, he crouched down and stretched out his hands, making an odd humming noise. Gussy came to a halt, looked at the man in front of him, tilted his head to one side, made an inquisitive sound, then lay down with his tongue lolling out. The African said a few words to him in an incomprehensible language, stroked his head, then straightened. 'Ladies,' he said, bowing.

'How remarkable,' said Melinda, rising from her curtsy, her eyes very round. 'He will obey no one except myself, normally. What did you do?'

'I showed him that I was no threat, and at the same time conveyed to him that his position is inferior to my own,' he replied. 'Will you come inside? It will not be worth visiting the lighthouse today, but the duke has other plans.'

They allowed him to usher them into the house. He snapped his fingers, whereupon Gussy obediently took his place at Abdas's heels, so that it would have been impossible for a stranger to detect to whom the dog actually belonged.

Their host entered the hall as they came in, greeted them and exclaimed, as he saw Gussy, 'Good God, man, what have you acquired there? A donkey?'

'He is a wolfhound and he belongs to me, Your Grace,' said Melinda, curtsying. 'I have never seen him so responsive with another.'

'Abdas has a way with animals,' he replied. 'Will you come into the drawing room? Our planned expedition cannot take place today for obvious reasons, so we must decide what to do instead.'

There was nothing to be seen of the fine view from the drawing room window beyond about twelve feet. 'It is usually possible to see the sea from here,' said Max. 'I fear that you will have to take my word for it, however.'

'It is always a source of regret to me that my uncle's house, though close to the sea in distance, has no view of it at all,' Constance told him.

Max nodded. 'When I first entered this room, I ran over to the windows like a child. I could hardly contain my excitement.'

The pleasures of outdoor walking would obviously be extremely limited that day, so the duke offered to show his visitors around the house, after which they would all be served with refreshments. 'No doubt your dog will need a walk, so, after we have eaten, perhaps we might walk down to the church,' he suggested. 'Who knows, the weather might even improve sufficiently to ensure that we catch sight of it before we bump into it!'

All of these suggestions were readily accepted and, after a glass of wine, the duke proceeded to escort his visitors around his home.

To begin with, they remained very much one party. As they reached the long gallery, they separated into two couples, Abdas taking a volume of maps from the shelf in order to point something out to Melinda, whilst Max and Constance looked at a painting that someone had done of the house and grounds a hundred years before. It was an imagined view from above, and appeared to depict an extensive estate.

'You know, I can't help thinking that the artist must have exercised his imagination to quite an extraordinary degree,' Max remarked. 'The property shown here must cover at least three hundred acres.' Lucy, after a cursory look at the pictures on the wall, went to look out of the window.

'Perhaps not,' Constance replied. 'Maybe an ancestor of yours gambled away half his inheritance.'

'No ancestor of mine, Miss Church,' said Max indignantly, then wanted to curse himself for his indiscretion.

Luckily, Constance took his remarks another way. 'No, of

course, I had forgotten that you inherited indirectly from the last baron,' she said. 'I know what it must be! Your estate must have extended out into where the sea is now. There was another village out there until the fourteenth century.'

'Indeed?'

'Oh yes. You can still see the ruins occasionally at very low tides. And of course' – and here her voice assumed sepulchral tones – 'when the sea is rough, you can hear the tolling of the church bell.'

'You terrify me!' Max declared, raising his hands in a gesture of submission. 'From now on, I shall sleep with a pillow over my head. You need not tell me, of course, that to hear it will be a certain omen of my own death.'

'Certainly not,' Constance answered, enjoying this banter rather more than she might have been prepared to admit. 'If you were to see Black Shuck, however, that would be a different matter.'

'Black Shuck? And what might that be?'

Lucy turned away from the window at this reference to a legend that she knew well. 'Black Shuck is a huge black dog with one burning eye, Your Grace,' she said. 'Isn't he, Miss Connie?'

Constance nodded. 'See him at night or hear him howling, and you may expect your immediate demise,' she intoned in the same sinister voice that she had used before.

'Good God,' Max exclaimed, pointing at Gussy. The wolfhound was stretched out on the floor next to his mistress, looking like one dead. Lucy knelt down to stroke the dog, who received this attention with a rhythmic thump of his tail.

Constance laughed. 'And you let him in! You were foolhardy indeed, Your Grace.'

'Undoubtedly,' he agreed, laughing himself. 'Do you know, I wish you would call me Max.'

'Certainly not! It would be most improper,' Constance replied, wishing she did not sound like someone's maiden aunt. 'Besides—'

'Well, Miss Church? "Besides" what?'

Constance paused, then went on reluctantly, 'I had gained the distinct impression that you enjoyed your exalted rank.'

'You are mistaken, ma'am,' said Max. His tone was still pleasant although his gaze had lost its former warmth. 'I play the duke because I must. Believe me, I find nothing agreeable in my position.'

'Nothing?' Constance echoed, wrinkling her brow.

Max looked back at the picture for a few minutes before speaking. 'The dukedom is a valuable one, both a blessing and a burden to the man bearing responsibility for it.'

She looked at him curiously. 'You speak as though it had nothing to do with you.'

There was a tiny pause before he answered. 'The title of duke has but lately been bestowed upon me,' Max replied. 'I have yet to discover all that it entails. And yet—' His voice died away.

'And yet?' she prompted him.

He looked straight at her. 'And yet I would willingly forgo it all for the chance to have this little piece of paradise,' he said. Suddenly, as their eyes met, it felt as if he was not really talking about Beacon Tower at all.

The murmur of voices, followed by gentle laughter from Melinda, broke the spell. Constance glanced towards the other couple, glad of something that might divert the duke's attention from her flushed cheeks. 'Gussy has definitely taken to Mr Okoro,' she said, indicating the still-recumbent Gussy.

'He has an affinity with all animals,' Max replied as they walked from the painting of the estate to the next, which portrayed a stout, rather bad-tempered-looking woman in Tudor dress. 'We were attacked by an enormous dog in the back streets of Portugal on one occasion. He crouched down and, well, crooned to it in some kind of way. In no time at all, the brute was lying down next to us, its tongue hanging out.'

Constance nodded, remembering what had happened in the drive a short time before. 'You must have been very relieved,' she remarked.

'It was damn … dashed inconvenient,' Max said frankly. 'The brute refused to leave us, and stood whining on the quayside as we rowed back to the ship.'

'He is a remarkable man.'

'What's more, I suspect that his blood might be bluer even than' – Max paused, then added smoothly – 'than mine. Shall we rejoin them?' Constance went with him to look at the book of maps that Abdas and Melinda still had open in front of them. She found herself wondering under what circumstances an English aristocrat might find himself exploring the back streets of Portugal.

Chapter Fifteen

Although the mist lifted slightly, the day was still quite hazy, so after Max had completed his guided tour, they enjoyed some delicious food, prepared by Mrs Hays. She had accepted employment at Beacon Tower, begun immediately, and had treated with contempt any suggestion that she might need time to settle in. They then took a walk down to the church, whilst Lucy, who had happily eaten some bread and cheese with Mrs Hays, ran back to The Brambles.

Keeping their earlier pairings, Max walked with Constance whilst Abdas gave Melinda his arm. Gussy darted here and there, investigating what seemed worthy of his notice, and always returning to his mistress. Like Constance, Melinda, too, had explained the legend of Black Shuck to her companion. 'It's to be hoped that no one mistakes your dog for the hellhound,' Abdas observed, only half in jest.

'I am very careful with him,' Melinda replied frankly. 'Although it is a foolish legend, some do lend credence to it, so he is never allowed outside the perimeter of the farm on his own, for instance, and particularly not at night.'

'The reputation of the phantom would be enhanced, if someone actually died of fright after seeing him,' Abdas pointed out.

'What a thing to have on one's conscience, though.' She paused. 'Are there dogs in ... in your country?' she asked him tentatively.

'How can you ask me when you have one yourself?' he replied.

'I meant Africa – the country where you came from.'

'Africa is not one country; it is many states; but it is no longer my home.' She said nothing, looking at him with a puzzled expression.

'What makes a home, Miss Grayleigh?' he asked her.

She looked around. 'The countryside,' she said. 'Knowing a place so well that you could find your way around with your eyes shut. But that's not really it. It's Mama and Papa and my brother Stephen; and Gussy of course; and my friends; our servants; Connie—' Her voice faded.

He looked back down at her, his expression bleak. 'The people,' he said. 'What do you think happened to my people when the slave traders came? There was some resistance; those who resisted, like my father, or who were too old to be of any value, were slaughtered there and then.' Melinda gasped, her hands going to her mouth. He went on, as if she had made no reaction. 'My mother also perished. Those of us who were young and strong were herded together and put in chains. The last thing we saw as we left was our village being burned to the ground. There are no places for me to explore with my eyes shut, Miss Grayleigh.'

'Mr Okoro, forgive me; I should not have been so crass as to remind you,' said Melinda.

'We were walked to the ship across many miles,' he continued. He was looking ahead, recalling the horrors of the past and not seeing what lay before him. It was as if now that he had begun to tell his story, some inner compulsion bound him to continue. 'Some perished on the journey. Others were lashed to make them keep walking. Once on the ship, the nightmare was only just beginning. Have you seen what a slave ship is like, Miss Grayleigh?'

She nodded, her eyes filling with tears. 'I saw a print of the diagram made by Mr Brookes for Mr Clarkson,' she said. 'I cannot believe that there are those who would treat human beings in such a way.'

'Believe it,' he said grimly. 'We were loaded like so much meat for sale, kept under a grille so we could not venture forth into the light of day. Many others perished in the foul conditions.' He paused. 'My wife was one.'

'Your wife!'

'She was expecting a child, so she was vulnerable.' Melinda caught hold of his hand, and he squeezed hers in return. She glanced briefly at Max and Constance, who had moved ahead whilst Gussy had been indulging in a prolonged sniff at something of great interest. They were not looking back.

'So how did you escape?' Melinda asked. 'I remember you telling us how Mr Persault saved you from the water; but if there was a grille across the hold, how did you get out when the boat sank?'

Abdas shrugged. 'There is good and bad in everyone,' he said. 'The call came to abandon ship. All the men ran to scramble into the rowing boat. I watched their running feet and knew despair. Then I saw one man pause and hesitate. He came back to unlock the grille, risking his own place in the boat.'

'Oh, God bless him for that,' Melinda cried. 'I do pray that he was spared.'

'I must admit to hoping that if any were saved, he was among them,' Abdas agreed.

'And what of the others?' Melinda ventured.

'My people?' Abdas asked, his voice anguished. 'I know not. Some drowned. Others managed to cling to the wreckage. I was able to help just two others to stay afloat until we were spotted by the crew of the *Lady Marion*. What kind of a … a man am I, to save just two and myself?'

'A truly remarkable one, I do believe,' Melinda responded. Then, after a moment, she added in a low tone, 'If only I could make it up to you for all that you have suffered.'

He stopped again and covered the little hand that rested on his sleeve with his own. 'Your kindness and sympathy are balm to my soul,' he assured her. 'Come, we must not get left behind.'

They caught up with the others as they reached the church. Scarcely had they exchanged half a dozen remarks when Melinda cried out, 'Look up there! Isn't that someone on the roof?'

They all glanced towards where she was pointing. A small figure was indeed clinging to the roof of the church. 'Let us investigate,' said Max.

They walked through the lychgate to see a small group of people gathered together, looking upwards, among them the vicar. 'What's to do?' Max asked him.

'Tommy Spencer, a lad from the village, has managed to climb onto the church roof by means of yonder tree,' said Mr Mawsby.

'Good heavens, why?' Constance asked.

'Because he's a boy, I expect,' Max answered good-humouredly. 'I suppose the silly lad can't get down now.'

'He did try a few minutes ago,' the vicar answered, 'but he slipped, and now refuses to move either way. In any case, as you see, it is far easier to drop from the tree onto the roof than to climb back up from the roof to the tree again.'

'What is being done to rescue him?' Max asked.

'Some long ladders are being fetched,' the vicar answered. 'A steeplejack could go up there easily. Unfortunately, there is no such man living near here, and the boy is getting more nervous by the minute.'

'Abdas,' said Max. The African went to his side, and the two men looked up at the roof of the church. The lad's position did indeed look most precarious. He was about halfway between the tower and the opposite end. As Max looked at the lad, he could see something of the pallor of his complexion and his general demeanour.

He had come across something like this before, in tragic circumstances. He had chanced to be on board another man's ship, about some long-forgotten errand. It had been a cold day in March, with a wind blowing across the Atlantic that cut right through into your bones. There had been a storm brewing and a young lad had been sent to climb the rigging to secure one of the sails more firmly. The boy had looked very unsure and nervous, and had had to be told more than once, 'Get aloft, you young varmint!' As he had climbed, the master had told Max that this was his first voyage.

Given the nature of the day and the lad's inexperience, in the master's place Max would have been inclined to send another more confident boy, and allow this youngster to learn his work when the conditions were less hazardous. He had held his tongue. It was not his ship, after all, and he barely knew the master, who was much older and more experienced than himself.

Whilst they had been attending to other matters on deck, they had been alerted by a cry from above their heads. The boy had managed to climb so far, then had missed his hold and was hanging on precariously, his face white, his eyes glassy with panic. Instinctively, Max had begun to strip off his coat, preparing to go up after the boy. He had only had time to get his arm out of one sleeve, when the lad's hold had failed him, and he had fallen to his death on the deck at their feet.

As Max remembered that incident, his jaw hardened. The ladders might arrive too late. He wasn't going to see another boy perish if he could help it. He cupped his hands, and with a voice that had often been raised to carry across the deck of a ship mid-ocean, he called out, 'Hold on, lad. We're coming.'

There was a window in the tower, perhaps eight feet above the roof on which the boy sat, and Max pointed to it. 'Go to that window with a rope, and talk to the boy. Don't let him move; I'll retrace his steps.' Abdas nodded, and immediately turned to the vicar to make sure that the door to the tower was unlocked, whilst Max made for the tree, halfway between a stride and a run.

'Your Grace?' Constance ventured, hurrying beside him. Along with everyone else, she had been watching the drama unfold. Every day since the duke's arrival, she had been obliged to revise her original impression of the man. Now, if she was not mistaken, he was about to embark on an adventure which would be positively heroic.

For a moment or two, Max was barely aware of having been addressed. These days of languor and inactivity had not suited him at all. He was a man of action. Now, he had an opportunity to put aside the part that he had been obliged to play and be true to himself. Again, he measured the distance from the window to the roof with his eye, and then looked carefully at the tree to see how the youngster had managed to cross from its branches to the roof. Courage and daring were two things; foolhardiness was quite another. He had no wish to provide someone else for the villagers to rescue with their long ladders!

'Your Grace?' Constance said again. Max looked at her this time. For a brief moment, he could not remember why she was calling him by a title that was not his.

'What are you going to do?' she asked him. By now, they had reached the foot of the tree.

He jerked his head in the direction of the stranded youngster. 'Go and get him down,' he replied easily.

'But it's so high,' she answered.

'Fearful for me, Miss Church?' he asked. Max had dressed in his best to entertain the ladies, and he could not possibly climb in such a well-fitting coat. What was more, he now realized that whilst he would have been able to throw off a coat of his own choosing with ease, he actually needed someone to help him off with this one; that is, if he were not to pull and tug at it and turn the sleeves inside out in a somewhat farcical display. 'Ma'am,' he said, 'I hate to ask you, but—'

'But no doubt my hands are by far the cleanest of anyone around here,' she suggested, with a twinkle.

She had only intended to offer for the sake of being useful. Now, she found that there was something exceedingly intimate in helping a gentleman off with his coat. It did not seem to be possible to do it without touching him, and in doing so, however fleetingly, her awareness of his muscular physique was heightened. She coloured slightly, thankful that his back was turned towards her. Once his coat was in her hands, he shed his waistcoat and then his cravat, and also entrusted them to her. Using the tree as a support for his back, he pulled off his boots. He then looked at the tree and set about finding the best way up.

Impulsively she said, 'Surely it would be best to wait for the ladders.' Even as she said the words, she looked at his face, and saw what was in his mind. The ladders might arrive too late. 'Go, then,' she said. 'Do be careful.' He turned briefly to look at her and knew an impulse to kiss her anxious, upturned face. 'Is there anything else I can do?' Constance asked him, breaking the spell.

'Blankets for the boy,' said Max, as he found the foothold he was searching for and climbed into the tree. 'He'll be shocked and cold.'

'Be careful,' she said again.

He turned his head and looked down. He was all buccaneer now, in his shirtsleeves, his eyes flashing in his swarthy face. 'I always am,' he responded, before resuming his climb. As Constance watched him, at last she located the elusive memory that had escaped her until now. The duke, and the man on horseback who had seen her at the window of the Scotts' house and had blown her a kiss, were one and the same! He *was* playing a part! Which was the part, and which the real man?

The sound of voices from behind her made her aware that she was staring up into the tree like a halfwit so, remembering her errand, she turned back to make sure that blankets were fetched for the terrified boy. Of the hazardous nature of the duke's next move, she hardly dared to think.

Those assembled in the churchyard were now looking up at the roof where the boy still crouched, apparently unable to move. There was no sign of the African or of Melinda. In response to her question, the vicar informed her that they had both gone into the tower. 'Miss Grayleigh's father employs the lad's uncle, so she knows him,' he explained. 'She thought that a friendly face might reassure him. A stranger, especially one who is obviously' – he cleared his throat – 'a foreigner, might cause him to panic further.'

Constance nodded. She was not sure how Mrs Grayleigh might feel about her daughter being left unchaperoned in such a way. Even so, now was not the moment to insist that someone else go up the tower to play propriety. She was certainly not going to do so! Instead, she passed on Max's message, and stood watching the roof. A glance to the right showed her both Melinda's and Abdas's faces at the window. To the left, she detected a sway of the tree's branches, then Max emerged, looking for a way to descend to the roof, which was a short drop below him.

'He'll be killed for sure,' said one woman, her tone one of dread tinged with not a little excitement. 'Big funeral for a duke, I shouldn't wonder.'

'There'll be another change at the Tower then,' remarked another lugubriously.

'Oh, do be quiet if you can't say anything useful,' Constance snapped. In that instant, Max dropped to the roof. Despite a gasp from the crowd, his stance did not waver for an instant. Slowly, but confidently, his arms outstretched for balance, he made his way to where the boy was crouched, and, before the lad could grab hold of him, he sat astride the roof and took him in his arms. There was another gasp from the crowd, this time one of relief. Nobody spoke; everyone understood that the next step would be just as hazardous.

Now, Abdas emerged from the window with a rope, one end of which was attached to the window whilst the other was in a coil over his shoulder. He made his way along the roof as lightly and as easily as Max had done and soon reached the other two figures on the roof.

'You didn't need to come down,' Max said. 'You could have waited in the tower and pulled us up from there.'

'You would deny me my chance to shine in front of a lady?' Abdas asked him, grinning.

Max glanced up to see Melinda looking down at them from the tower. 'I see,' he murmured. 'Well, let's get the lad to safety and earn our plaudits.'

The most difficult part of the whole business was to persuade the boy to put his confidence in them. To begin with, he was gripping Max so tightly that it was almost impossible to move. A few minutes' talking to him and building up his confidence was time well spent. The rope, though quite unnecessary as far as Max and Abdas was concerned, represented a lifeline to the boy, and once he had it tied around him, he became much more co-operative.

To everyone's relief, they soon reached the tower, whereupon Abdas climbed the rope with ease, pulled the lad up, then let the rope down again so that Max could follow.

On the ground, as soon as the boy was pulled to safety, there was a hearty cheer in which Constance joined, and she was conscious of a surge of relief so powerful that it took her by surprise.

She now realized that he was neither a dandy nor a brute but definitely a buccaneer; certainly not the kind of man that she ought to be hankering after, if she had any sense! It was quite a lowering thought to discover that in that case, clearly she had no sense at all.

Chapter Sixteen

The day after the lad's rescue being Sunday, Mr and Miss Fellowes, together with their niece and her guest, attended the morning service. The duke and his secretary were there in the Beacon Tower pew. Their presence was now accepted among the village populace. Even those who had never seen anyone with dark skin before were now used to the sight of Abdas. Some of them had even been heard to say that he was 'no worse than plenty of foreigners and a good deal better than most' – meaning, of course, anyone who came from the other side of Aylsham.

The willingness of the villagers to accept both men had, of course, increased tenfold after their daring rescue of Tommy Spencer. The lad's mother, once she had given him a good hiding for his foolishness, had recounted the story of his rescue to anyone who had not witnessed if for himself. There was even a smattering of applause for the two heroes of the hour as they entered the church, hastily quelled by disapproving looks from the more pious members of the congregation.

After the service was over, the duke invited the Fellowes party to eat with them, by way of paying Miss Fellowes back for her hospitality, and they were delighted to accept. The mist from the previous day had blown away completely, and the day was sunny, if rather breezy, so the walk from church was followed by a stroll in the gardens.

'I wonder at your spending so much time here, when you have much bigger estates elsewhere,' Constance remarked, as she walked at the duke's side. The walled garden afforded protection to its many plants from strong winds from the sea. It was here that she had seen the duke fighting with Abdas. How different the nobleman looked today! Yet there was a vigorous energy about him, even in repose, which – or so it seemed to Constance – must surely be obvious to anyone with eyes to see.

Max shrugged. 'A whim,' he drawled.

'I wish you wouldn't do that,' Constance replied.

'Do what?'

'Play the languid aristocrat.'

'Play?' he murmured. 'And what makes you think that I am playing, Miss Church?'

'Yesterday's events for a start,' Constance replied. 'You climbed that tree and walked along the roof as if you encountered such hazards every day of the week. *And*,' she went on, when he looked as though he was about to interrupt her, 'I saw you in Diss.'

'Diss?' he queried, drawing his brows together as if puzzled.

'You were on horseback,' Constance declared. 'Later, I saw you fighting with a group of men.'

Max stared at her in consternation. 'When did you realize that it was I?' he asked her.

'Something at the back of my mind kept telling me that I had seen you before,' she told him. 'When you looked up at me in the gig, the angle of your face seemed familiar. I ought to have realized when I saw you fencing, only—' She broke off. How could she admit that she had been flustered at the sight of him in his shirtsleeves? After a moment, she continued rather lamely. 'Only I did not. Then when you climbed the tree in that devil-may-care fashion, I knew.'

He raised his hand. 'Ah, no,' he responded. 'I may climb with confidence, but being "devil-may-care" at great heights is never wise.'

'Neither is taking on several men in the open street,' she pointed out.

Max sighed. 'Would you believe me if I told you that I had been finding my new responsibilities rather irksome?' he said ruefully. 'I needed to escape for the evening. Barnes is inclined to be – protective, shall we say? – of the ducal reputation. It was easier to slip away secretly than try to explain myself to him.'

'People do not always understand one, do they?' Constance

replied. 'And sometimes, the people closest to one can find it the hardest.'

'Very true,' Max agreed. 'I suspect that you too have secrets, Miss Church. Are your uncle and aunt aware of your acquaintance with the writings of Thomas Paine, for instance?'

'How did you—?' She broke off abruptly.

'You quoted him the other day, remember?'

'Hoist with your own petard, then, Your Grace,' she declared triumphantly, making a swift recovery. 'You must be acquainted with them yourself in order to have recognized the quotation.'

'A nobleman has a duty to identify traitors in the midst.'

'Mr Paine is not a traitor,' she said indignantly.

'He's been convicted of seditious libel,' he pointed out. 'He's also a member of the French Convention. *And* he advocated the separation of the American colonies from Britain.'

'I am sure that he is a good man and an honest one,' she protested, then coloured as she realized what she had revealed.

'You have met him, then? Under what circumstances?'

'It was in London. I went with Papa and we met him at the house of a mutual friend.' She described her father's study in Cambridge, the lively company, the discussions and the debates. 'I missed it terribly after Papa died,' she confessed. 'It opened up a world for me; a world of intellect, in which questions and challenges were welcomed.'

'Questions and challenges; or a room full of men with radical views simply agreeing with each other?'

'That's a hateful thing to say,' she said hotly. 'Just because most of them would ... would—'

'Would dispense with such as myself at the drop of a hat?' he suggested.

'I wasn't going to say that,' she replied, flushing.

'No, I'm sure you were not. That was intolerably crass and ill-mannered of me.'

'Yes it was,' she agreed.

'No doubt you would send me to the guillotine for such remarks. In my defence, I would like to remind you that crassness and ill manners are not solely the province of the aristocracy.'

'No indeed; buccaneers are capable of such behaviour too.'

'*Touché*,' he responded, raising his hand in a fencer's gesture. 'Shall we go inside now? I suspect that dinner might be nearly ready.'

It was only as they were walking back to the house that Max said provocatively, 'You didn't mention *everything* that you saw me do when I was in Diss.'

Constance felt the colour flooding into her cheeks. 'No, I did not,' she agreed, trying for a touch of bravado. 'I dare say you do the same when you catch sight of any female at a window.'

'Oh no,' Max answered. 'I only blow kisses to pretty ones.'

It was as well that they reached the house at this point, for Constance had no idea how to respond to this audacious comment.

Max conducted them to the dining room, where the table was laid ready for dinner. The furniture had been polished to a shine, likewise the silver, and the curtains and carpet, whilst somewhat worn, had obviously been cleaned. Either Barnes and Davis had been exceedingly busy, or more servants had been employed. 'We have two young women who walk here from the village each day and report to Barnes,' the duke informed them.

After the splendid dinner cooked by Mrs Hays, the visitors took their leave. As they did so, Max said, 'Shall we go to the lighthouse tomorrow, if the mist does not foil our plans again?' Constance glanced towards Melinda in order to discover her opinion. It had not escaped her notice that whilst she had been walking with the duke, her friend had been in close conversation with his secretary. It was no great surprise, therefore, when Melinda nodded in agreement.

Constance woke early the following morning, with a feeling of excitement that she told herself firmly was solely due to the fact that the coming visit would be an interesting one. Of course, she told herself, it could not have anything to do with the fact that her escort had called her pretty! She knelt on the window seat in her room, watched the sun rise in the midst of a red glow, and remembered the old saying, 'Red sky in the morning, sailors take warning.' There might be sailors in sore need of a guiding light before the next day came.

Constance and Melinda walked to Beacon Tower as before, accompanied by Miss Fellowes with her sketchbook and, of course, Gussy. They were met on their arrival by Max, superbly dressed as always, today in a dark-blue coat with a light-blue waistcoat and buff breeches. Abdas was at his elbow.

'Good morning, ladies,' he said, bowing as he ushered them into the house. 'Would you care for a glass of wine, or shall we set off immediately?'

The ladies opted for the latter course, and were soon being handed into an immaculate open carriage. Constance, sensing the power in the duke's arm as he assisted her with his hand under her elbow, asked, 'Do you ever drive yourself, Your Grace?'

'Occasionally. I prefer to ride, I must admit.'

'Do you drive, Mr Okoro?' Miss Fellowes asked.

The African inclined his head. 'It is a pleasure I have acquired since' – he paused briefly – 'since coming to this country,' he concluded smoothly.

'Are there any horses in Africa?' Melinda asked him.

'Now, that I cannot tell you, Miss Grayleigh,' Abdas replied. 'All I can say is that I have never seen any there, although I have seen lions and elephants.'

The ladies were enthralled at this revelation, and begged him to tell them more. Max sat back easily in his seat, and listened as the African wove a spell with his honeyed tones. Miss Grayleigh was well on the way to being utterly entranced with him. At any rate, no one would be able to say that she had fallen for his fortune. Doubtless, he thought cynically, her parents would be much better disposed when they discovered that he was a ship owner with some handsome investments and a neat estate, rather than a secretary to a great man.

He stole a glance at Miss Church and saw that she was watching him curiously. She, too, was in for a surprise. She thought him a titled man with lands and riches. How would she feel about him when he was revealed to be a mere 'mister', comfortably off rather than wealthy, and with no property to his name? The fact that she despised the aristocrat that he had pretended to be gave him some hope.

About her radical sympathies, though, he was conscious of some disquiet. Miss Church's opinions were no different from those held by many intellectuals. If she was amongst those whose politics caused them to desire a revolution in England such as was currently taking place in France, however, then at all costs he must make sure that she knew nothing of Alistair's exploits.

Although she had been surprised at his activities in Diss, she had said nothing to indicate that she did not believe him to be the duke. Nor had she exhibited any suspicious behaviour so far. Unfortunately, his mind kept going back to the moment when he had asked Alistair what he should do should he suspect anyone of endangering the mission. His cousin's instructions had been quite clear. 'Kill them,' he had said.

Max knew that Alistair had a ruthless streak which meant that he would be more than capable of cold-bloodedly carrying out such a grim task. He himself had killed before, in the heat of the moment, in defence of his own life or that of someone else. He looked at Constance Church and knew that he could never do it. What was more, because of the way that he had come to feel about her, he would do all in his power to protect her.

He caught himself up sharply. Why was he thinking of hopes and feelings? How did they fit into his encounters with Miss Church? Whatever relationship existed between them would disappear once Alistair arrived to take his rightful place. He looked away from the woman sitting opposite him and gazed at the sea. Would to God he were out there now with his ship under him and this whole masquerade behind him. For all that it had been undertaken for honourable reasons, he felt like the grossest deceiver.

Constance's thoughts were much as he had imagined. At first completely absorbed by Abdas's stories, she had soon started to wonder at the haughty nobleman who allowed his employee to take centre stage whilst he himself played the part of an onlooker. Had there ever been a duke who behaved in such a way?

The lighthouse was the other side of Cromer from West Runton, built on a piece of land called Foulness. From its eminence, the party were able to look down on the town, which looked very small, with its few dwellings chiefly clustered around the lofty parish church.

'My uncle tells me that although the lighthouse tower has been here for over a hundred years, the man who built it could not afford to have the fire lit,' said Constance.

'That would not appear to be very sensible,' her friend murmured.

'Don't believe it, Miss Grayleigh,' Max said. 'A day mark in itself provides a valuable beacon, giving a point of identification – something not readily come by at sea. Shall we go in, ladies?'

The lighthouse was tended by two young women who greeted them with curtsies, and not a little curiosity, especially when confronted with Abdas Okoro. They were very happy to allow the visitors to look round, and adjured them strictly not to interfere with the light. 'Them up at London'd have our hides if we allowed any harm to come to it,' said one of them.

Having promised to leave it alone, the party ascended the spiral staircase, Max going first, and Abdas bringing up the rear, with the ladies in between for safety's sake. Gussy took one look at the spiral staircase and flopped down outside the door to await his mistress's return. Miss Fellowes, too, declined to climb the tower. 'It is some time since I made a sketch from this perspective,' she declared, preparing to sit on a rug that was being spread out by a groom.

Max was the first to enter the chamber where the light was held. When he looked at what was before him, he could not help exclaiming in awestruck tones, 'By God, Abdas, just look at this!'

'By God, indeed,' the African replied, obviously similarly impressed as he came into view. 'Wonder upon wonders.'

'What is this wonder?' Melinda asked.

'It is the light, ma'am,' Max replied, gesturing towards the mechanism before them. 'Up until now, lighthouses have depended on coal-fired lights to keep them lit. Here, you see oil lamps and reflectors on a revolving frame.'

'I can see the benefit of oil lamps over coal, but why should the frame revolve?' Constance asked.

'The idea is still in its infancy,' Max responded. 'It is only the second such installed by Trinity House, to which this lighthouse now belongs. The effect of the frame revolving is that the light flashes.'

Constance frowned. 'Forgive me; I still cannot see the advantage.'

This time it was Abdas who answered her. 'The frame can be constructed so that the timing of the flash varies,' he explained. 'When new lighthouses are built, the timing could be different for each one.'

Constance's brow cleared. 'I see! So a list could be made of all the different lighthouses and their light patterns! A mariner would then be able to discover where he was by the pattern of the flashing light.'

'Exactly so!' Max declared. 'We will make a sailor of you yet, Miss Church. Believe me, when you have been at sea after a storm with your mast gone and only the pole star to guide you, anything that might give such a clear indication as to where you are would be a real boon.'

'I can imagine,' she replied. She was remembering how Max had spoken in a languid tone about the need to find something to do on board ship. Such a circumstance was beginning to sound unlikely in the extreme.

The view from the lighthouse covered a large expanse of sea. They stood admiring it, commenting idly on its blueness on such a fine day, the sparkle of the sun on the water, and the white, fluffy clouds. 'There's a boat out there,' said Melinda, pointing. The others turned to look.

'Where? I cannot make it out,' said Constance, screwing up her eyes to try and see it.

'Perhaps I can help,' said Max, producing a brass folding telescope from inside his coat. 'Allow me to locate it first.' Within a very short time, he had found the boat in question, and offered the telescope to Constance, who struggled at first to find anything at all.

'At one moment, I think I almost have it, then it's gone,' she confessed, laughing,

'And the lighthouse isn't even moving,' Melinda reminded her. 'What on earth must it be like at sea, with the whole vessel rocking beneath one's feet?'

'It's an acquired skill,' Max said. 'Remember that everything is magnified, so a tiny movement of the instrument itself makes a big difference to what is seen at the other end. Other reference points help, too. Do you see that cloud near the horizon – the one with a curly edge at the bottom, a little like a 'w' ? The vessel is just below and to the right of it.'

'It will probably have sailed all the way to America by the time I've found it,' Constance grumbled.

Max laughed. 'Something of that size? I doubt it's more than a fishing smack. Here, let me help you.' He found the vessel again, and by dint of holding it steady for her with his left hand and guiding her with his right, he enabled her to locate it.

'I've got it!' she exclaimed with triumph, turning her head to look at him and then blushing furiously as she realized how close he was. Why, she was practically in his arms! 'I shall never find it again now that I have looked away, of course,' she went on, making a recovery. 'Melinda, would you like to have a look?'

As Constance held the telescope out to her friend, she noticed that there were some letters engraved on it. 'To M.P. with fondest love, M.P.' How odd, she thought to herself. The donor has the same initials as the recipient.

Profiting from the instructions given to her friend, Melinda managed to locate the boat with Abdas's help. Unlike Constance, she appeared to be utterly unembarrassed at the proximity of the duke's secretary. 'Amazing how something so distant can appear to be so close,' she remarked, as she returned Max's telescope.

'Not so very distant,' he replied with a smile. 'Abdas?' he added, holding the instrument out to the other man, who, like Max, found the vessel with ridiculous ease.

After they had looked their fill and the gentlemen had once more admired the advanced mechanism of the light, they descended the stairs and went back outside, passing the two curtsying attendants, whose shy smiles broadened as they received the coins that the duke put into their hands.

They sat on blankets, eating their picnic, chatting idly, and looking out to sea, whilst Gussy, reunited with his mistress, lay in blissful relaxation at her feet. Most of the conversation was supplied by Abdas and Melinda. Max and Constance, although not silent, seemed to be more preoccupied, whilst Miss Fellowes only snatched a few moments to eat, before returning to her sketch.

After they had enjoyed their food, they were not sorry to return, for the sun had gone in and what had been a breeze was becoming more substantial altogether.

'Wind's getting up,' Mr Fellowes remarked, as the gentlemen dropped the ladies off at home. 'I shouldn't be surprised if we were to have a storm tonight. You'll hear it up at Beacon Tower, I shouldn't wonder.'

'No doubt,' the duke answered.

'Heaven help any poor souls who are out at sea in it,' said Miss Fellowes.

'Amen,' responded Abdas and Melinda, who spoke at the same time, then shared a long exchange of looks.

Chapter Seventeen

Mr Fellowes's prediction proved to be correct. During the evening, the wind increased, accompanied by driving rain, and by the time Melinda and Constance retired, it was bidding fair to become as bad a storm as either of them could remember. 'I fancy that we can hear the sea, even though I know that we cannot,' said Melinda with a shudder, as they sat looking out into the night from Constance's bedroom window. 'Just fancy Abdas – I mean, Mr Okoro – and the duke out in a storm in such weather!'

'No doubt the duke would be snugly tucked up in a hammock whilst the mariners aboard the same ship were fighting to preserve his life,' said Constance.

'Do you really think so?' Melinda asked her.

Constance sat for a moment deep in thought. There was a time when she would have answered this question unhesitatingly in the affirmative. 'I don't know what I think about him any more,' she said frankly. 'What of you?'

'What of me?' Melinda wrinkled her brow.

'What do you think of Abdas – I mean, Mr Okoro?' Constance asked teasingly.

After a long pause, Melinda said, 'I've never met anyone like him before.'

'No, I don't suppose you have,' Constance replied.

Melinda stared at her. 'I don't mean the colour of his skin,' she said, adding indignantly, 'I don't see him as some kind of ... of novelty, like something at a fair.'

'I never thought that you did,' Constance assured her.

Melinda was silent for a moment, something about her

expression indicating that she was picturing the African in her mind. 'If you really want to know, I think that he is absolutely beautiful. His colour is part of that, although it's something that I hardly notice now, any more than I notice the colour of your hair. It is his character that draws me, Connie. For all that he has suffered – and he has lost so much, more than you could imagine – he is not bitter. He is loyal and brave, and full of *joie de vivre*. His mind is so quick and intelligent, so interested in everything – even in me, and I have been nowhere and done nothing in comparison. It's true,' she went on, when Constance would have protested. 'He listens to my opinions. He has a fine mind.'

'Combined, of course, with a manly physique,' murmured Constance provocatively.

'Needless to say, you are utterly unaware of the duke's physical attributes,' Melinda retorted, proving that she could give as good as she got. The consequence was a modest pillow fight.

The following morning dawned bright and clear, the wind appearing to have blown itself out in the night. Mr Fellowes took himself off down to the seashore to discover whether the hazardous conditions had caused any tragedy to occur. He came back with an exciting tale to tell. 'Apparently a ship got into difficulties about two miles out from the shore,' he said. 'As often happens at such times, a group of men gathered together in order to try and give assistance. They launched a boat and rowed out amid punishing waves, determined to rescue as many as they could.'

'Such brave lads!' exclaimed his sister.

'Gallantry is often thought of as a characteristic of the nobility,' Constance agreed, 'But surely none could be so gallant as those who risk their lives for others.'

'I'm glad to hear you say so,' said her uncle, grinning. 'For your dandy-brute duke was one of them.'

'He was?' Constance exclaimed. A week ago she would have been more surprised.

Her uncle nodded. 'They had to make three journeys altogether. The first time, they got so far, only to be beaten back by the force of the waves. The second time, they reached the vessel and rescued a number of folk, including the captain's wife and baby son. On their return, Haslingfield and Okoro were waiting—'

'Mr Okoro too!' Melinda interrupted.

Mr Fellowes nodded. 'They were both waiting and took the places of the most exhausted men. The boat went out to the stricken vessel once more, took off another group and brought them safely back to shore.'

'Was anyone hurt?' Melinda asked. Constance knew that she was thinking of Abdas.

'Amazingly, almost everyone was saved,' said Mr Fellowes. 'Three men had lost their lives earlier when the ship first got into difficulties. After the boat had taken its second load of survivors, the remaining crew, including the captain, managed to launch the ship's rowing boat, and make for the shore.' He chuckled. 'They did have some help.'

'What do you mean?' his sister asked.

'Apparently, Haslingfield gave instructions for the boat to be brought alongside the ship. With Okoro directing operations, they stood by whilst the duke was helped aboard.'

Constance's hand flew to her mouth. 'He actually went aboard the sinking ship?'

'I had it from one of the men in the rowing boat,' her uncle answered. 'Then, under his leadership, they launched the ship's boat and rowed for the shore.'

'And no one was hurt, you say,' Constance pursued. If Melinda had been thinking of Abdas earlier, she was now thinking of the duke.

'They are a little concerned for the young child, having been exposed to the elements for such a period of time. Other than that, there was nothing more than cuts and bruises. They were taken to the Red Lion to get dry clothes and food.'

'From where had the vessel come?' Miss Fellowes asked.

'It was a Swedish craft, apparently. The captain speaks English and the wife has a smattering; the rest don't understand a word. A mercy he was rescued, really, otherwise heaven knows how they would have communicated.'

'I wonder whether we ought to go and see if we can be of any assistance?' Melinda said diffidently.

'Do you speak Swedish then, my dear?' Mr Fellowes asked with a twinkle.

'Well, no, although I do speak French,' she said doubtfully. 'Actually I was wondering about the poor mother and the baby and whether she might like some help.'

'The vicar has been informed about what occurred,' Mr Fellowes responded. 'He might know whether any help has been sent to her already. You don't want to overwhelm the poor woman.'

'We could go to the vicarage and see if any help is needed,' Constance suggested.

'Find out if they have enough blankets,' said Miss Fellowes. 'We can easily spare some if necessary.'

'Amazing how the day can be so bright and sunny, almost as though the storm had never been,' Melinda commented as they left the house, having fetched their bonnets.

As Constance nodded in agreement, a group of three men from the village came into view, knuckling their brows as they saw the two young ladies. 'Just going to ask for more blankets from Miss Fellowes, miss,' said one of them.

'We were going to ask the vicar if he wanted any,' said Constance. 'Are the poor folk dreadfully cold and distressed?'

'Hard to tell, miss, seeing they're foreigners,' the man replied lugubriously. 'Glad to be alive, though.'

'Unlike the poor souls who perished in the storm,' said Melinda.

'Have they ... have they found...?' said Constance tentatively.

'Two of them were washed up this morning,' the man answered. 'No sign of the black, though.'

Suddenly, Melinda lost all her colour. Her hand went to her throat. 'He was ... lost at sea?' she ventured in a thread of a voice.

'Aye, miss. No sign of his corpse as yet.'

'Abdas!' she murmured; then, without another word, she gathered up her skirts and ran in the direction of the village.

'Melinda, wait!' Constance cried. She turned back to the man who had been speaking. 'A black man was lost, you say. Was this the duke's secretary – Mr Okoro?'

'Him what was in church, miss?'

'Yes, that's right,' Constance answered hastily, looking to where

Melinda was running away from them, her petticoats a flurry of white, Gussy galloping at her heels.

'Why no, miss, he came back safe and sound; one of the bravest men I've ever seen, what's more.'

'Thank you,' said Constance, beginning to run in pursuit of Melinda. Although Mr Fellowes had told them that Abdas was safe, Melinda's heart was now obviously ruling her head. 'Don't let me keep you from your errand,' she called back to them. The men glanced at one another, not a little mystified, then carried on towards the Fellowes's cottage.

Melinda had been a country girl all her life, and having had a brother to compete with, was fleeter of foot than her friend. All she could think of was to run to where Abdas had last been seen. If his body had not been washed up, then perhaps he had not been lost after all. Perhaps he had managed to swim to shore further along the coast. Perhaps he had been injured and was even now struggling to make his way back.

As she ran, the different times when she had encountered him kept going through her mind: the strength in his arms as he had carried her into the cottage when she had first met him; the teasing expression in his warm brown eyes as they shared a joke; his keen interest as the lighthouse was examined and discussed; his courage at the rescue of Tommy Spencer; his anguish as he described the loss of his family and his tribe. Surely heaven would not permit him to have been saved from the waves only to allow him to perish so close to the shore?

She ran all the way to the church in a state of blind panic. Once there, it occurred to her that she had no idea where to look, or what to do next. Remembering that the vicar had been judged to have some involvement with those who had been shipwrecked, she cut through the churchyard in order to make her way to the vicarage. She paused briefly to look up at the roof of the church. There at that window, she had watched Abdas make his way to the boy; there, in the church tower, she had helped him to prepare the rope, their hands had touched, and clung together briefly, and they had exchanged more than one glance. Was this to be the most precious memory that she would ever have?

Choking back a sob, she dashed her hand across her eyes, picked up her skirts again and circumnavigated the church, only to run headlong into a man coming the other way. 'Miss Grayleigh! What is this? You are distressed! Can I help you?' he said, catching hold of her elbows in order to prevent her from jarring herself against his solid bulk.

She looked up in astonishment. There before her stood Abdas Okoro, quite unharmed, looking down at her in some concern. 'Abdas,' she exclaimed, tears starting to her eyes. 'I thought you had perished! They told me—'

Gently, he gathered her into his arms. 'Ssh, be still now,' he said in soothing tones. 'There is no need to cry. You see, I am quite well.'

It was no good. The tears, held back in her headlong flight, had to come, although now they were tears of relief. All the time he held her close, crooning to her, whilst Gussy flopped down on the grass and lay there panting.

At last, her tears subsiding, Melinda caught hold of his lapels and looked up at him, her heart in her eyes. 'If anything had happened to you,' she said tremulously, 'I don't know what I would have done.'

'The waves would never have claimed me, for I would fight against far greater odds to return to you, my heart,' he responded. He drew her closer and lowered his head until their lips met.

Constance, running to catch up with her friend, paused just inside the lychgate. She watched as Abdas pulled Melinda into a closer embrace, and her arms slid around his neck. Smiling, she turned away, and walked on alone to the vicarage, going by the road so as not to disturb the lovers.

Mrs Mawsby welcomed her, apologizing for the vicar's absence, and she was very happy to share all that she knew about the previous night's rescue over a cup of tea. Like Mr Fellowes, she was full of praise for the two gentlemen from Beacon Tower. 'His Grace's gallantry has proved any early unfavourable reports of him to be nothing but malice.' Constance sipped her tea, whilst Mrs Mawsby told the story in her own words. Although it gave her a secret pleasure to hear how gallant the duke had been, she could not help feeling embarrassed at the thought that the 'malicious reports' had chiefly come from her!

After the tea had been drunk, she walked slowly back to The Brambles, thinking about Abdas and Melinda. How would Mr and Mrs Grayleigh view the match? Would they disapprove of a marriage with a man of another race? Constance suspected that they would be more concerned about Abdas's prospects. Would the duke make it possible for him to marry – perhaps find him a post where there would be accommodation for a wife as well? The duke that she had first met – the dandy brute – would never have done such a thing. What of the man that she had come to know since then? She had wondered how she might feel had the duke perished beneath the waves. Now, with Melinda's experience fresh in her mind – her look of anguish, her headlong flight – she realized that the death of the duke would have been just as intolerable to her. Imperceptibly, he had come to matter to her more than she knew.

When had it happened? She could not tell. At the beginning, she had stigmatized him as a dandy brute, albeit one who, much to her annoyance had made her heart beat faster. She had told herself that his arrival in the neighbourhood was calamitous and had encouraged others to shun him. He had soon revealed finer qualities. His behaviour towards Abdas, Mrs Dobbs and others had shown him to be a man who treated others with consideration; whilst his rescue of Tommy and of the shipwrecked mariners had shown him to be quick-thinking, resourceful and courageous. Far from hating and despising him, like Melinda she had tumbled into love.

What of her future prospects? Did she have any more chance of happiness than Abdas and Melinda? She doubted that she even had as much. At least it was plain that they were besotted with one another. She had no idea how the duke felt about her. Even if he was drawn to her, how could a duke possibly make a match with an ordinary girl of no fortune whose aunt and uncle lived in a cottage? She would do much better to put him out of her mind.

Abdas and Melinda appeared half an hour later, looking very happy, Melinda holding tightly to his arm. He bade them a formal farewell, lifting Melinda's hand to his lips, before heading back towards Beacon Tower.

'He has asked me to marry him,' Melinda told Constance, her expression softening as she remembered the kisses and vows of love that they had shared. 'He has gone to fetch the gig from Beacon Tower, then he will drive me home so that he can ask Papa for my hand.'

'Oh, Melinda, I'm so happy for you,' said Constance, embracing her friend. 'Will your father be amenable, do you think?'

'I believe so,' her friend answered. On the way back from the church, Abdas had told her in strict confidence that he was only acting as the duke's secretary temporarily as a personal favour to his friend Mr Persault. In fact, he had a snug property of his own, and a merchant ship which earned him good money, as well as some useful investments. He would be very well able to provide a wife with the elegancies of life as well as its comforts. Mr Grayleigh need have no fear for his daughter's welfare.

'I suppose this means that your stay is at an end,' said Constance regretfully.

'Yes, I'm sorry,' Melinda replied.

'No, you aren't,' said Constance, smiling.

'I'm not sorry that Abdas has declared himself; I'm sorry to be leaving you,' Melinda clarified. 'Will you please give your uncle and aunt my apologies that I had to leave without thanking them personally for my stay?' Constance had arrived home to discover that her uncle and aunt had both gone out in the gig, surrounded by blankets.

'Yes, of course. They will be sorry to have missed you. I'll not tell them about Mr Okoro. Your parents should be the first to know.'

Melinda nodded. 'I shall come again soon. I know that Mama will want to talk everything over with me. She will certainly want to go to Aylsham, if not Norwich, for my bride clothes. I will ask her if you can come too, for you must be my bridesmaid, dear Connie, as we have always planned.'

'That will be lovely,' said Constance warmly.

By the time they had packed Melinda's things, Abdas had returned, and soon Constance was waving them off. She was glad that her aunt and uncle had both gone out. She would not have wanted them to see that she was very close to tears.

'Pull yourself together, my girl,' she said out loud in stern tones, rubbing vigorously at her tears with her handkerchief. 'Anyone would think that they were leaving for some distant estate of the duke's already.' Of course they were not; nevertheless a voice inside her head whispered, Melinda is your best friend. How will you do without her?

She was about to go inside when a voice called out, 'Miss Church! How pleased I am to have found you at home!' It was Colin Snelson.

'Mr Snelson! Good day,' she replied, smiling more because she was glad of the diversion than from the pleasure of his company. 'Have you just arrived back? You have missed the excitement of the storm last night. Has anyone told you about it?'

'I have heard something of the drama,' he answered seriously. 'Miss Church, there is a matter that I need to discuss with you in private.'

'You sound very solemn,' she responded. 'Would you like to walk in the garden?'

He frowned. 'I would prefer to go into the house,' he answered.

Constance frowned as well. She considered herself to be beyond the age of needing a chaperon. What was more, she knew that her aunt's approval of the young bailiff would guarantee that Miss Fellowes would consider a private interview inside to be perfectly permissible. She thought guiltily of the smiles that she had bestowed upon him in Aylsham. He could not know that her actions had been motivated by a desire to make the duke notice her. Fearing that allowing him to be with her alone in the house would give him altogether too much encouragement she said, 'My aunt and uncle are both from home, so you will have to make do with the garden.'

They walked around to the back of the cottage where they sat down on a bench beneath a large apple tree. Constance hoped devoutly that he was not going to propose. Now that she had acknowledged to herself where her affections lay, the notion of even thinking about his proposal seemed absurd. He sat with his hands clasped between his knees, and she waited for him to speak. 'You may remember that when we met at Aylsham, I was on my way to Cambridge.'

Constance nodded. 'Yes, I do remember.'

'Having set everything in order here, I went to visit some relations near Cambridge. They had summoned me to attend to a family matter. You must not think that I left my post without permission, Miss Church,' he added earnestly. 'Perhaps you did not realize that the terms of my employment permit me to take a holiday if all my duties are discharged. In ordinary circumstances, of course, I would have asked my employer, had he been to hand.'

'Oh! I see,' she responded. Guiltily, she realized that she had given very little thought to where he had gone, or why.

'Before I returned, I thought that I would take the opportunity of visiting the Duke of Haslingfield's principal estate.'

'You knew that he had inherited, then?'

'Yes, I knew, but had no expectation of ever seeing him.'

'Is the Cambridgeshire estate very extensive?'

'What? Yes, it is a large estate; that isn't what I wanted to say.' He paused then looked directly at her. 'As soon as I arrived at Beacon Tower, I sought the duke out in order to introduce myself to him and explain my absence. Miss Church, I do not know who that man might be, but of one thing I am quite certain: he is not the duke.'

Chapter Eighteen

'Not the duke? Don't be absurd,' said Constance. 'I witnessed his behaviour on the journey. You have never seen such an arrogant performance. The way he treated his servants was an absolute disgrace!' She had said the words before, originally with conviction, later with a twinge of unease; never before, as now, with a feeling of downright disloyalty.

'That may be so; but he is not the duke. Of that I am quite certain.'

'How can you be so sure?' Constance asked him, conscious of a sinking sensation.

'Whilst I was Haslingfield, I had the opportunity of looking round. It's enormous, Miss Church – Beacon Tower is nothing to it. It's more like a palace than a house – and as for the grounds!'

'You can tell me all about it on another occasion,' said Constance, containing her impatience with some difficulty. 'What of the duke?'

'Ah yes. Whilst I was there, I had the chance of looking at a number of portraits of the family.'

'If you are going to tell me that he is unlike other family members, then I must tell you that that means nothing,' said Constance. 'My parents were both dark, but look at me!'

'If it were only that, then I would agree with you,' said Snelson heavily. 'However, I was shown a portrait of the young man who was to become the duke. He is tall and slim, with fair hair and a somewhat pale complexion – quite unlike that swarthy fellow up at Beacon Tower.'

'Surely there must be some mistake. Heirs can die and more distant men come into an inheritance. In fact, the duke himself has said that the position is unfamiliar to him.'

'I'll wager it is,' said Snelson in a cynical tone. 'He looks more like a damned pirate to me.'

Constance turned pale. Had she not herself called the man a buccaneer? Now, at last, Snelson's words hit home. 'Then if he is not the duke, who is he? And where is the real duke?'

'I have a very real fear that this man may have made away with him,' said Snelson after a long pause.

Constance gasped. 'No!' she exclaimed. 'I won't believe it.' When her companion looked dubious, not to say surprised, she went on, 'You have not been here in recent days. He joined in a rescue at sea and many men were saved. He, together with his secretary, brought a lad down from the church roof. He is not a murderer, I am convinced of it.'

'Well then, perhaps he has simply secured the real duke for a time until he can achieve his own ends.'

'And what might those be?'

There was another silence. 'What if he were to be in league with the French, in order to facilitate an invasion?'

'Here? In Norfolk?'

'There is a good harbour at Wells. Or what about Weybourne, just along the coast? It is deep enough there to bring big ships in, and what better place? Especially if there is an ally close by in a big house to take them in.'

Constance opened her mouth to protest, then closed it, recalling her uncle's words. She remembered, too, how at first the duke had made out that he had little interest in the sea, then betrayed his knowledge and seamanship. She thought of how he had produced a telescope and had been so adept in its use, easily finding and identifying a small boat. What if Cromer lighthouse were to be used by someone as a signal for an invasion fleet, as well as a safety marker for British sailors? How delighted the duke had been to discover that the pattern thrown by the light was so distinctive! Would he pass this on to enemies of England? She did not want to believe that he was a traitor; unfortunately, too many things indicated that he was not what he seemed. What was she to believe?

'What do you intend to do?' she asked eventually.

Snelson's face took on a resolute expression. 'I will go to Aylsham and speak to the magistrate. He is a family acquaintance and has some volunteers at his disposal. I shall put my case before him and urge him to bring some men to arrest this fellow.'

'Oh pray,' exclaimed Constance, much disturbed by this disclosure. 'Surely such a drastic measure is not necessary!'

'What do you suggest instead?'

'Well … could we not just go and ask him?'

He looked at her pityingly. 'Do you have the smallest hope that he would tell you the truth? Besides, if he really is a traitor, the last thing that we should do is put him on his guard.'

'I suppose so,' she agreed reluctantly. 'But please do not go yet. Take a little time to get to know him. You may find that there is a perfectly innocent reason for— '

'Exactly,' he said grimly. 'What innocent reason could there possibly be?'

'I don't know! There must be one, surely? Please, wait for a day or so. Don't do anything in haste.'

'While plots are being hatched against England?' He sighed.

'At least promise me that you will tell me before you take action.' He nodded reluctantly in assent, and said no more on the subject.

After he had gone – and he did not stay for long, the solemn nature of his suspicions rendering other conversation rather awkward – Constance sat in the garden wondering what to do. How she wished that Melinda was still there, so that she might consult her!

She wondered what role Abdas Okoro might have in this strange affair. He and the duke had never really seemed to play the parts of secretary and employer. What if Abdas were implicated in this business? He had no reason to love England and Englishmen, after all. What upon earth would Melinda do if the man she loved proved to be a traitor? She decided to ride over and speak to her friend the next day. She could not reconcile it with her conscience to keep quiet over such a matter.

'What a pity for you that Melinda was obliged to leave, my dear,' said Miss Fellowes to her niece as they were waiting for dinner to be announced.

Constance nodded. 'She was so sorry not to have been able to see you first,' she answered with perfect truth. In accordance with her promise, she had said nothing about her friend's romance. Instead, she had made up a story about Melinda's having received some news of her family, upon hearing which the duke's secretary had escorted her home.

'I do trust that it was nothing distressing,' said Miss Fellowes, as her brother came in. Even in correct evening dress, he always looked as though he might have been digging the garden. He had a note in his hand which he gave to Constance.

'This came for you,' he said incuriously, before turning to his sister. 'Were you talking about Miss Grayleigh's sudden departure?'

His sister made some response, and while the two of them were discussing the matter, Constance took the opportunity to read her note.

I have decided to waste no time and to ride to the magistrate tonight.
England's safety is more important than your scruples.

She gave an involuntary gasp which she managed to turn into a cough. Tonight! It had never occurred to her that he would act so quickly. While she was still taking in the contents of her note, the maid came to announce that dinner was ready, and she wandered in to the dining room behind her uncle and aunt, who were, by good fortune, still preoccupied with their own conversation.

During the meal, Constance managed to give enough attention to her relatives' remarks to avoid attracting notice. In reality, more than half her mind was preoccupied with the question of what she should do, given Snelson's actions. When she had begged him to take a little more time, she had had no idea of what course to pursue. If she had been honest with herself, she would have admitted to hoping that he would not do anything, so she would be saved from making any kind of decision. Now, plainly she had to do something and she had to do it tonight. The only possible course of action that came into her mind was to warn the duke of the danger in which he stood. She thought that she knew how it could be done; but she would have to wait until after dark in order to carry out her plan.

Mr and Miss Fellowes were never usually late birds. On this occasion, needless to say, when Constance was hoping for them to retire early, they seemed predisposed to stay up late, lingering over the tea tray until Constance was almost at screaming point. Then, just as it seemed as though they might go upstairs, Mr Fellowes said to his sister, 'What do you say to a game of chess?'

Constance only just managed to bite back a protest. Knowing, however, that this would only cause further delay and attract attention in precisely the way that she most wanted to avoid, she simply said 'Well, for my part, I am feeling quite sleepy, so I will bid you goodnight.'

'Goodnight, my dear,' replied her uncle as he set out the chess pieces. 'What was your note about by the way?'

Constance had had some time to invent an answer to this question. 'Just a suggestion from Miss Mawsby that we might go for a walk,' she answered casually.

In order to be certain that she would not be caught leaving the house, Constance waited for quite a whole hour after she had heard her aunt and uncle go to their rooms. When the house was quiet, she slipped a shawl around her shoulders, tiptoed down the stairs, and left by the back door, closing it softly behind her. That done, she hurried off to Beacon Tower. She was confident that the duke – or whoever he was – would still be downstairs. Ten o'clock at night might seem late to country folk; for someone used to town life, it would be rather too early to have retired.

It never occurred to her that she might have difficulty in locating the room in which he would be sitting. The night was clear and the moon full. Naturally, he would be in the saloon at the back with the splendid view of the North Sea. Cautiously she made her way around the side of the house, anxious not to arouse any other person.

She knew from local gossip that he had not taken on many servants. Mrs Hays lived in, but Davis walked up from the village with Jilly and the two young women who took their daily instructions from Barnes. As she rounded the corner of the building, the view that he would have from the saloon came into her line of sight, and she let out an involuntary gasp at its beauty. The moon, shining onto the sea from a cloudless sky, tinted the sea with shades of black, grey and silver; whilst the stars, dwarfed by the greater light, nevertheless filled the sky with a myriad of spangles.

'Good evening, Miss Church,' said the duke's voice from behind her, causing her to jump. 'Although you are, of course, more than welcome to admire the view from my garden, I am curious to know what you are doing here at such a time.'

She turned at the sound of his voice, and at once, her heart began to race. He was in his shirtsleeves without a cravat, the shirt open to partway down his chest. His own dark hair hung loose about his shoulders. Constance's mind had been doing battle with the suspicions voiced by Colin Snelson. Now, looking at him in the moonlight, it seemed quite impossible that he should be a duke. 'Who are you?' she whispered.

He looked down into her anxious face. 'Come inside,' he said, his voice lowered. 'You mustn't be seen out here.'

He led her into the saloon through the garden door, his hand under her elbow. Once the door was closed behind them, he drew her over to the window. The moon was still working its magic, transforming the world outside into a scene of extraordinary beauty. 'Now,' he said, 'what is this about?'

'*You* tell *me*,' she replied. 'Who are you?'

'What makes you think I am not what I purport to be?' he asked her. For a few moments she was tempted to take his words at face value. Then something about the way that he was looking at her, half quizzically, half speculatively, caused the fleeting hope that perhaps Snelson was mistaken to shrivel and die.

'Almost everything you say and do,' she answered in frustrated tones, watching him as he poured a glass of wine, which he offered to her, then drank himself when she shook her head. 'No arrogant aristocrat would treat his secretary as a friend in the way that you do. You say you know little of the sea, but you wield a telescope like an expert and play a major part in a rescue. Although you play the dandy, you are never seen in gloves; you even wear your most dandified clothes as if you were a swaggering buccaneer. Now, to cap it all—'

'Well?'

She took a deep breath. 'You look nothing like the portrait of the new duke.'

'I see,' he replied with a rueful grin. 'It does not occur to you that perhaps Mr Snelson – who is doubtless your informant – may have been looking at the wrong portrait?'

'It did occur to me,' she said carefully. 'But taken with everything else—'

'Taken with everything else, you have a man who neither looks like a duke nor behaves like one. Rather a tenuous foundation on which to build an argument, I would have thought. Not everyone who becomes a duke was brought up to occupy that position; nor do all members of a family resemble one another.' He looked at her curiously. 'Miss Church, I fully accept that you believe I have a case to answer. The question that I would put to you in turn is, why have you decided to confront me at this time of night?' He put his glass down and walked slowly towards her. She took a couple of steps backwards. Swiftly, he closed the gap between them and caught hold of her chin. He was now all buccaneer. It struck her that he could be a very dangerous man. She met his gaze squarely, hoping that he could not feel that she was trembling.

As if he could read her thoughts, he said, 'Did it not occur to you that if I were indeed the villain that you think me, you are now in my clutches? I could easily make away with you – or do something even worse.' He held her gaze with his own, and lowered his head; unmistakably, he intended to kiss her.

Much though her foolish heart might leap at the prospect, however, she could not afford to forget the reason for her errand. Before he could carry out his intentions she said quickly, 'Snelson has gone for the magistrate.'

'What?' he said, releasing his grip.

'Snelson believes that you ... you are a French spy or agent of some sort,' she said. 'He thinks that you are here to play your part in the enabling of an invasion fleet to moor nearby, perhaps at Weybourne. He has gone to Aylsham to see the magistrate, and bring back with him some volunteers to arrest you.'

For a moment, Max was tempted to laugh out loud at the irony of Snelson's suspicions. 'So you have come—'

'To warn you.' Becoming fully conscious of the enormity of her actions, she could feel herself blushing a fiery red.

'With what end in view?' he asked her curiously.

'So that you might escape.'

'You suspect that I am an enemy of England,' he pointed out. 'So why are you helping me?'

She turned away abruptly. 'You may be a traitor – a thing that I find quite abhorrent,' she said, her voice catching slightly. 'But I cannot believe that you are a bad man. You saved Tommy Spencer, and you rescued all those people who might have been lost at sea. I do not want you to ... to hang.'

He grinned wryly. 'I believe traitors are still hanged, drawn and quartered.'

She turned back towards him, her face as white now as it had been flushed before. 'Then for God's sake, go!' she exclaimed, clutching at his sleeve. 'Go at once, before they come.'

'That would be an admission of guilt,' he pointed out, 'and I haven't said that I'm guilty.'

'If you are not guilty, what are you doing here, pretending to be a duke?'

He looked at her for a long moment. 'I can't tell you that, I'm afraid.'

'Can't – or won't?'

'Can't,' he answered wryly. 'It's a matter of honour, my dear.'

'Honour!' she exclaimed, throwing her hands into the air. 'A fig for honour! It's a word men use whenever it suits them, to justify duels and gaming debts and all kinds of other things that only bring heartache to those they love.'

The last word seemed to hang in the air between them. He caught hold of her hands, and pulled her into his arms. 'Constance, my dear,' he murmured, as he lowered his head and this time, he did kiss her full on her mouth. She had been kissed twice before; once against her will by a gentleman who had overindulged at a garden party, and whom she had rewarded by pushing him into a nearby fountain. On the other occasion, she had permitted the familiarity chiefly in order to satisfy her curiosity. Neither of these experiences had been pleasurable. This time, however, she was conscious of a delicious invasion of all her senses, combined with a feeling deep down inside that this was where she belonged, and always desired to be.

Eventually he drew back, still holding her in his arms. 'So you want me to run?' he said.

'I want you to be safe,' she replied simply, her heart in her eyes.

'If I ran – would you come with me?' Before she could answer, he turned her to look out of the window, holding her against him gently, her back against his chest. 'Supposing all I had to offer you was a ship and a loyal crew, and the wide open sea?'

Even whilst her blood stirred at the picture he conjured up, there was suddenly no time for her to think, let alone answer, for at that moment, they heard the sound of a door opening, followed by cautious steps. Max released her and held up his hand for silence, directing her with a movement of his head to step into the shadows to the side of the door. Moments later, Snelson came into view, a pistol in his hand.

Seeing Max standing in the centre of the room, apparently alone, he said, 'Well, Mr Imposter; are you now ready to disclose who you really are? Or should I say "*monsieur*"?'

'Say what you like, but pray do not pollute my ears with that execrable accent,' said Max in his most languid tones.

'Execrable, is it?' asked Snelson. 'And how would you know?' He took a step closer to Max. 'It might interest you to learn that I have been to Aylsham to the magistrate.'

'How fascinating,' Max drawled, his hand going to his mouth as if to cover a yawn. 'Is this story taking us anywhere, Snelson? I must confess myself to be at something of a loss, both as to the purpose for this conversation, and, more seriously, for your reasons for being in my house at this time of night. Are you drunk?'

'Yes, you'd like that, wouldn't you?' said Snelson, taking a step closer to Max. Constance, much alarmed at the turn that events were taking, looked frantically about her, and caught sight of a bronze figure on the cupboard next to her.

'Like having my bailiff drunk in my saloon? Certainly not,' Max responded. 'Now get you gone before I become seriously annoyed rather than amused.'

'Amused? Let's see how amusing you find it when the magistrate arrives.'

At this point, Constance, who had picked up the bronze figure, lifted it above her. Max, seeing her intentions, raised a hand, saying, 'Wait!'

Snelson, thinking that he was being addressed, said sneeringly, 'For what?'

Before either of the men could say anything more, Constance brought the figure down on his head, so that he crumpled to the floor. 'Now will you flee?' she said, turning to Max.

'Indeed, I think that one of us should,' he said, taking one step towards the fallen man. Before he could examine Snelson's injury, however, he became aware that Constance had turned very white. The bronze figure slipped from her fingers, and fell to the carpet with a dull thud as she realized just what she had done.

'Dear heaven, have I killed him?' she asked, swaying alarmingly. He helped her to a chair, intending to look at Snelson as soon as she was seated. Before he could leave her side, Barnes appeared in the doorway, as dapper as always.

The valet bowed courteously to Constance. 'Good evening, Miss Church,' he said formally. 'I trust I see you well. Is your aunt in good health?'

Constance, suddenly overcome with a most unsuitable desire to giggle at the incongruity of this conversation, responded to both questions in the affirmative. He observed the body on the floor. 'Dear me,' he said in his usual calm tone. 'May I be of assistance in this matter, Your Grace?'

'Mr Snelson has met with an accident,' Max replied. 'I was about to take a look at him when Miss Church became rather distressed, and my first duty is to her.'

'Naturally,' said Barnes. 'Allow me.' He went down on his knees next to the fallen man in order to feel for a pulse in his neck. After a long moment, he looked up, his face solemn. 'I think it were as well that the young lady left immediately,' he said calmly.

Max nodded. 'I'll take her home,' he said.

'He is dead!' uttered Constance, aghast. 'Oh no, surely not! I never intended—'

'Of course not,' Max agreed, almost as shocked as she. 'Barnes, are you quite sure?'

'There can be no mistake,' Barnes replied. 'Indeed, Your Grace, it would be wise to take the young lady away at once.'

'Very well,' said Max. 'Come then, Miss Church.'

'You should be gone too,' she responded, pulling herself together with some difficulty. 'He had sent for a party to take you into custody, remember?'

'I remember,' Max replied. 'Let's deal with one thing at a time. The first task is to get you to safety.'

'So I should hope,' said Barnes with dignity. 'Allow me to help you on with your coat, Your Grace.' The valet retrieved the item in question from a chair where it had been carelessly thrown, and with a reproachful 'tsk tsk', held it out for Max to put on. 'I fear that I cannot see your cravat,' he murmured, looking around.

'No more can I,' Max replied dismissively. 'Are you ready, Miss Church?'

'Oh! Yes ... yes, I am ready,' Constance replied, feeling as if she was inhabiting some strange, other world which bore no relation to reality. 'But the magistrate ... and—'

'Fear not,' said Max reassuringly. 'Barnes is more than capable of coping with any circumstance that might transpire, aren't you, Barnesy?'

Something that might have been a faint wince crossed the valet's features. 'I trust so, Your Grace,' he said primly.

As soon as they were outside in the drive, Constance said, 'What now?'

'I'm going to take you home,' Max replied.

'Oh, for goodness' sake, as if that is necessary,' she answered impatiently. 'Your safety is far more important.'

'Nothing is more important than *your* safety,' he responded, taking her arm.

'I am perfectly safe here. My own home is barely half a mile away.'

'Ah yes, but we are to be invaded by a party from Aylsham at any moment,' he reminded her.

'And they will find—' Her voice broke. 'Oh God, what have I done?'

'It was an accident,' he said firmly. 'You were intent upon defending me from a man with a loaded pistol in his hand.'

'Yes, but Mr Snelson—'

'There is nothing that we can do to change matters,' he reminded her. 'I will take the blame. Snelson came to the house at an unexpected hour. Thinking that he was a housebreaker, I struck him over the head. Barnes will bear out my story.'

'But you did not do it, I did! Why should you take the blame for something that I have done?'

He stopped and turned her to face him. 'Because nobody must know that you were ever there. Besides, somehow you have become my responsibility.'

'Like a ... a horse, or a dog, or—'

He pulled her closer to him. 'No, not like any of those,' he replied, brushing his lips briefly against hers. 'Come, we must get you home. I cannot rest easy until you are safe, and I need to get back and help Barnes.'

'Yes, poor Mr Barnes—' She paused. 'Does he know who you really are?' she asked him, her eyes narrowed.

'Barnes knows everything about me,' he assured her.

'How can he if you only met him on the way here?' she asked, before going on slowly, 'That meeting was all a pretence, wasn't it?'

'I've already revealed far more to you than I should,' he said.

'Then why can't you tell me the rest?'

'Out of loyalty to another, I can't say more; believe me, as soon as I can, I'll tell you everything.'

'And in the meantime, you'll keep yourself safe; you'll not allow them to arrest you?'

'I'll do my best to guard against such an eventuality.' They had reached the garden gate. Fortunately, owing to her uncle's diligence in maintaining his property, it opened without a sound. 'Will you be able to get back in?' Max whispered.

'By the back door,' Constance replied. He went with her around the back of the house, treading carefully so as not to disturb the sleeping inhabitants. She set her hand on the door handle, then turned to look at him. His face was in shadow, making it quite impossible for her to read his expression.

She found herself completely at a loss. She had set off that evening, determined to warn him of Snelson's intentions. She had expected him to be alarmed; even dismayed; perhaps angry at the thwarting of his plans. She had not expected him to stand and bandy words with her! Her warning had been given more than half against her conscience; and yet, when it had come to making her choice, she had without hesitation brought a heavy weight down on the head of a poor, blameless man, making of herself a murderess so that the dandy-brute duke might go free!

Amongst all of the thoughts swirling around in her head, the one that kept coming back to her was the moment when he had said, 'If I did run, would you come with me?' He had not asked her again. Had he really meant it, or had it been a kind of joke, intended to torment one who had found him out? She felt her face colouring all over again, for in her confusion, she had actually voiced something of her thoughts.

'Of course I meant it,' he said, leaning closer and catching hold of her by her shoulders. 'Will you be ready if I come for you?'

'Yes. Oh, but pray be careful!'

'I will.' He bent his head and pressed one brief, hard kiss onto her lips. 'Don't fear for me – or for yourself. All will be well, I promise you.' He paused briefly, then went on. 'You have asked who I am; all you need to know is that my name is Max, and that I am in love with you.'

Her heart leaped. 'And you will come for me?' she said breathlessly.

'I give you my word.'

He stepped back, ran his hands down her arms, caught hold of her hands, lifted first one then the other to his lips. Then he released them, sketched a brief salute, and melted into the shadows. She wanted to ask him, 'When? Will you come for me here? What should I bring?' She even opened her mouth to tell him that his sentiments were returned. It was too late: he was gone.

Chapter Nineteen

'What do you mean, he's not dead?' Max asked wrathfully. After leaving Constance, he had hurried back reluctantly to Beacon Tower. Whilst he had been obliged to kill on occasions (never without regret), and he had learned how to come to terms with his actions, Constance had not. The last thing that he had wanted to do had been to leave her alone with her inevitable feelings of guilt and self-blame. On this occasion, however, he had been left with no alternative. Whilst he might have no compunction about rousing the Fellowes household in order to provide Constance with some support, he knew that this step would blast her reputation more completely than anything else. She had enough to deal with without having that on her plate. What was more, the house-breaking story would do very well, only if he were there when the magistrate arrived. The best way of protecting Constance would be to play the part of an outraged aristocratic householder right up to the hilt.

He was thinking about some of these matters when he entered the drawing room and found Barnes awaiting him with the news that Snelson was in fact very much alive.

'The young lady's blow was not sufficient to kill the gentleman,' Barnes explained, in response to Max's question.

'Then why in God's name did you say that he was dead?'

'If you will recall the incident, I did not exactly say as much,' said Barnes carefully.

'Damn you, Barnes, you knew perfectly well what you were implying!'

'It seemed to me, Your Grace, that it were best to get the young lady out of the way as quickly as possible,' the valet explained. 'As long as she knew that the gentleman was merely injured, she would insist on ministering to his hurts; especially since—' He paused delicately.

'Since what?'

'Apparently, Mr Snelson has been courting Miss Church. She might consider herself bound to him.'

'The devil she does,' Max returned shortly, thinking that if such were the case he might as well go and finish the man off himself. He remembered with some disquiet that although he had told her of his feelings, she had not said that she returned them. 'What have you done with him?'

'At present, he is upstairs,' said Barnes. 'I have bathed his head and dressed his wound. However, he has left us with a little problem. It would in fact be much more convenient if the man were indeed dead.'

'How very disobliging of him,' said Max, his ready sense of humour rising to the surface despite himself.

'Indeed, Your Grace. The housebreaker story is all very well if we have a corpse. If, on the other hand, he is able to tell of his suspicions—'

'Yes, I see. Very awkward. And we can't very well say that I struck him down if he can say later that I was standing in front of him.'

'I have a solution to that problem, Your Grace.'

'I hope it's one that leaves Miss Church out of the matter.'

'Of course. I shall say that I came into the room and saw Snelson holding you at gunpoint. Not having met the man before, what else was I to think other than that he was a housebreaker?'

'Or some other kind of villain. Very good, Barnes. Much better that they don't speak to him, though, don't you think?'

'Undoubtedly. He is in a room in the tower, under the influence of a sleeping draught, with a groom in attendance.'

'So when our visitors ask after him, we can take them up to see him, if they insist.'

'They won't, Your Grace. In the meantime, I suggest that you put on your dressing gown and prepare to meet them.'

They hurried upstairs where Max allowed the valet to help him into a nightshirt – which he never normally wore – and his most opulent dressing gown. 'Don't think I'm not grateful for what you've done,' Max said as he slid his arm into the rich blue brocade sleeve. 'I'm still very annoyed with you, none the less.'

'Why, Your Grace?'

'Because Miss Church is even now sitting in her chamber, her spirits oppressed by the belief that she has killed a man,' Max replied in exasperated tones. 'She is suffering quite needlessly.'

'Consider, Your Grace, how relieved she will be when she discovers that all is well.'

Max looked at him doubtfully. He remembered how years ago, his sister Ruth had gone to play with some young relatives of the rector in the village without telling her mother where she was going. Mrs Persault had not heard about the visitors to the rectory and had not thought to make enquiries there, whilst Ruth had blithely assured the rector's wife that of course her mama knew where she had gone. By the time Ruth eventually returned, a search party had been organized and Mrs Persault had become quite frantic. Of course, she had been relieved that her daughter was safe; but these feelings were soon replaced by fury that she should have been caused so much needless worry. Ruth had spent several days in her room on a diet of bread and water. She had also been made to write letters of apology to all those whom she had inconvenienced, including the gardener's boy, who had taken part in the search (although the housekeeper had been obliged to read it to him, since he could not read it for himself). Recalling these events, it occurred to Max that Miss Church's relief at Mr Snelson's survival might quickly be succeeded by justifiable anger at the distress that she had been caused. Heaven send he could speedily put an end to her misery.

Before he could give this any further thought, they heard the unmistakable sound of horses approaching. 'The men from Aylsham,' said Barnes.

'Then let us go downstairs,' said Max.

Barnes held up a hand. 'No, Your Grace. A man in your position would not come downstairs in his night attire to greet such men.

Better to remain here whilst I open the door, then you can descend when you hear the commotion.'

Max nodded, acknowledging the justice of this suggestion. He waited in the doorway of his chamber, listening to the sound of forthright knocking on the door, followed by the measured pace of Barnes as he crossed the hall. There then followed a conversation of some sort, a voice raised in protest, and the clatter of feet indicating a number of persons entering the hall. Judging that this might be an appropriate moment for him to make an appearance, Max took a deep breath and thought of Alistair. Then he began to stroll down the passage, deliberately slowing his pace from his more natural energetic stride. He touched the pocket of his dressing gown, tracing the outline of his pistol. Although he trusted that he would not need it, it was good to know that it was there.

He had the opportunity of noting the number and condition of the individuals gathered in the hall. There were eight men in the party, whose ages were probably between eighteen and fifty. Most of them gave the impression of being on a huge treat. They had possibly never entered such a house before and were obviously bent on taking in everything in order to tell an interesting tale when they got home. A large, gangly youth, probably the youngest present, stood a little apart from the others, waiting by the door with a vacuous grin on his face. A stout, red-faced man with the appearance of a gentleman farmer seemed to be leading the band.

'Disturb His Grace when he has only just retired?' Barnes was saying in outraged tones. 'It's more than my place is worth.'

'It'll be more than your life's worth if you're found to be harbouring a traitor,' the red-faced man retorted, his voice carrying a slight Norfolk burr.

'Aye, he's a Frenchie,' added one of the others.

'Now we don't know that,' said their leader. 'But Mr Snelson – whose judgment I've never had cause to doubt – was quite insistent that the man residing here is not the Duke of Haslingfield.'

'Did someone mention my name?' murmured a voice from above their heads. Max came slowly down the stairs. He had slipped back into his chamber in order to pick up a lace handkerchief. This he extracted from his pocket – taking care not to disturb the pistol

– and held it to his nose. 'I take it that there is a good reason for my being disturbed? I do not like to appear unreasonable, but there seem to be a number of persons in my hall who – really, one does not like to seem rude, who have neither been invited' – by now, he had reached the last landing, where he paused – 'nor, indeed, were ever likely to be,' he concluded, rather pleased to have steered his way successfully through a number of clauses to the end of his sentence.

The leader of the visiting party bowed instinctively, and those with him followed suit, bobbing their heads and touching forelocks. 'Forgive me for disturbing you, sir,' said the red-faced man. 'My name is Sir Godfrey Glennis, and I have the honour of being a magistrate in Aylsham.

'I'm Haslingfield,' said Max. He completed his descent and held out his hand to the baronet, in much the same way that a king might extend his hand to a subject. Glennis, who had been to court once and had been utterly overawed by the whole experience, managed to resist an urge to go down on one knee. 'From what you were saying as I was coming down the stairs, I understand that you have had tidings of a traitor in this locality. If you need to use my house as a base whilst you search, you are more than welcome.'

The baronet now found himself completely at a loss. In the heart of rural Norfolk, the threat of invasion from the French seemed, for the most part, to be very distant and unlikely. Indeed, it had been the last thing on Sir Godfrey's mind as he had completed the day's business in order to join the vicar for their weekly bottle of port which they shared over a game or two of chess. Snelson's anxious demeanour had struck an incongruous note when he had been admitted to the baronet's bachelor establishment, and his host might have dismissed the whole matter from his mind had it not been for one circumstance.

Just two days before, he had chanced upon an article in his newspaper in which the writer had described the cunning displayed by spies, traitors and the like. The same article had gone on to say that a lack of vigilance at time of war might easily prove to be the country's undoing, and had described the bucolic stupidity of a country squire who had allowed the opportunity of snaring a French sympathizer to slip through his fingers. Sir Godfrey had no desire to be ranked among such company. What was more, he had always found Snelson to be a sensible man, not inclined to be carried away by far-fetched tales. The deciding factor had been when the vicar had sent a message to say that as he was required to attend at a death-bed, their game of chess would have to be postponed. Snelson had returned to the coast in order to make sure that their quarry did not escape, leaving Sir Godfrey to assemble some local volunteers.

Had Sir Godfrey been questioned as to what he expected to find when he arrived, he would probably not have been so foolish as to describe a shifty-looking individual muttering '*Zut alors!*' under his breath whilst Snelson held him at gunpoint. On the other hand, he would certainly never have envisaged this lordly, assured-looking man who invited him into his home and offered him every assistance. Furthermore, Snelson, who had promised to meet him here, was conspicuous by his absence. In addition to all this, Tom Seekings, who was standing by the door, his face adorned by its usual vacant expression, kept interjecting the word 'zur' into the conversation, whilst bobbing up and down in the manner of one who needed to relieve himself. What was to be done?

Again, Max took the initiative. 'If you have come from – Aylsham, did you say? – you will be ready for some refreshment. Might I suggest that you accompany me into my book room so that we may discuss this strange affair further? Your – er – company might be more comfortable in the kitchen, I fancy.'

The band of men, who had been shifting rather uncomfortably from one foot to the other during this exchange, glanced at one another with expressions of relief, whilst Seekings muttered 'zur' for perhaps the sixth time.

'That is very good of you,' said Sir Godfrey, glancing round. 'I must own, I had expected to be meeting Snelson here.'

Max raised his brows. 'It would appear to be rather a strange hour for you to be calling upon my bailiff in my house,' he murmured. 'However, I believe that my valet may be able to shed further light on this matter.'

Barnes's face took on a mortified expression. 'Shall I return to give my account of tonight's events after I have taken these men to the kitchen, Your Grace?' he asked humbly.

'Indeed, I think you should.'

The party obediently followed him, except for Seekings, who now came and tugged at the baronet's sleeve. 'Zur,' he said urgently.

'Go with the rest, boy,' said Sir Godfrey irritably. 'Someone will show you where to ... to ... you know.'

'No, zur, t'ain't that,' the lad said. He pointed to Max. 'I seed him afore.'

There was a moment's quiet. The party halted on its way to the kitchen. Max casually slid his hand into the pocket of his dressing gown to touch his pistol, his expression unchanged.

'Have you, lad?' Sir Godfrey asked, looking at Max. 'When was this?'

'I seed 'im in Aylsham,' said Tom. Now aware that he was the cynosure of all eyes, he was determined to make the most of his moment. 'Dressed up like a prince, 'e were, in a fine carriage. *And* 'e 'ad a black servant.'

'Yes, what the lad says may well be true,' Max agreed languidly. 'I passed through Aylsham quite recently, and my secretary, who is from Africa, was attending me. Perhaps some of these others might have been told of the incident?'

After a brief pause, a sensible-looking man with greying hair said, 'My brother goes to the Black Boys most weeks. He said as how there was someone staying there so grand that they called him "Your Grace".'

'That was indeed where I stayed,' said Max in a bored tone. 'Is there anyone else with observations to make upon my movements, or my person? No doubt Barnes could furnish you with my exact itinerary, should you deem it to be necessary.'

Sir Godfrey flushed. 'No, indeed, Your Grace,' he said, for the first time addressing the man in front of him in the correct form.

'Then let us repair to our refreshments,' Max replied, ushering the baronet into the book room. He poured them both a glass of brandy, and invited his guest to be seated, making polite conversation the while about the quality of the spirits in front of them, and of the difficulty of obtaining good brandy by legitimate means.

The topic was almost exhausted when there was a soft knock on the door, and Barnes entered. 'Well now, Barnes,' said Max, 'perhaps you had better tell the magistrate about your part in this evening's sorry affair.'

'Magistrate?' said the valet in anxious tones. 'Oh pray, Your Grace, don't let him take me to prison. I was only doing what I thought was right.'

'Indeed, Barnes, and I am convinced that someone as perspicacious as Sir Godfrey plainly is will give you credit for it.'

'Yes, certainly,' said the baronet, visibly pluming himself at this praise. 'Speak up, my man.'

'Perhaps I had better give my side of the story first,' said Max. 'Being unable to sleep, I came downstairs in search of a book. I was in here leafing through' – he picked up the volume on the table in front of him – '*The Widow of Malabar* by Mariana Starke, when I felt sure that I heard the sound of someone entering the house.'

'Good Gad, sir!' the baronet exclaimed.

'Exactly so,' Max murmured. 'Naturally, I feared that we were under attack by housebreakers. I was unarmed, so as you might suppose, I was feeling very vulnerable. Some of these fellows are desperate rogues.'

The magistrate shook his head. 'There is no need for you to tell me so,' he said. 'You would be shocked at the number of scoundrels I have to deal with in the course of my duties. But I have interrupted your story.'

'Imagine my surprise when Mr Snelson entered the room, waving a pistol in the air, and talking wildly. I could not imagine what he was doing in my house at that hour, and said so.'

'Did he explain himself?' Sir Godfrey asked.

Max looked at Barnes. 'I'm afraid he did not have the opportunity,' the valet admitted in sheepish tones. 'I heard the noise of an intruder, and on coming into the room I saw a man whom I did not recognize threatening His Grace.'

'You did not recognize him?'

'Snelson was not here when I arrived with Barnes,' Max explained. 'He only appeared a day or so ago, and Barnes had not met him.'

'Very well. You saw him threatening the duke, you say?' said the magistrate.

Barnes nodded. 'I had no weapon myself, and Mr Snelson was brandishing a pistol. I took hold of that bronze ornament yonder,' he went on, indicating the object with which Constance had struck the bailiff, 'and hit him on the head. Oh pray, Sir Godfrey, believe me, if I had had the slightest idea of who the man was, I would never have struck him.'

'Very well, Barnes,' Max replied. 'I'm sure that Sir Godfrey understands that you acted in good faith.'

'Yes indeed,' Sir Godfrey agreed. 'Where is young Snelson now?'

'Upstairs in bed,' Max replied. 'Do you wish to see him? I'm afraid he won't be able to talk to you, as he has been given a sleeping draught.'

The baronet made a dismissive gesture. 'No need, no need. And your man may go back to his duties. He was obviously acting in defence of his master. It is plain to me that young Snelson let his enthusiasm run away with him.'

'Off you go then, Barnes,' said Max. Then when the valet had gone, he turned to his visitor again.

'Now, to the purpose for your visit. As I came downstairs, I overheard talk of a traitor. Can you tell me any more? It is a matter which interests me exceedingly, since I am told that the question of the security of the realm has been raised in the House. I have not yet spoken since I came into the dukedom, and might make this the topic of my maiden speech. Should you object if I were to mention your name as my source of information?'

'No; no indeed,' the baronet replied, his head full of dizzy visions of himself being pointed out as the man who had featured in an important political debate. 'However,' he went on with some regret, 'I confess that I do not know a great deal about the business. My chief informant was Mr Snelson.'

'Snelson has a cottage of his own. I wonder why he arranged to meet you here?'

Sir Godfrey looked rather embarrassed. He fiddled with the stem of his empty brandy glass, which Max chose to take as a hint that he would like to have it refilled. 'Well, you see, he came to me with a tale of a man who he was sure was not who he was pretending to be.'

'An imposter of some sort? Your good health, Sir Godfrey.'

'Oh ... oh yes, and yours too, Your Grace.'

'And Snelson suggested that you consult me, presumably? Very proper, of course, but at this hour?'

If anything, Sir Godfrey's embarrassment increased. 'Not exactly,' he said, failing to meet Max's eyes.

By now, Max was enjoying himself so much that he was able to produce a genuine laugh without the slightest difficulty. 'Good God! Snelson actually suggested that I was the imposter, didn't he? Didn't he? Don't deny it. My dear sir, it's written all over your face!'

The baronet looked at him then, half puzzled, half relieved that this haughty aristocrat appeared to be unbending at tidings which might have been expected to arouse his wrath. 'Well, I have to admit—' he began.

'I knew it!' Max exclaimed. 'And you arrived, only to have my identity vouched for by your own men!'

The baronet did chuckle then. 'That was a stroke of luck for both of us,' he agreed.

Max nodded. 'What did he say to you? How did he convince you that I must be an imposter?'

'He said that he had been to Haslingfield, your principal seat. Apparently, the portraits that purport to be of the duke are nothing like you.'

'I should be very surprised if they were,' Max remarked, pouring another generous measure of brandy into the baronet's glass. 'I only came into the dukedom a few short weeks ago. I'm from a junior branch of the family, and don't have the height and colouring that is normally found in those that hold the title.'

'Ah, that would explain it,' said Sir Godfrey, relaxing under the influence of several generous measures of spirits.

'I think that perhaps he had an additional motive,' Max went on. 'He has been courting a young lady in the village who has so far been spurning his advances. Perhaps the notion of looking like a hero in front of her encouraged him to rash action.'

'Very likely,' agreed Sir Godfrey, gesturing rather more expansively with one hand than he had intended, and nearly losing hold of his glass with the other.

'Sadly, tonight's escapade will make him look rather foolish in front of her. That, coupled with the fact that he has placed me in a very awkward position, will be enough to make him want to play least in sight when he has recovered.'

'Perhaps the young lady will take pity on him when she sees his broken head; eh? Eh?' put in the baronet.

'Yes, perhaps,' Max agreed, smiling slightly. 'Well, I must not detain you further. Now that you have satisfied yourself as to my identity, you will no doubt wish to take your men back to Aylsham and their beds.' He got to his feet. It was not part of his plan to have his unexpected guest drop off in the book room.

'Yes, indeed,' the baronet agreed, setting down his glass with some reluctance, for it had been exceedingly fine brandy. 'When young Snelson comes round, I trust you will oblige me by giving him a flea in his ear for bringing me out on this wild goose chase?'

'I will do so, of course. No doubt his intentions were good, but he must learn to get his facts straight.'

After the unwanted visitors had gone, Max went back into the book room in order to finish his glass of brandy. Although he had appeared to fill his glass as frequently as Sir Godfrey's, he had in fact drunk very little, feeling that he needed to keep alert. Now, he decided that he deserved a little more.

The book room was set at one of the corners of the house, overlooking a quiet part of the garden. The man who had built the house originally had clearly wanted to be able to walk out into his garden at a moment's notice for, like every other room on the ground floor, it had a door which led directly outside. The curtains in this room had been closed earlier, giving it a feeling of cosiness. It was as Max was crossing the room to pick up his glass that he heard a noise outside. Swiftly, he blew out the candles set on the mantelpiece, and moved stealthily to the outside door. Taking out his pistol, he threw the door open, then stepped to one side, saying, 'Show yourself, damn it. I've had enough cloak and dagger for one night.'

'And so have I,' said a faint voice from outside. 'For God's sake, let me in, Max – if you've finished peacocking about in that dressing gown.'

'Alistair?' Max exclaimed, putting his gun back in his pocket and stepping outside. His cousin stood just to the right of the door, leaning against the wall. His manner could have passed for his usual nonchalance, until it became apparent that he had one hand pressed to his shoulder. 'Come on, inside with you.'

It was not until he had helped his cousin into the house that Max realized another man had followed them. 'This is Anders,' said Alistair. 'He's one of us.'

Now that they were in the light, Max could see the bloodstains beneath Alistair's hand. 'Good God, what happened here? Have you been followed?' His hand went to his gun once more.

Alistair shook his head. 'Winged as we left the French coast. This has largely dried up, but I'm feeling devilish weak.'

'Your mission?' Max asked as he helped his cousin into a chair.

'Compromised,' Alistair responded. 'Dead in the water before it even began. Someone was on to me, that's for sure. Where's Barnes?'

'Seeing our other visitors off the premises.'

Alistair closed his eyes. His naturally pale complexion was chalky white. 'Max, the mission might have failed but there are papers ... vital information ... they must go to Hampson ... I—'

At this fortuitous moment, the door opened to admit Barnes. 'Your Grace!' he exclaimed when he saw Alistair. Max grinned. Barnes had served him well, but there was no doubt where his deepest loyalty lay. Alistair opened his eyes then. 'Barnes,' he murmured with the ghost of a grin. 'Now I shall do.' Then turning to Max he said, 'You'll go?'

'At once,' Max replied. Half an hour later he was heading for London on horseback with Alistair's precious papers in his pocket.

Chapter Twenty

On reaching her room, Constance found herself completely at a loss as to what to do next. Going tamely to bed was unthinkable. Max had not said when he might come for her. For all she knew, he might be back as soon as the magistrate had gone, which might be in one hour or in three. She had visions of his throwing stones up at her window in order to catch her attention. Then it occurred to her that he would not necessarily know which window was hers. For a short while, she sat at the window with the candle burning, until she realized that anyone who chose to snoop about would see her there and wonder at her actions. So she blew out the candle, leaving the curtains open. This meant that she was unable to read – not that she could set her mind to anything other than the events of the evening.

She tried to concentrate on Max: on his laughing eyes, his promise, his kiss, even his declaration; anything other than that dreadful moment when Colin Snelson had fallen beneath her blow. She had not imagined that it could be so easy to kill a man; and yet the bronze ornament had been very heavy. She could still hear the sickening thud as it had fallen on his unprotected head. Hurriedly she pushed that thought to the back of her mind and again began to think of Max. Was he all right? Had he managed to make believable enough excuses to the magistrate? Was he even now being carried off in shackles? She sprang up and began to pace about, only to return hastily to her place at the window, in case he should come and find her absent.

Eventually she closed her eyes, and leaned her head back against the window frame. She schooled her mind to think of events earlier in their acquaintance. She remembered him fencing with Abdas, walking with her in the garden, looking at the lighthouse. At last, the excitement of the day and late evening took their toll, and she drifted off to sleep where she was.

By the time she woke, the day had begun. Before she opened her eyes, she could hear sounds of movement in the house, and came to, for a moment not remembering why she had fallen asleep fully dressed and sitting by the window. She stretched, feeling an unaccustomed stiffness in her back, and was slowly returning to full awareness when the door opened softly and Lucy the maid put her head around the edge of it.

'Why, Miss Connie!' she exclaimed. 'Never say you've been there all night!'

Constance was about to deny it, when she realized that the evidence of her creased clothes, let alone her untouched bed, would give the lie to such an assertion. 'The moonlight was so strong last night that I couldn't sleep,' she said, glad that there had been a full moon and a clear sky. 'So I sat here to look at it and must have dropped off eventually. What time is it?'

'It's still early, Miss Connie,' Lucy told her. 'Not quite seven o'clock. I'd just stepped out into the garden for some herbs for Mrs Dobbs and I saw that your curtains were open. Do you want your water and your chocolate now, or shall I help you out of your things so you can sleep in your bed for an hour or two? You must be that stiff!'

Constance looked at her bed. It did seem inviting. Max would hardly be throwing stones up at her window now that the household was stirring. 'Just for half an hour then,' she replied, turning so that Lucy could unlace her. 'If anyone asks for me, you must come and tell me at once.'

She closed her eyes, not expecting to sleep at all. To her astonishment, a comfortable bed and a warm coverlet, coupled with an exceedingly poor night, meant that the next time she opened her eyes, it was almost eleven o'clock.

Lucy must have been on the alert for any movement, for as soon as she set her feet to the floor, the maid appeared.

'Lucy, you should have roused me before this,' Constance

exclaimed. 'Whatever must my aunt and uncle think?'

'Oh, don't you fret about that, miss,' Lucy replied. 'I told them you'd had a poor night and were catching up. Shall I fetch your hot water and your chocolate now?'

'Yes, please.' Then, before the girl left, she added craftily, 'No doubt I've missed all kinds of excitement.'

'Oh no indeed, miss,' Lucy replied guilelessly. 'Nothing's happened that I'm aware of.'

'And nobody's asked after me?'

No, miss,' Lucy answered, looking at her a little curiously, for this was the second time that her young mistress had referred to such a possibility.

As breakfast was long since over, Lucy brought toast and marmalade with the morning chocolate. Constance, who would have protested that she had lost her appetite eternally after the previous night's goings-on, ate both slices under Lucy's watchful eye and, to her surprise, felt better for it.

As she prepared to go downstairs, her imagination got to work in the most morbid of ways. She imagined herself present in the parish church at Colin Snelson's funeral. For some strange reason, the coffin would be left open during the service; the vicar would preach on the wickedness of those who had struck him down; then, as the service drew to a close, the corpse would dramatically sit up and point at her with an accusing white finger.

Nonsense, she told herself. You were acting to defend another; but Max had gone and, despite his promise, had not yet returned. He will, she told herself. He *will* come, surely? Doubts arose in her mind, despite a determined effort to suppress them.

Although she would have been glad of conversation to divert her thoughts, she was not to be so fortunate. Her uncle had walked into Cromer to meet someone, and her aunt, preparing a canvas for a new painting, showed no desire for conversation, or even curiosity about her late appearance, simply remarking that she hoped her niece now felt more rested.

She went out into the garden, her eyes not taking in the beauty of the beds on which her uncle worked so hard. Part of her wanted to walk to Beacon Tower and find out what was going on; yet the very idea of going near the place where she had committed murder made her feel quite sick with dread. It would no doubt have been a virtuous act to go to the church and pray for her victim's soul. As she thought about doing so, however, she saw in her mind's eye that same picture of Snelson, ghastly pale, sitting up in his coffin, and shuddered.

She wondered whether she would ever be able to sit in that church again with peace of mind. Perhaps she ought to seek the vicar out and make her confession? Yet how could she do so without implicating Max when she did not know where he was, and what he might have said or done since she had last seen him? It was whilst her thoughts were in such turmoil that the vicar came into view, almost as though she had conjured him up. He appeared to have come from the direction of Beacon Tower and, although he waved cheerfully enough, his face wore a solemn expression.

'Good morning, Miss Church,' he said politely. 'You are taking the air, I see.'

'It is such a lovely day,' she replied, not with perfect truth as although there was some fleeting sunshine, the day promised to be a cloudy one.

'Oh indeed, indeed,' the vicar responded. 'At least fine weather takes my mind off my sombre task.'

'Your sombre—' Her voice faded away.

'Task, yes,' he concluded heavily. 'Arranging obsequies is always distressing, I find; particularly when the person was comparatively young, and with no family in the vicinity, either.'

'Of course,' Constance replied, feeling for the gatepost because she was conscious of a sudden giddiness. Colin Snelson's nearest relatives were in Cambridge. How shocked they would be to hear of his death so soon after they had seen him! 'I suppose you ... you went to Beacon Tower in order to ... to make arrangements.'

'It seemed only right,' the vicar agreed. 'The incident having occurred within the duke's jurisdiction, so to speak.'

'And did you see the duke?'

'No, I spoke to his manservant,' the vicar replied. 'Apparently, His Grace is indisposed. He did at least give permission for me to carry forward the arrangements that I already had in mind. Ah well,

I had best get home and start to write an address for the occasion. What on earth does one say, though?'

'Perhaps that he was faithful in ... in fulfilling his duty,' Constance suggested faintly.

'Ah yes, that might be suitable. Good day, then, Miss Church.'

After he had gone, Constance walked into the back garden and sat on the grass with her back to a tree. Her conversation with the vicar had almost caused her to bring back what little she had consumed for breakfast. Would she ever become accustomed to the shocking knowledge that she had killed a man? Heretofore, she had had the luxury of a comparatively clear conscience. Would she now be obliged to go through life with this stain upon it?

She had no more idea of what she ought to do next than she had had when she woke up that morning. What had happened to Max? What was this indisposition from which he was suffering? He had certainly not been injured when she had last spoken to him. If he had been hurt resisting arrest, then he would have been carried off to be locked up somewhere, unless he had somehow escaped and Barnes was hiding him. However could she find out what was going on without betraying her close involvement in the affair?

She was so deep in thought that her aunt had to call her name three times before she answered. 'Connie! Are you there?'

'Yes, Aunt,' she answered, scrambling to her feet. 'I'm sorry; I was in a brown study. Do you need me for anything?'

'Why yes,' her aunt responded. 'I was wondering whether you would go to Annie Habgood on my behalf? I was intending to do so myself, but—'

'But you cannot wait to get started on your new painting,' Constance said, finishing her sentence. 'Yes of course. I'll get my bonnet.' Truth to tell she was thankful for any means of diverting her morbid thoughts.

Annie was a relation of Mrs Dobbs. Her husband, who was at sea, always took care to leave his wife adequately provided for. Unfortunately, Mrs Habgood had never really mastered the art of managing, and often had to be helped out by friends and neighbours. Mrs Dobbs, very conscious of her own position at The Brambles, would as soon fly to the moon as ask for assistance, so

Miss Fellowes always made sure that visits to the Habgood household took place without her foreknowledge, so as not to embarrass her.

When Constance arrived, she found that Mrs Habgood was surrounded by the usual chaos. She had seven children, one of whom was now in service in one of the farms in the local area, whilst another had been taken on as a groom at an inn in Cromer. Although only five were still at home, there always appeared to be more, because they were never properly supervised, Mrs Habgood having the habit of throwing her apron over her head and howling whenever things became too much.

The first thing that Constance did was to set about getting the children washed, instructing the older ones to help their juniors. This done, she sat them down at the table for a breakfast of bread and dripping. Then, after they had eaten, she sent them out to play whilst she helped Annie to wash up and tidy the house. After two hours spent cleaning, washing and baking, the house looked very different, and Constance was left with the satisfaction of knowing that the family would be adequately fed and clothed for the rest of the week, at least.

Perhaps because for a brief period her mind had been taken off the previous night's troubles, she instinctively took a different route home, longer, and with some attractive views. To her surprise and dismay, she looked up to find herself only a few steps away from Snelson's cottage. 'Oh, no!' she gasped, the horror of what had happened hitting her like a blow that temporarily deprived her of breath.

What would happen to his cottage and his things, she wondered to herself? She took a few steps towards it. She hoped that measures had been taken to secure his property. It would be dreadful if some vagrant wandered in and made free with his belongings. She hesitated. Should she try the door herself, or refer the matter to the estate office? Telling herself not to be foolish, she walked towards the cottage. She was almost at the door when it opened, and in front of her stood Snelson, his face rather pale and surmounted by a bandage.

She had never fainted in her life, not even after she had struck

Snelson over the head and thought that she had killed him. She almost did so now when confronted with a dead man, and had to steady herself by clutching at the doorpost. Would he point at her with a white finger, as she had imagined him doing from his coffin?

'Miss Church!' he exclaimed. Constance opened and closed her mouth without any sound coming out. 'Come inside,' he said quickly, ushering her in and pulling out a chair for her to sit down. After another swift look at her face, he crossed the small sitting room, which opened out directly from the front door, and took a serviceable decanter from the top of the sturdy sideboard under the window. He poured a measure of brandy into a glass which he then placed in her hand. After a brief hesitation, during which she looked up at his face, she took a sip and choked slightly.

'That's better,' Snelson said a moment or two later, when he saw the colour begin to return to her cheeks. 'Now tell me what has occurred, for the plain truth is that when I opened the door to you, you looked as if you had seen a ghost.'

For a moment she could not think how to answer. How could she say that she had thought him to be dead because she had struck him? 'I ... I had not expected to see you,' she confessed eventually.

'Not expect to see me in my own cottage?' Fortunately, because she could not think how to respond to this objection, he answered the question himself. 'Oh, I expect you thought that I would still be engaged with the magistrate.'

'Yes ... yes, that was it,' she replied, thankful for the breathing space given by his mistaken assumption. 'Did ... did you go? What transpired?'

'As to that, I am not very sure,' he answered, wrinkling his brow. 'Do you mind if I sit down? As you can see, I have sustained a blow to the head and I am still feeling a little unsteady.'

'Please do,' she answered, suddenly overcome anew by feelings of guilt.

'I did indeed go to Aylsham. I spoke to Sir Godfrey, and tried to impress upon him the seriousness of the case. He told me that it would take him some little time to assemble the men, so I offered to return here and keep watch. It then occurred to me that the imposter might make off before they arrived, so rather than meekly waiting for them, I decided to detain him myself. I cornered him in Beacon Tower, and he looked pretty fearful, I can tell you! But even while I had my pistol trained upon him, someone – one of his confederates, no doubt – struck me down from behind and rendered me unconscious.' Constance raised her hand to her mouth. Snelson, glancing at her, evidently perceived it as a sign of shock. 'My dear ma'am, I am distressing you with this account, so I will say no more.'

'No indeed,' Constance exclaimed. Then realizing the infelicitous nature of this expression, she corrected herself hastily. 'I mean, yes. It is very distressing! Pray tell me, how did you make your way from Beacon Tower to here? When did you come round?'

'I would hazard a guess that I was carried here late last night or in the early hours of the morning,' Snelson said thoughtfully. 'I have a vague memory of coming round in a daze, and being given a draught of some sort. I suspect that it may have been a sleeping draught, probably to make sure that I was unable to intervene when the magistrate arrived.' Here his voice took on a bitter tone. 'No doubt that imposter spun him some plausible tale, making me out to be a foolish country yokel, in order to persuade him to go away again.'

'No doubt,' Constance murmured. 'So what do you plan to do now?'

'I cannot fetch Sir Godfrey again,' Snelson replied. 'I expect I am a laughing-stock the length and breadth of Aylsham by now. I will have to return to Beacon Tower and secure him properly myself; and this time, I will have no compunction about shooting to kill, if necessary.'

'Oh, pray wait until your head is better,' Constance begged him, horrified at the notion of more violence.

He paused, thoughtfully. 'I will wait until my head has recovered,' he agreed eventually. 'At the moment, I feel as though I could be overpowered very easily.'

'I will ask my aunt to send you some broth,' Constance promised, getting to her feet. All kinds of thoughts were crowding into her head and she needed solitude in order to examine them.

'You are very kind,' said Snelson, also rising and taking her hand. 'A veritable angel of mercy.'

'One very much in disguise,' she said ruefully, removing her hand before he could kiss it. It had after all been the one with which she had struck him down.

She left his cottage deep in thought, and wandered home by a circuitous route, not really conscious of her whereabouts. What exactly had been going on the previous evening? At the time, she had felt as though everyone involved, including herself, had been taken equally by surprise by what had transpired. Now, as she looked back, she began to wonder how many of the evening's events had been carefully orchestrated for her benefit. She was sure that she could acquit Colin Snelson of deceit. Why, he had been so unsuspecting of her own motives that he had told her of his intention to summon the magistrate, never dreaming that she would betray him.

What of Max? Her opinion of him over the time of their acquaintance had see-sawed wildly between contempt, fascination, admiration, and finally love. Last night, she had even consented to fly with him. Had she not been waiting for him to come for her? He had never appeared.

She had been so relieved that Snelson was not dead that she had not thought any further about who had arranged for him to be transported to his cottage. Now, it occurred to her that Barnes must have lied when he said that Snelson was dead. Had his master known all along that the bailiff had only been stunned? Even if he himself had been deceived by Barnes, the valet must have enlightened him when he returned to Beacon Tower. Max had known how much she had been affected by Snelson's supposed death. He must have guessed how she would be racked by guilt; yet he had allowed her to pass an entire night in the belief that she had been responsible for the death of a man.

She remembered her meeting with the vicar. Doubtless the funeral of which he had spoken was to be for one of the drowned sailors. Furthermore, the news that he had given concerning Max's indisposition had almost certainly come from Barnes, who was now revealed to be untruthful. It was far more likely that whilst she had been tossing and turning, tortured mentally by what she thought she had done, Max had either been enjoying an undisturbed night's sleep, or running away in order to save his own skin.

'How could he be so cruel?' She declared out loud. She could no longer fool herself with regard to the nature of the man; he was all deceit, all lies; and, fool that she was, she had actually fallen in love with him! Well, that was where her folly would end. He would never cozen her into trusting him again! What was more, she would go to Beacon Tower this instant in order to give him a piece of her mind.

Chapter Twenty-one

The walk that took her there, far from calming her temper, whipped it up so that when Barnes opened the door to her, she was blazing with fury.

'Miss Church; may I be of assistance?' The dapper little man's very courtesy fanned the flames of her indignation.

'Certainly,' she responded, stalking past him in a manner which seemed to say that if he did not move, she would walk over him. 'You may tell me what I have ever done to you to merit being treated in such a barbarous way,' she demanded.

Barnes stepped back in surprise. 'Barbarous? Madam, I—'

'Barbarous,' she repeated. 'You knelt by Mr Snelson's body and allowed me to believe that I had killed him. How could you?'

'May I be permitted to know how you have discovered that he still lives?' Barnes asked her.

'The man came to his own front door! That would constitute a pretty robust case for his not being dead, would you not agree?'

Barnes inclined his head. 'I deemed the subterfuge prudent, madam,' he said, regaining most of his equanimity.

'Prudent! What of my feelings in this matter? How could you do such a thing, after my aunt and I had extended the hand of friendship to you on the journey here? Oh, but I am forgetting,' she went on, her tone heavy with sarcasm. 'All of that was a lie, too, was it not? You were not newly acquainted with the duke; you knew him very well indeed.'

'No, madam,' Barnes insisted. 'I had never met him before that day.'

'You will understand, I am sure, if I keep to my own opinion on that matter,' she replied. 'However, I am reminded that I did not come to bandy words with you. I have come to speak to that ... that pitiful excuse of a man who pays your wages.'

It was at this point that the normally imperturbable Barnes found himself in a real dilemma. The man whom the wrathful young lady in front of him had known as the Duke of Haslingfield had gone to London on a vital mission; the real Duke of Haslingfield was even now upstairs. At no point had anyone informed him, Barnes, whether it was now safe to reveal the presence and identity of the genuine nobleman. Seeking to temporize, therefore, he said, 'His Grace is not available, I fear.'

'Not available? What upon earth does that mean?'

'It means that he cannot speak to you at present,' said Barnes. 'Rest assured, Miss Church, that when I next speak to him, I will inform him of your visit. No doubt he will do himself the honour of waiting upon you when he has the opportunity.'

Obviously insisting on speaking to him was not going to get her anywhere. Doing what she wanted to do, namely, storming through the house and flinging all the doors open in search of the man, was unthinkable. She thanked Barnes with as much civility as she could muster, then went home, where she gave vent to her feelings by indulging in such vigorous pursuits as giving assistance with the laundry, sorting out the attic – a task which she had been putting off for months – and weeding for her uncle. Although these tasks did not entirely succeed in diverting her mind, they had the merit of tiring her out. Thanks to her busy day, the relief of having a clear conscience, and the wakefulness of the night before, she fell asleep as soon as her head touched the pillow.

Constance had always been accustomed to knowing what needed to be done and getting on with it. It was with a sense of weary disillusionment that she awoke yet again in an indecisive frame of mind. Whilst part of her wanted to make a second visit to Beacon Tower and demand an explanation, she dreaded looking like one of those women who are forever to be found chasing after a man. Yet for how long was she expected to sit here whilst Max decided when to be 'available' to see her?

Before she could fret herself into a headache, Colin Snelson arrived at The Brambles with a much smaller bandage around his head, looking very much more like himself, and clearly wanting a word with her. This objective was not accomplished very easily, as by now her aunt and uncle had heard a rumour concerning his misfortune. This rumour appeared to be confirmed by the bandage he wore, and consequently they were very concerned.

'Is it known who struck you?' Mr Fellowes asked. 'Was it a housebreaker, do you suppose?'

'Who can say?' said Snelson. 'I was attacked from behind so did not catch a glimpse of the villain.'

'Housebreakers?' exclaimed Miss Fellowes. 'Oh, merciful heaven, might they still be in the vicinity? Brother, we must check all the doors and windows, and make sure that we are not an easy target.'

After Miss Fellowes had ushered her brother insistently out of the room – for even in her agitation, she did not forget the desirability of thrusting her niece and the bailiff together – Snelson said, 'Forgive the subterfuge.'

'Subterfuge?' Constance echoed, not certain at first to what he might be referring.

'The housebreaking story. I was no more struck over the head by housebreakers than by ... by you,' he declared, seizing upon the most unlikely assailant that he could imagine. Fortunately, his agitated pacing meant that he was not looking at her as he spoke. 'I have no doubt that I was struck by some confederate of his – possibly that secretary whom I have not yet seen. It makes me all the more determined that their plan should be foiled.'

'How ... how do you intend to do that?'

'I intend to go to Beacon Tower.'

'Is that wise?' Constance asked him, wrinkling her brow.

'What could be more natural? I am the estate bailiff, after all. I wonder, would you care to accompany me? After what happened last time I went to Beacon Tower, I would prefer to have you behind me.' Wincing slightly at the irony of his words, Constance agreed and went to fetch her bonnet.

There was no question of not being admitted on this occasion.

Mr Snelson was employed by the estate and had as much right to be on the premises as Barnes himself. 'In fact, in some senses the security of the property is more my province than yours, Mr Barnes,' he said, as they were standing in the hall. 'I would like a word with His Grace, if you please, so that I may receive his commands.'

'As I told Miss Church yesterday, I am not sure whether that will be possible,' said Barnes.

It was at this point that another voice spoke from above them. 'Most things are possible, my dear Barnes, if one will only make the effort,' it drawled. Just as Sir Godfrey and his magistrate had observed Max descend the stairs in his dressing gown the previous night, so now the occupants of the hall saw another gentleman, as fair and pale as Max was dark and swarthy, and clad in the same garment. 'It would appear that I have visitors, and at an early hour,' he went on, as he continued his descent. 'You must forgive my undress; I have sustained a little – ah – mishap.' He drew their attention to the fact that one arm was supported by a sling. 'Whom might I have the honour of addressing?'

They stared at him for a brief moment, at a loss for words. Barnes obviously knew him although he was a stranger to both of them. Whoever he might be, he was an aristocrat to his fingertips and he looked to be very much at home. A small quizzical smile twisted his lips. 'If I might, ah, establish my credentials first, I am Haslingfield. And you are—?'

Of the two visitors, Snelson was the least surprised. He had after all seen Alistair's portrait. Constance, on the other hand, had been clinging to the hope that Max really was who he had claimed to be. Confronted with this utterly authentic aristocrat, she found herself deprived of speech. Snelson glanced at her pale face and cleared his throat. 'This lady is Miss Church, who is one of your nearest neighbours, Your Grace; I am Snelson, your bailiff.' Constance curtsied automatically. She dreaded new revelations and would have liked to turn tail and run. Aside from the impropriety of such actions, she was conscious that her limbs were trembling almost too much for movement.

The languid gentleman bowed with casual grace. 'Let us go into the book room so that we may examine this affair,' he said. 'Barnes, arrange for coffee if you please.' Barnes opened the door into the book room and they all went in, Constance first, waved through by the duke, who followed just ahead of Snelson. Once the door was closed, their host said, 'Now, you must tell me in what way I may serve you. It must be something uncommonly urgent if it has summoned me from my bed before the day has properly begun.'

Snelson looked at the duke, then at Constance. 'Well, Your Grace,' he began eventually, 'I find myself at a bit of a loss. I came here to expose an imposter, but ... well—'

'Yes?' prompted the duke, inviting Constance to sit down and taking a seat for himself before waving a languid hand at another chair for the bailiff.

'Your Grace, there has been another man living here and masquerading as you,' Snelson continued.

'And you thought to unmask him,' put in the duke. 'Did you believe him to be some sort of villain – a spy, for example?'

Snelson coloured. 'I did, Your Grace,' he agreed, his chin high. 'I'm still set on catching him if he is an enemy of England.'

'Very public spirited of you, I'm sure,' the duke remarked. He sighed. 'I suppose I do owe you an explanation.' The door opened to admit Barnes with a tray. 'Ah, coffee. Miss Church, will you pour?' After the valet had gone, he went on. 'I would much prefer brandy, but Barnes denies me such comforts. He says it may inflame my wound.'

'I hope you are not seriously hurt, Your Grace,' said Constance, managing to speak as she poured for all of them, the activity helping her.

'Barnes is inclined to mother me,' he replied. 'My hurts are largely superficial, I thank you, and I am making good progress.' He took a mouthful of coffee. 'Now, where were we? Ah yes, your imposter, Snelson. His presence here and my wound are connected. You will know that I inherited only recently. My man of business has never really understood the expectations that people have of one who is – oh dear, I really feel that I must be somewhat indelicate and describe myself as a man of the town! I had become entangled in a rather messy – ah – situation, and needed time and space to bring the matter to a conclusion. Unfortunately, there were those who took exception to my behaviour, and I blush to confess that I found myself obliged to take part in a duel, and then go to ground so as to avoid arrest. In order to throw others off the scent, my cousin Max agreed to take my place until I was well enough to rise from my bed. He was experiencing a little bother of his own with gaming debts, I believe, so he was glad of an excuse to disappear.'

As Constance listened to his tale, she could feel disgust and contempt welling up inside her. 'So your cousin took your place as a kind of … of jest?' she asked, trying not to let her feelings show.

The duke smiled ruefully. 'I was trying to avoid the use of that word,' he admitted. 'For our excuse, I must tell you that he and I have often indulged in such japes. They really mean nothing at all.'

Constance put her cup down with a hand that was not quite steady. She had agonized over Max, fallen in love with him, been ready to kill for him, fly with him, and he had only been there for a jest! 'How exquisite humour is in London these days,' she remarked, quite surprised when her voice did not tremble. 'I should never be able to keep up with it, I fear.' She rose to her feet and the men did the same. 'Thank you for enlightening us, Your Grace. I fear I must be on my way now.'

'It was my pleasure,' he replied. 'I trust that you have been entertained.' Had she been looking at him at that moment, she would have seen his eyes narrow.

'Oh, excessively,' she answered with an unconvincing laugh. 'How surprised the local populace will be when they discover that their duke has changed heads.'

'I doubt I shall be here long enough for anyone to notice,' the duke replied. 'Snelson, do you have other business to bring to my attention?'

'No, Your Grace.'

'Before you go, I believe I must commiserate with you.'

'Your Grace?'

Haslingfield pointed to the other man's bandage. 'I understand that I am not the only sufferer. I believe you were struck down whilst attempting to detain my cousin as a spy.'

'Yes, Your Grace.'

'Do you know who struck you?'

'I was struck down from behind, so I cannot say,' Snelson stammered.

'From behind! How dastardly!' the duke exclaimed. 'Shame on him! Would you not say so, Miss Church?'

Luckily, since Constance was quite unable to locate her voice, Snelson murmured something about escorting her home. 'Miss Church is understandably shocked,' he explained.

'Of course,' the duke replied. 'You must forgive my maladroitness at mentioning such a matter in her presence. I am certain, Miss Church, that you are in no danger of being struck down by the same person.'

'The story is beginning to get round that I was struck by house-breakers,' said Snelson.

'Then let that story stand. Doubtless one of Max's servants was responsible, and he may deal with your assailant in whatever way he believes to be appropriate.'

'I *knew* that that other man was not the real duke,' Snelson exclaimed as soon as they were out of earshot of anyone in the house. 'I *knew* it! Why, the fellow looked exactly like some sort of cut-throat. Did I not say so?'

'Yes, yes, you said so,' Constance answered in a distracted tone.

'Now the man we met today, well, I would have known him for a duke at the very first glance. He is just like the portrait that I saw at Haslingfield, although older, of course. And then there was his bearing. It was just what one would expect of a true aristocrat. Did you not think so?'

'I suppose so,' Constance agreed in much the same manner as before.

'I must say, I don't think much of this jest they played together, do you? That rogue must have been laughing up his sleeve the whole time. When I think … '

Not knowing what to think herself, and only certain that she did not want to have her ears assailed with Snelson's reflections on the matter, she stopped walking and turned to face him. 'Mr Snelson, there is no need for you to walk home with me. I am sure that you have a great deal to do.'

'I am quite happy to do so,' he assured her. 'Indeed, I would be happy to escort you anywhere you wanted to go,' he added in earnest tones.

'You are very good,' she replied, trying hard to keep hold of her temper, 'but just now, I would be glad to have simply the company of my own thoughts.'

'Miss Church, in view of your recent shock, I—'

'Oh, pray just go away!' she shouted at him, finally at the end of her tether. She turned and picking up her skirts, ran in the direction of The Brambles, heedless alike of his voice calling to her, or of the tears coursing down her cheeks. Her nerves and her conscience had both been in shreds, and it had all been done for a jest! If only she could disappear from this vicinity and never come back!

Chapter Twenty-two

Max's journey to London went without a hitch. He would have liked Abdas beside him, especially in view of the vitally important papers which he carried inside his coat. Abdas was still at Melinda's home, however, and to go and collect him would have added valuable time to his journey, as well as probably attracting unwelcome attention.

He set off from Beacon Tower at ten o'clock, riding Filigree, his own trusty stallion. They travelled for four hours, rested for four, then travelled on for four more. Arriving at a decent inn at six in the morning, he entrusted Filigree to a sleepy-looking stable lad, and made a careful pick of the horses for hire to take him on the next stage. After yet another change and hardly any rest, he eventually arrived at Hampson's office at five o'clock in the evening.

Hampson displayed very little surprise at his appearance, and received the papers that he handed over with a word of thanks, leafing through them with an unchanging expression. 'Your presence would indicate that your cousin has been detained in some way,' he remarked in matter-of-fact tones.

'The bullet that winged him has rather hampered his activities,' Max agreed. His tone was similarly even, but his eyes were cold.

'Mercifully, though, he was able to pass these on to you,' Hampson replied, turning in order to lock the documents into a safe set in the wall behind him. 'I trust that he will recover.'

'It's to be hoped that your trust is not misplaced, sir,' Max replied, 'since if he perishes I will hold you directly responsible.' Not feeling capable of conversing further with the man, Max left immediately after this and went to Brooks's in search of congenial company. To his surprise and delight, he found Sir Stafford Prince ensconced in an armchair, a book in his hand.

'My dear boy!' Sir Stafford exclaimed. 'This is most unexpected.' He beckoned to a waiter and ordered wine. 'How did your business work out? It *was* Spain whence you were bound?'

In the time that the baronet took to ask his second question, Max had recalled the story that had been concocted to account for his absence. 'Everything went well,' he replied, taking a chair opposite his stepfather. 'I don't think I was really needed, though. I'm sure they could have managed without me.'

'Sometimes, all that it takes is for one to be present in order to make a difference. Have you dined?'

Max had in fact eaten very little that day. Indeed, all his eating had been done in a hurry, if not whilst still on his feet. He was very happy, therefore, to accept Sir Stafford's invitation, and soon the two men were tucking in to a fine beefsteak pie.

While they ate, their conversation did not touch upon Max's activities. Max was so hungry that he allowed his stepfather to bear the greater part of the conversation, which was chiefly about the estate, Lady Prince, Ruth and the two boys. When they had finished, Sir Stafford invited him to come back to his house and share a bottle of brandy. 'I've something rather fine which I think you will like,' he said. 'You can stay the night if you have made no other arrangements.'

'I'd be delighted,' Max replied. 'I must be up betimes, though. I—' He almost said that he needed to return whence he had come, and stopped himself just in time. Instead, he went on, 'Have a commitment tomorrow that cannot be broken.'

'Then let us make the most of this evening,' said Sir Stafford after the tiniest of pauses.

Once in the privacy of Sir Stafford's house, Max told him all about what had occurred whilst he had been in Cromer, ending with his recent ride, much of it by moonlight. Alistair's comment that his mission had not prospered had caused the baronet to shake his head. 'I fear the remaining members of the royal family are doomed,' he said despondently. 'The papers you've taken to Hampson may tell a different story, but I doubt it.'

Max's only omission from his story was any mention of his feelings for Constance. Something must have conveyed itself to the baronet, however, for when they bade each other goodnight, he said, 'If you intend to rise with the lark, I don't suppose I'll see you in the morning. Have a good journey.'

'Thank you, sir,' Max replied. 'And thank you for—'

The older man waved his hand dismissively. 'It's nothing,' he said. 'Just make sure you take the young lady to meet your mother as soon as may be.'

Although the return journey to Cromer could not have been said to have the same urgency as the one to London, as far as Max was concerned, haste was certainly of the essence. He had set off on Alistair's behalf without a second thought, carrying with him little more than a change of clothes, enough money for his needs and the precious papers. He had had neither the time nor the opportunity to call upon Constance and to reassure her, both as to Snelson's survival and his own intentions. As far as the bailiff's condition was concerned, he could only hope that Barnes would pass the news on to her. For the rest, he would have to speak for himself, and pray that his sudden departure would not cause her to lose all faith in him.

Throughout his journey, different scenarios jostled about in his head. His favourite was the one in which, thankful for Snelson's recovery and relieved concerning his own safety, Constance cast herself into his arms. Unfortunately, the one which seemed to come into his head more frequently was that in which she blamed him for the mistake over Snelson, berated him for disappearing without even so much as a note, and refused to speak to him ever again. Consequently, although he had time and opportunity to rest, he scarcely slept any more than he had on the way to London.

When he arrived back in the vicinity of Cromer at around ten in the morning, some sixty hours after setting out, his first instinct was to go to The Brambles in search of Constance. He had steeled himself for reproach and accusations; it came as something of an anticlimax to be told by the maid that none of the family was in, and that Miss Church had 'gone a-visiting'.

As this could mean anything from a half-hour's local excursion, to a day out in Aylsham, and as the maid did not seem to know which of these Constance's 'visiting' might be, Max left a message to say that he had called and would return. He then made his way to Beacon Tower. Here, he was able to report to Alistair the safe delivery of the papers, much to his cousin's satisfaction.

'I travelled halfway across France and got myself winged in their defence,' he declared. 'I should hate to think that you had mislaid them on a mere canter to London.' The real Duke of Haslingfield sat at his ease, clad in a pewter-coloured waistcoat embroidered in silver and just a suggestion of pink, and light-grey breeches with gleaming hessian boots. As his sling was still in evidence, his superbly cut coat of midnight-blue brocade was worn negligently across his shoulders.

Max grinned. 'I see that you are much recovered,' he observed. 'You're better than I expected.'

'Loss of blood and fatigue were the main culprits,' Alistair answered. 'A night's sleep and some good red meat made a lot of difference. Barnes tells me that tomorrow, I should be able to wear a light enough bandage so that I can get my coat on properly.'

'I don't suppose you can tell me anything more about the papers with which I was entrusted,' said Max, as his cousin stood up in order to pour him some wine.

'Not a chance of it,' Alistair replied. 'Instead, you might tell me how you have been occupying yourself, and what you think about this, the smallest and most isolated of my holdings.'

Max obliged, recounting the various things that had happened to him since his arrival. He also gave as full a description as he could of the small estate of which Beacon Tower was the hub. As he did so, he could not help betraying his keen interest in the local area and the people. Alistair made a mental note of this, and said nothing.

It was also inevitable that Constance's name should come up. 'I have met Miss Church, as it happens,' said the duke when Max had finished his tale.

'Indeed?'

'Yes, she came here yesterday with Snelson. I found the interview most entertaining, I confess.'

'Entertaining?' Max queried, his face rather set.

'Why yes,' Alistair replied. 'Barnes, you see, had told me that it had been Miss Church who had struck my good bailiff over the head, a fact of which he was plainly unaware. I had an amusing few minutes at their expense.' He paused, glancing briefly at his cousin before going to refill his glass. 'I dare say once he knows, she will have to give him her head for washing before she is forgiven. They tell me that every marriage has such stories.'

'You are mistaken,' said Max shortly. 'She is not engaged to Snelson.'

'Is she not? Then indeed, I must be mistaken, as you say.'

Max grunted. Then, after a moment or two, he said curiously, 'What brought them here in the first place?'

'They wanted to see the Duke of Haslingfield,' Alistair replied.

'Snelson had worked out that it wasn't I,' Max told him, momentarily diverted. 'In fact, he persuaded the Aylsham magistrate to turn out with some volunteers to arrest me. He came first to make sure that I didn't run away. Constance – I mean, Miss Church – struck him over the head to silence him. Then when the magistrate came, I put on the performance of a lifetime, and so did poor Barnes, who pretended that it was he who had struck the bailiff, thinking that he was defending me from housebreakers.'

Alistair laughed. 'Now that I *hadn't* heard! Barnes would be pleased. He enjoys amateur dramatics.'

Max nodded. 'He certainly seemed to. So when they came, you introduced yourself. What reason, then, did you give for our exchange?'

'Naturally, I couldn't tell them the truth; so I said that it had been a jape that we had fashioned between us.'

'For what reason?' Max demanded, beginning to become alarmed.

'We both needed to show London a clean pair of heels,' Alistair replied. 'I was fleeing the wrath of a cuckolded husband, and you were evading your creditors.'

'Oh dear God!' Max exclaimed. 'Well, I suppose it was marginally better than the other way round. But do you realize what you have done?'

'My dear fellow—'

'This is the lady that I have been hoping to make my wife,' said

Max. 'Despite doubting my identity, she rushed to warn me of the magistrate's coming, which is why she struck Snelson over the head. In order to get her away quickly, Barnes told her that she had killed the man, and I, in my anxiety to protect her, did not look for myself to see if it was true, fool that I was! Then with all the business of the magistrate coming, your arrival and the urgency of your errand to London, I was obliged to hurry off without sending her word that Snelson was only stunned. God alone knows what agonies of mind she has gone through; and now I find that you have told her it was all for a jest!' He stared at his cousin for a few moments before striding to the door.

'Where are you going?' Alistair asked him.

'To find her, wherever she may be, and try to sort out this bloody mess.'

Alistair raised his glass. 'Good luck with that,' he murmured to empty air.

Max strode off to the stables in search of a mount. There were plenty of horses that he could use whilst Filigree enjoyed a well-deserved rest. Logic dictated that he ought to rest himself. He had had one decent night's sleep over the past three, and even that – the one that he had spent in London – had been short, owing to his desire to set off in good time. What was more, he had no idea where to begin to look for Constance. None of these considerations counted for anything when weighed against the need to find her, in order to dispel the erroneous impression that Alistair had given. The safety of the realm could go hang; he needed her to know the truth – or at any rate, as much of it as he knew himself.

He turned the corner to walk into the stables and stopped short; for she was there in front of him, stroking Patch and thanking the groom for his assistance. All at once, from being desperate to tell her his story, he was lost for words.

Constance had just returned from visiting Melinda's home. Unable to sleep, she had set off in good time that morning in order to solicit her friend's opinion. Her visit had not been well timed, although Mrs Grayleigh had been very pleased to see her. 'Dear Abdas has taken Melinda for a drive,' she disclosed, thus providing some heartening reassurance with regard to her attitude to her prospective son-in-law. 'I have been so excited about preparing for a wedding that I have quite worn her out, I fear.' She had no idea of their destination, confiding that they had told her not to expect them until later in the day.

There was clearly no point in waiting, so after a brief chat with Mrs Grayleigh, Constance had set off back to Beacon Tower. It was fortunate that she knew the journey well, for she drove largely by instinct, giving no attention to her surroundings. The hoped-for opportunity to discuss Max's behaviour with Melinda had failed to materialize, and she felt no more settled than before. She did not know what to do or where to turn.

Then, as she was on the point of walking home, having finished her conversation with the groom, she turned and saw Max coming towards them. 'Miss Church,' he said, bowing with more energy than grace.

Ever since Max's departure, she had felt as if she was living a strange half-life; rather like someone trapped in a corridor, with the door of the room that she had just left locked behind her, whilst the door that she wished to open also resisted her entry. Guilt over Snelson and anxiety about Max had, with each new revelation, turned to an overwhelming sense of betrayal. She had gone through so many emotions that she felt as if she had been run through the laundry maid's mangle; and all because of a jest!

She opened her mouth to acknowledge his greeting. As she did so, however, it suddenly occurred to her that she did not know how to address him. She took a deep breath. 'You will forgive me for not returning the courtesy, sir,' she said, offering a curtsy so perfunctory as to be almost non-existent. 'You have the advantage of me, since I have no idea who you are.' She turned her back, and set off at a brisk pace.

'My name is Max Persault,' he said, moving quickly to her side and keeping step with her. 'I am the cousin of—'

'The Duke of Haslingfield; yes, I know,' Constance interrupted. 'He told me all about it.'

'He did?' For a tiny moment, Max was conscious of a surge of relief that perhaps Alistair had actually told her the truth about their masquerade. Then as he looked at her stormy face, he realized his mistake.

'Oh yes,' Constance replied, her tone rather brittle. 'He has explained everything to my satisfaction.'

'He has?' said Max cautiously.

'As soon as I saw him, I understood why I had never really believed that you were a duke,' she answered. 'He has the word *aristocrat* written all over him; whereas I knew you to be a dandy brute right from the very beginning.'

Her words brought back to him all the memories of how ludicrous he had felt in his adopted role, and he could not suppress a chuckle. From the moment that it left his lips, he knew that he had made the crassest possible mistake. She whirled round to face him. 'Of course, you would laugh! It has all been so terribly amusing, has it not? Fooling a whole community of honest people for a jest!'

'A jest! How could you think it?' he asked incredulously, forgetting for a moment how plausible Alistair could be when he chose.

'Oh no, of course, I was forgetting; you were running away from your creditors. Another set of honest people of whom you have made game!' She turned to continue her journey; he stopped her by catching hold of her arm.

'Now who is being dishonest?' he demanded. 'You talk of all these people whom I have let down; what you really mean, Miss Church, is that you are angry because you think I was making game of *you*. You are simply annoyed because your pride has been hurt.'

For a moment, she felt almost unable to breathe. 'My pride? Do you really think that that is what this is about?' She took a deep breath. 'I was torturing myself because I thought that I had been the cause of Colin Snelson's death; and all the time, you knew that he was still alive.'

'I didn't know; I swear,' he replied.

'I don't believe you,' she said swiftly, pulling her arm from his grip and walking on.

'It's true. Think, Constance; Barnes examined him; I did not. You know that this was so. When I brought you home, I, too, believed that he was dead.'

'And when you went back to Beacon Tower?'

'I'll admit that I did discover then that he was alive; but by that time, the magistrate and his party were arriving, and I had to deal with them.'

'You could have come and told me afterwards. You knew how anxious I was.'

He looked at her for a long moment. 'I was obliged to go on an errand for Alistair,' he answered.

'Conniving at his illicit activities, no doubt,' she said.

'No,' he said decisively. 'I have not been honest with you, I admit; and for that I apologize. But my activities have not been dishonourable, I swear.'

She paused and turned to him again. 'The ironic thing is that if you had told me from the beginning that you were in debt, I would not have condemned you. I have some funds of my own; I would even have tried to help you.' Another shadow passed across her face. 'Was that why you asked me to ... to...? No, of course not,' she concluded bitterly. 'My small inheritance could never cover your debts. No doubt your suggestion that we go away together was yet another jest. Have you shared it with your cousin? I'm sure he, with his predilection for amorous intrigue, would find it vastly amusing.'

'It was no jest, I promise you,' Max declared, catching hold of her by both arms, this time, and pulling her against him. 'We can go now if you wish it: today; and I will prove to you that I am worthy of your trust.'

Again, she pulled herself away. 'Too late, Mr ... what was your name, again?'

'Persault.'

'Mr Persault. Goodness, what a mouthful! If I cannot remember it, I doubt if I should ever learn to spell it! No, you are too late, I fear. Mr Snelson has long been a suitor of mine, and thanks to your outrageous conduct, I now perceive his worth.'

'Does he know yet that you hit him over the head?' Max asked suspiciously.

'True love always forgives,' Constance replied, her head held high, quite proud of the fact that her colour did not change as she practised this little economy with the truth. 'We are anxious to have the banns read as soon as possible. You may come and hear them if your conscience is sufficiently clear.'

'And what of *your* conscience?' he demanded, venturing to catch hold of her again, this time by the wrist. 'Does it permit you to marry one man whilst you are in love with another?'

'In love?' she echoed scornfully. 'Perhaps I was naïve enough to believe it for a few brief hours; blame the romance of the moonlight. Now, I hate and despise you, more than I have ever despised anyone. Go back to your gambling and your posturing, for I have no desire to see you ever again as long as I live!'

They stared at one another for a long moment, before she whirled round and ran in the direction of The Brambles. Max watched until she was out of sight before walking back to Beacon Tower.

Constance's satisfaction at having given him a piece of her mind lasted until she got back to her room. 'I won't cry over him again,' she said out loud. 'He's not worth it.' Nevertheless, despite her words, her eyes filled with tears at her disappointed hopes. That might be the last time that she would see him. He had thoroughly shed his duke's disguise and could not be mistaken for anything other than some kind of adventurer. His dark hair had been confined imperfectly at his neck, and his clothing had been practical and hard-wearing rather than elegant. His hands.... She thought of his hands gripping her shoulders. As usual, he had been without gloves. On the little finger of his right hand, he had still been wearing the signet ring of the Duke of Haslingfield. Obviously, he had not yet given it back.

This thought took her back to one of the first times she had seen him. He had been getting out of the carriage, accompanied by Field, the dismissed valet. Then, too, he had been without gloves. He had been sporting the same signet ring. He had also been wearing one of rose gold, inset with a pearl. It had not been on his hand today.

Mentally, she gave herself a little shake. What did it matter how many rings the man wore? she told herself severely. Most probably, he had pledged it whilst gaming with somebody. She tried to dismiss the subject of the rings from her mind, but it would not go away. She had seen someone else wearing the rose-gold ring, and quite recently, too. When had that been? Could it have been Max on a previous occasion – when they had been at the lighthouse, for example? Rack her brains as she might, she could not recall.

Chapter Twenty-three

After having been summarily rejected by Constance, Max walked back slowly. A man with more experience of women might have taken some comfort from the vehemence of his dismissal. Max's knowledge of the female of the species was somewhat limited. The majority of his time was spent at sea in an exclusively male environment. On shore, he generally had business matters to attend to, after which he would usually pay a visit to his mother and his sister. Whilst there were always females who, for a consideration, would attend to a man's physical needs, romantic attachments had never played much of a part in his life. He therefore was inclined to take Constance at her word. She hated him; she never wanted to see him again. He could see why. Very well then; he would not pester her with his unwanted presence. He would bid farewell to his cousin, return to London and get back to sea as soon as could be managed. At least the *Lady Marion* was one female who would not break his heart.

He found his cousin at the desk in the book room, making some notes. Haslingfield looked up and eyed his face dispassionately. 'You don't look like a man for whom the phrase "I wish you joy" would be entirely appropriate,' he remarked.

'Perceptive of you,' Max answered, heading straight for the decanter and pouring himself a glass of brandy, which he swiftly emptied and refilled.

'A bath and a change of clothes after your long ride might have made a difference,' Alistair murmured.

'Alistair, are you fond of these glasses?' Max asked in an even tone.

'As I saw them for the first time the day before yesterday, I'm largely indifferent to them,' he replied.

There was a shattering sound followed by tinkling as Max's glass smashed against the fireplace. 'Any more bloody stupid remarks of that nature, and the decanter will follow it,' said Max.

'Oh, pray don't do that,' said Alistair, looking up at his cousin. He had displayed no reaction to the sound of breaking glass. 'The brandy in it is rather good.'

Max gave a bitter chuckle, took two more glasses and poured brandy into both then took one over to Alistair. 'Would that my troubles could be solved by filling a bath with water,' he said. 'No, she is now convinced that I am a heartless deceiver. What's more, you were right about Snelson. She has engaged herself to him and even invited me to stay for the banns.'

'Which invitation you refused, I take it.'

Max shook his head. 'I'll not stay and see her wed another,' he declared. 'I'll trespass on your hospitality this evening, if I may, and then be gone by first light.'

'Stay for as long as you please,' Alistair replied. 'Only for God's sake, have a bath and dress yourself properly.'

Max did as his cousin suggested, reflecting that this would probably be the last night that he would spend at Beacon Tower. The two men had never been in the habit of frequent visiting. Chances were that the next time they met it would be in London, or perhaps at Haslingfield. Playing the duke had had its amusing side, apart from the damage done to his personal life. All in all, though, Max decided it was probably a blessing that he was not a duke in good and earnest. He would be neglecting his principal seat in preference for this much smaller residence overlooking the sea.

He had never felt the need of a home apart from his ship. Here, at Beacon Tower, he had begun to feel the desire to settle, preferably in a place like this. It was not to be. Constance's decision had seen to that. He would have dinner with Alistair, then retire in reasonable time and leave early the following morning.

'I won't promise to see you off,' Alistair remarked as they sat over their brandy after the excellent meal prepared by Mrs Hays. 'Will you go straight to London from here?'

Max shook his head. 'I must ride over and bid farewell to Abdas,' he replied. He had told his cousin the story of Abdas's courtship. In so doing he had revealed more about his own feelings than perhaps he realized. Alistair sat at ease, his legs crossed negligently, asking the occasional judicious question, and all the time working on the information he received with a brain that was far more acute than most of his London acquaintances would ever have supposed.

'This agonizing confirms me in the belief that I am much better off having no heart at all,' he concluded eventually. 'Believe me, coz, when eventually I marry, it will be entirely for my own convenience. Anything else is just too uncomfortable to contemplate.'

In the event, Alistair did bestir himself to join his cousin for breakfast, wandering down negligently in his dressing gown. Max was not able to set off as early as he would have liked, owing to the fact that he was to call upon the Grayleighs. 'Farming family or not, they will hardly be pleased if you knock on the door at seven in the morning,' Alistair pointed out.

His departure was very different from his arrival, Max reflected, as he rode out of the stable yard dressed in comfortable riding clothes, the essentials packed into two saddle-bags. 'Barnes will send the rest on,' Alistair had promised. 'To where should he address them?'

'To the *Lady Marion* in the Port of London,' Max had replied. 'Or you might as well keep them if you wish. When would I have cause to be so dandified on board ship?'

'They wouldn't fit me,' Alistair had declared frankly, 'unlike your ring, to which I have become rather attached. Quite the only thing of taste that I can remember seeing you wear of your own volition.'

Alistair stood on the doorstep until Max was out of sight. He was about to go back inside when a man who bore all the appearance of a working farmer approached, having walked up the drive. Engaging in conversation on his threshold when not properly dressed was not normally an activity in which Alistair indulged. He nodded distantly to the man, said, 'You'll be wanting the stables, no doubt,' and turned to walk into the house.

'Sir? Beg pardon, sir?'

To be hailed in this way was even more unusual, and Alistair's curiosity was piqued. He turned round. 'Yes?' he said.

'Beg pardon, sir, but I was hoping for a word with His Grace,' said the man, turning his head to look in the direction in which Max had gone.

'You are speaking to him,' Alistair replied. 'How may I be of service?'

The man looked round again, hesitated and turned back, twisting his hat in his hands. 'Well, I ... beggin' your pardon, sir, I'm sure you're a very fine gentleman an' all, but—'

'But?'

'But I was 'opin' to speak to His *real* Grace, if you know what I mean.'

There was a short silence. 'As opposed to the counterfeit one,' Alistair murmured. 'Today is not convenient for ... ah ... "His real Grace". Come back tomorrow.' Turning his back on the mystified tenant farmer, he walked back inside, ascended to his bedchamber and rang for his valet. 'Ah, Barnes. Have a message sent to ... Bramble Cottage, is it?'

'The Brambles, Your Grace.'

'Ah yes, The Brambles. What would I do without you to put me right? Have someone go there to find out who is within. If the aunt and uncle are there, get them out of the way with some message; it doesn't matter what.'

'For how long, Your Grace?'

'Long enough for me to deal with Miss Church,' Alistair replied in an even tone. 'My cousin has been rather careless. She knows far too much for her own good.'

Shortly afterwards – for in fact, His Grace could be dressed and out of the door far more swiftly than he pretended – he was to be seen strolling gently in the direction of The Brambles.

A message had proved to be unnecessary, as Mr and Miss Fellowes had gone out for one of their occasional long walks. They had invited Constance to go with them but she had chosen to remain at home, pleading letters that needed writing. She had not wanted to spend a whole day with her uncle and aunt. Her feelings were still too raw to risk that kind of exposure.

She could not stop thinking about Max. To enter the drawing

room of the cottage brought back memories of the visit that he had paid them when he and Abdas had dined. Walking to the sea only reminded her of how he had held her as she had attempted to use the telescope. She could not bear to look in the direction of Beacon Tower. To divert her thoughts, she walked into the garden to pick some flowers, but as she came back inside with her basket, she paused on the threshold, remembering how he had bade her farewell there, on the night when she was sure that her love was returned. 'Fool!' she said out loud, as she went in search of a vase, then had to reassure Mrs Dobbs, who looked at her in some surprise.

She had only just filled her vase with water, when she heard the door knocker, followed by the maid's footsteps. 'Leave those to me, and go and attend to your visitor, Miss Constance,' said Mrs Dobbs.

Constance was not anticipating a call, and the last person that she had expected to see was the real Duke of Haslingfield; yet there he was, having been admitted to the drawing room. In contrast with Max, he looked nothing like a brute. Although there was certainly a good deal of the dandy about him, there was something about his slim, upright carriage and alert stance that spelled concealed strength and danger.

'Miss Church,' he murmured, bowing gracefully.

'Your Grace.' Constance's curtsy was only just the right side of courteous. She had not forgotten that it had been this man's misbehaviour that had set in train all the events that brought about her broken heart.

Alistair's lips twitched slightly. They stood staring at each other briefly before he said, 'May I sit?'

Constance flushed. However she might feel about this man, he was the most powerful landowner in the vicinity and she had been less than hospitable. 'Forgive me, Your Grace, my aunt and uncle are from home,' she said. 'Was it my uncle whom you wished to see?'

'I should be glad to make his acquaintance; however, my business is with you,' he replied.

'With me?' Constance's voice came out as more of a squeak than she would have liked.

The duke inclined his head. 'I feel that I was less than courteous when you called,' he told her. 'I would be glad if you would stroll up to Beacon Tower, so that I might be able to explain matters.' When she did not answer him, he went on, 'Max is not there, if that is what concerns you.'

Mention of Max unlocked her anger, and with it, her tongue. 'I cannot imagine what you might have to tell me concerning your libertine career or that of your spendthrift cousin that would interest me in the slightest,' she said forthrightly, adding 'Your Grace' impertinently on the end.

'By my "spendthrift cousin" I assume you mean Captain Max of the *Lady Marion*,' Alistair murmured. He looked across at Constance, who was staring at him, her anger forgotten. 'Yes, I thought that would get your attention,' he added, half to himself. He glanced around the room. 'Might I pour for you, Miss Church?' he asked, indicating a wine decanter on a table by the window with an elegant gesture of one white hand. 'You look a little ... *distraite*.'

She looked, not at the decanter, but at his hand, and captured the fleeting memory that had eluded her before. 'The ring,' she gasped. 'You were Field!'

His smile disappeared. 'Come, Miss Church; let us go to Beacon Tower.'

She raised her chin. 'And if I won't come?'

His hand hovered over the pocket of his coat in which he carried a small pistol. 'I'm afraid that I will really have to insist,' he said, as his smile returned.

'You are certain that you do not require my presence?' Abdas asked. The Grayleighs had all been up when Max arrived; indeed, Mr Grayleigh and his future son-in-law had been at work already, and had had to be summoned from the fields, where they were moving the bull. Evidently the farmer had discovered the African's ways with animals, and was employing them to best advantage.

Max shook his head, smiling. 'I can see that you are well settled here, and have no desire to drag you away,' he said. 'For my part, I must visit my mother and my sister, then I'll get back to sea.'

'You must be sure to come to our wedding,' Melinda insisted.

'Of course he must; for I want no one else to stand up with me,' said Abdas.

'I will do my best,' Max replied, smiling slightly. In normal circumstances, he would have moved heaven and earth to oblige his friend; on this occasion, he wasn't so sure. Constance, he knew, would be at the wedding. How would he endure it if, as he suspected, she was by then Mrs Snelson?

After taking some refreshment with the family and staying for as long as courtesy demanded, he took his leave. Abdas walked out with him to his horse. 'My friend, why not make your peace with her?' he said as Max put his foot in the stirrup.

'She has made it quite plain that she will not forgive me,' Max replied. 'Besides, she has cast her lot in with Snelson.'

By this time, Melinda had come out to join them. 'Mr Snelson?' she echoed. 'I don't think so.'

'Miss Grayleigh, she told me so herself,' said Max.

'Forgive me for sounding dubious, but I am her closest friend,' Melinda replied. 'I really think that if she had affianced herself to Mr Snelson, I would have been one of the first to know.'

Max frowned. 'Yes, perhaps,' he agreed. 'All the same.'

As he was speaking, they heard the sound of hoofbeats approaching at speed, and moments later, a large bay horse entered the yard with Barnes on his back. The valet looked highly agitated. 'Thank God I caught you, sir,' he said. 'You must come back with me at once.'

'What is it, man?' Max asked him.

'It's Miss Constance; she's in mortal danger,' the valet replied.

'From whom?' The valet stared at him for a long moment, and Max lost some of his colour. 'My God,' he said, remembering the conversation that he had had with Alistair. Foolishly, he had supposed that with the end of this particular adventure, the need for secrecy would be over. He had forgotten that his cousin's life and those of others often depended on successful subterfuge. Although this would, please God, be the last adventure of the kind for him, it would not be for Alistair. Without hesitation, he dug his heels into his horse's sides and set off, the valet in pursuit.

'Abdas,' said Melinda, her eyes large with worry.

'We'll go after them,' he assured her, running to harness the gig.

Chapter Twenty-four

'Where has the bastard taken her?' Max asked grimly as they rode.

'He was going to bring her to Beacon Tower,' the valet replied, his bay keeping pace with Filigree.

'I'll bet he was,' Max ground out. Max had no illusions about Alistair. The duke was fond enough of his cousin in his cold-hearted way. Since Constance had cast her lot in with Snelson, however, he would see no reason to spare her for Max's sake. Presumably, Mr and Miss Fellowes would have been lured away on some pretext. Alistair, cunning fox that he was, would make sure that no one saw him take Constance to Beacon Tower. There would be a hue and cry when she failed to return. Later, no doubt, she would be found at the foot of the cliffs, apparently the victim of a tragic accident.

On arriving at Beacon Tower, Max threw himself off his horse, thrusting the reins at Barnes, and ran in through the front door, which, strangely enough, was slightly open. Where would Alistair have taken her?

Almost as if the other man had read his mind, a voice called out, 'In here, Max. I assume those distinctive footsteps are yours?' Following the direction of the voice, Max entered the book room, to find his cousin standing next to the fireplace, his boot on the fender, his arm along the mantelpiece. 'Subtlety really isn't your strong suit, is it, my dear fellow?'

'Where the hell is she and what have you done with her?' Max asked, his feet apart, his fists clenched.

'I rest my case,' Alistair murmured. 'However, I'm at a loss to understand the reason for your hasty return.'

'I told you,' Max replied, taking another step towards his cousin. 'What have you done with Constance? If you've harmed a hair of her head, by God I'll—'

'Pray do not do such violence to your feelings. I am persuaded that it must be bad for your constitution.'

'If you don't tell me in the next five seconds, I shall do violence to *your* constitution,' Max declared furiously.

Alistair sighed. 'Oh, very well,' he murmured. 'She is unharmed. Really, my dear fellow, I am at a loss to understand why you should be so concerned. After all, you told me that she has plighted her troth to another.'

'She might be engaged to another man, but I happen to be in love with her,' Max answered. 'And if it hadn't been for falling in with your schemes, I wouldn't have been obliged to fill her ears with untruths which destroyed her faith in me.'

'If it hadn't been for my schemes, you would never have met her,' Alistair pointed out. He paused. 'She is not and never has been engaged to Snelson, and she now knows the truth about your masquerade. Really, coz, she knows far too much for someone who is not a member of the family. It's high time you attended to that, I think.'

'Not engaged?' Max echoed, homing in on what seemed to him to be the most significant piece of information. Slowly, hope began to dawn in the expression on his face. 'Alistair, where is she?'

His cousin smiled. 'You know, I may be old-fashioned, but I have always understood that a lady prefers to have a declaration from a man when he is in the same room as she is, rather than hearing it shouted from next door.' He nodded towards the door which led into the drawing room overlooking the sea.

Max entered the room to find Constance standing in the centre of it, looking in his direction. His anxiety had been extreme. Part of him had believed that Alistair would never hurt Constance. Unfortunately, another part of him, knowing his cousin's ruthless streak, had feared that he might indeed have found a way to dispose of her. Now, seeing her safe and sound, he felt momentarily deprived of speech and the use of his limbs.

Constance had been untroubled by such fears. She remembered

the moment when Alistair had taken out his pistol in order to demonstrate to her the seriousness of the mission on which he had been engaged. They had then walked to Beacon Hill where the duke had told her as much as he could about the exchange that he had persuaded Max to make. She had listened, her feelings swaying between disappointment in herself at her lack of faith in Max, and a similar feeling towards him for not trusting her enough to tell her the truth.

Both had things that they wanted to say. Any need or desire for talk disappeared, however, as each caught sight of the other. Apologies or explanations would have to wait as he ran to meet her, and caught her up in an embrace which she returned with equal fervour.

'I thought I'd lost you,' he said, his voice not quite steady.

'Oh, so did I,' she replied with fervour.

'Constance, I must tell you—' he began.

'It's all right; your cousin has told me everything,' she assured him.

'Thank God.' Then their lips met in a long kiss filled with tenderness and with passion too. Their last kiss had been one of farewell. This was much more by nature of a beginning, with misunderstanding put behind them.

'Tell me truly, did he hurt you?' he said eventually, holding her a little away from him and looking into her face. 'If he has done so—'

'No indeed, he didn't,' Constance replied, returning his gaze directly. 'He brought me back here so that he could tell me the real reason for your masquerade. But how do you come to be here? I thought that you had left for London.'

'And imagined that I was going to take part in more reckless gambling, no doubt,' he suggested provocatively.

'I didn't know what to think,' she confessed. 'You said that you would come for me on the night when the magistrate came, and then you disappeared. When I went up to Beacon Hill, I was confronted with a completely different duke.'

'I had to go straight off to London to deliver Alistair's papers. I was hoping that he would tell you all about our exchange then; instead, he spun you that tale about excessive gambling.'

'He was not aware at the time that you … that I—' Her voice faded away.

'That you were the love of my life?' Max suggested, pulling her close to him once more. 'No, he would not know that, because I hurried off on his errand before we had a chance to talk.'

'So why did you come back today?' Constance asked him.

'I'd left Beacon Hill, and had just stopped off at the Grayleighs to say goodbye to Abdas. Barnes came galloping up with a story of how Alistair intended to kill you because you knew too much.'

She gasped. 'You could not really have supposed that he would do such a thing.'

Max hesitated before replying. This was not the moment to disclose quite how ruthless his cousin might be if pressed. 'He would not care how much he frightened you if he could only get his way,' he answered eventually.

'He was very kind, and ready to explain everything to me. Oh Max, I have been accusing you of being a dandy brute, and all the time you were engaged upon the defence of your country!'

Max shook his head. 'Not really,' he said. 'Alistair was the one putting himself in danger. I was just peacocking about in fine clothes and using a title that wasn't mine.'

'I thought that you were an aristocrat of the worst kind; rude, arrogant, heartless and idle. I didn't like you at all at first.'

'The dandy-brute duke; I remember,' he said with a smile. 'The only trouble was, I wasn't very good at staying in role.'

'No,' she agreed. 'You were always much more of a buccaneer; and the more that you revealed your real character, the more intrigued I became.'

He took her hand and drew her over to the window, then held her with her back against his chest, so that they could both look out to sea. This was how they had stood on the night when she had come to warn him about the magistrate.

'Will you enjoy coming buccaneering with me?' he asked her, his arms wrapped around her.

'Is this an improper suggestion?' she asked him, looking teasingly over her shoulder.

'Certainly not,' he replied indignantly.

'Oh. I wasn't sure,' she returned, looking away.

He released her, turned her to face him, and went down on

one knee. 'Damn it, Constance, you have just heard me say that I love you to distraction. I've never given much thought to marriage before; now, I can't think of anything else. Say you'll marry me, Constance. I have no home to offer you, save the *Lady Marion*, but I have sufficient to—'

She did not allow him to finish. Taking his face between her hands, she bent over and kissed him on the lips. 'Oh, yes please,' she said. 'Captain Max,' she added softly. 'It suits you.' In reply, he stood up once more, pulled her into his arms, lowered his head and kissed her as ruthlessly as the buccaneer that she had always known him to be.

'I love you, Max,' she said, as soon as she was able.

'Even though you have now discovered that I am not a duke and that I do not have lands and a vast fortune at my disposal?'

'That is a disappointment, naturally,' Constance replied with mock seriousness. 'I am not quite sure how I will become reconciled to it.'

'Perhaps with more kisses like these?' Max suggested, claiming her mouth again.

Eventually, he led her over to the doorway and into the book room, where Alistair had been joined by Abdas and Melinda.

'She said yes,' said Max, grinning, as Constance ran over to embrace Melinda.

'Thank heaven for that,' the duke replied. 'I've already ordered champagne and glasses. I think that you've left me just enough unbroken ones for a toast.'

Mr and Miss Fellowes were delighted to receive the news of the proposal, and at once gave the happy couple their blessing. Bearing his stepfather's advice in mind, Max took the earliest opportunity to escort Constance to meet his mother and sister, who were both very happy with his choice. 'Perhaps he will be less at sea, now,' said Lady Prince hopefully. Privately, Constance doubted whether Max would ever want to spend a great deal of time away from the sea, although he had assured her that this need not be the case. He had taken to the North Norfolk coast, and as Constance had no family other than Mr and Miss Fellowes, they both decided that they would look for a property in that area.

As soon as Constance and Melinda had had a chance to put their heads together, they decided upon a double wedding. His Grace of Haslingfield offered Beacon Tower for their use for the wedding breakfast. After a brief stay there he had moved to his principal residence near Cambridge. No one expected him to visit again for some considerable time.

'A pity,' the rector remarked to Mr Fellowes as they were playing chess one evening. 'It was so good for the neighbourhood to have the house occupied.'

After the wedding, Abdas planned to take his new wife to his own estate in Hampshire. The duke had offered Haslingfield to Max and Constance for their honeymoon whilst he remained at Beacon Tower. Later, as the celebrations were still going on, however, the duke appeared dressed for travelling and took Max on one side. 'There's been a change of plan,' he said, handing his cousin a sealed packet. 'I'm taking the carriage, and you remain here. This is for you. Don't open it until I've gone; and be happy.'

Before Max could protest, or do more than wring his hand warmly, he had run lightly down the steps, climbed into his carriage and driven away at speed.

'What's that?' Constance asked, joining him. 'I thought your cousin was staying.'

'So did I,' Max replied. 'Apparently we are to stay here instead. I wonder what this is?' He opened the package carefully, and scanned the papers that it contained. He looked at his new wife, his eyes aglow. 'Connie, it's the deeds of this house. Alistair has given us Beacon Tower as his wedding gift.'

Constance looked down at the papers that he was holding. 'Oh Max, such generosity; and I didn't have chance to thank him.'

'He didn't want that,' Max replied, putting a protective arm around her shoulders. 'We can thank him later; for now, let's go back inside. After all, it is our home.'